MY TIME WITH THE PRINCE

To my beyond supportive family and friends, without whom you wouldn't be reading this book today.

To my fellow trans people. You who have found love, found strength, found truth despite the voices that said you could not. This is for you.

CONTENT WARNING

This story contains themes of attempted rape, bigoted remarks and domestic abuse.

Reader discretion is advised.

TABLE OF CONTENTS

<u>ONE</u>

"So, what are your interests?" She asked as she took a sip of her wine. She stared intently at her date, waiting for him to answer the simple question. After a moment of silence, he cleared his throat and wiped his lip with a napkin. "Well, I- I like many things." Anastasia kissed her teeth at his response and took another sip of wine. "Anything.. in particular?" She asked, her patience wearing thin. She watched as his eyes darted around the dimly lit room. He looked at all the other couples, at the servers, even out the windows. He looked at anything but her.

Finally, his gaze met hers and he stopped eating. "What is this, an interrogation or a date?" He chuckled, to which she had no reaction. "Tough crowd.." He said wryly and began to eat once more. Anastasia sarcastically smiled at him before drinking the rest of her wine. "Well, if I had to pick something. It'd definitely be your perfectly feminine skin. Tell me, how long have you been out?" Anastasia cleared her throat and shifted in her seat, clearly uncomfortable. "I- I don't really know if I wish to talk about that on a first date." She muttered, starting to sweat. "Y'know, I'm an ally. You're safe with me. I'm very accepting. You're actually more beautiful than most *real* women I know so it's not difficult." Anastasia's grip tightened around the stem of her wine glass, her knuckles whitening as she forced herself to keep her expression neutral. The word "real" echoed in her mind, sharp and cutting. She set the glass down carefully, her fingers trembling slightly as she folded her hands in her lap.

"Real women?" she repeated, her voice calm but laced with an edge. "What exactly do you mean by that?"

Her date leaned back in his chair, seemingly oblivious to the shift in her tone. He smirked, as if he thought he was being charming. "Oh, you know what I mean. You're just... different. Special. It's not a bad thing—it's a compliment." Anastasia's stomach churned. She could feel the heat rising to her cheeks, but she refused to let him see her falter. "A compliment," she echoed, her voice flat. "Right."

He nodded enthusiastically, clearly misreading her reaction. "Exactly! I mean, it's not every day you meet someone like you. You're so confident, so... unique. I admire that." Anastasia's patience was wearing thin, but she forced herself to take a deep breath. "Right," she said again, her tone sharper this time. "So, tell me—what exactly is it about me that you find so... unique?"

Her date hesitated, his smirk faltering for the first time. He glanced down at his plate, pushing a piece of food around with his fork. "Well, I mean... it's obvious, isn't it? You're just... not like other women." Anastasia's chest tightened, and she felt the familiar sting of anger bubbling beneath the surface.

She leaned forward slightly, her eyes narrowing as she fixed him with a pointed stare. "Not like other women," she repeated, her voice low. "Care to elaborate?"

He shifted uncomfortably in his seat, his confidence visibly waning. "Look, I'm just saying... I think it's amazing that you're so open about who you are. It's brave. And honestly, it's... kind of hot."

Anastasia's jaw clenched, and she had to resist the urge to throw her napkin in his face. Instead, she leaned back in her chair, crossing her arms over her chest as she regarded him coldly. "Brave," she said, her voice dripping with sarcasm. "Right. Because existing is such a courageous act."

Her date blinked, clearly taken aback by her tone. "I didn't mean it like that," he said quickly, his voice defensive. "I'm just trying to say that I respect you. I mean, I've always been an ally, you know? I've got nothing but love for people like you."

"People like me," Anastasia repeated, her voice icy. She could feel her heart pounding in her chest, but she refused to let him see how much his words had affected her. "You mean trans women." He hesitated, his eyes darting around the room again as if searching for an escape. "Well... yeah," he finally admitted, his voice barely above a whisper. "But that's not a bad thing! I think it's amazing. You're amazing."

Anastasia stared at him for a long moment, her expression unreadable. Then, without a word, she reached for her purse and stood up. Her date's eyes widened in surprise, and he scrambled to his feet, nearly knocking over his chair in the process. "Wait, where are you going?" he asked, his voice panicked. "Did I say something wrong?"

Anastasia turned to face him, her expression calm but resolute. "Yes," she said simply. "You did." And with that, she walked away, leaving him standing there in stunned silence.

Slamming the hotel room door behind her, Anastasia tossed her bag onto the carpeted floor with a thud, the straps flopping uselessly onto their side. The sound echoed faintly in the quiet room as she leaned her back against the door, exhaling sharply.

"God," she muttered under her breath, "why do I always pick the frogs?" Her voice was heavy with self-annoyance as she pushed herself off the door and trudged over to the bed. She flopped down unceremoniously, arms sprawled out across the duvet. Her mind replayed snippets of the evening in vivid, excruciating detail. She groaned loudly and rubbed her forehead with both hands, as if she could physically erase the memory of it.

"Yet another red flag... and I walked right into it," she muttered bitterly. "Great job, Anastasia. You've really outdone yourself this time." For a few more moments, she lay there, scolding herself silently. Then, with a sharp sigh, she sat up and yanked off her heels, wincing as she massaged her aching feet. The shoes clattered to the floor as she tossed them aside, and without bothering to change, she crawled under the covers. Sleep, mercifully, didn't take long to come.

Bzzzz. Bzzzz. Bzzzz.

The piercing vibration of her phone jolted Anastasia awake, and her hand shot out instinctively, smacking blindly at the nightstand. Her fingers fumbled over the glass surface, swatting the phone until she finally hit the "Snooze" button. She muttered something unintelligible and slumped back into her pillow, hoping to drift off again. But the damage had been done—she was awake now.

Her mind was still sluggish as she swung her legs off the bed, her bare feet brushing against the cool carpet. The hotel room was bathed in soft, early morning light filtering through the thick curtains. The air felt stale, and she sighed as she pushed herself off the bed, moving toward her suitcase.

She rifled through its contents with no real enthusiasm, pulling out the teal dress she'd worn to last night's disaster of a date. She stared at it for a moment before tossing it unceremoniously to the floor. "Not today, Satan," she muttered under her breath.

Dragging herself to the bathroom, Anastasia turned on the shower and waited for the water to heat up. She leaned against the sink, glancing at herself in the mirror. Her reflection looked as tired as she felt—dark circles under her eyes, her hair a chaotic mess. "Morning, gorgeous," she said wryly, her lips quirking into a half-smile.

Once she finished, Anastasia wrapped herself in a towel and pawed through her suitcase again, pulling out the first thing she saw: a loose sweater and a pair of faded jeans. "Practical. Low effort," she muttered, slipping them on.

She paused in front of the mirror again, considering her options. "Makeup?" she asked aloud, tilting her head at her reflection. "Yeah, no. Absolutely not." Her face looked back at her with the same deadpan exhaustion she felt. "You'll survive."

Satisfied with her minimal effort, she padded back into the bedroom and began to gather her belongings. The mess from the night before—her bag, her discarded heels—lay scattered across the room, a reminder of the evening she'd rather forget. With a deep sigh, she threw everything back into her suitcase, zipping it up with more force than necessary.

Finally, Anastasia grabbed her phone from the bed, glancing at the screen one last time. No new messages, no missed calls. No surprise there. Slinging her bag over her shoulder, she left the room without looking back, heading out into the uncertain morning and toward whatever awaited her at Elsmere Manor.

She stopped the car at the top of a winding path, leading into wild and untamed bushes. The drive had been long and quiet, the winding roads of the English countryside occasionally flanked by towering oaks and sprawling fields that seemed endless. Anastasia tightened her grip on the steering wheel as the car rattled down the dirt path leading to Elsmere Manor. The tall iron gates were already swung open, creaking faintly in the wind. Anastasia couldn't help but glance at them uneasily as she drove through. They seemed too heavy, too imposing, to have been left open on their own. The manor emerged slowly from the mist ahead, its silhouette towering and jagged. Even in its neglected state, it held an undeniable majesty, as if demanding admiration despite the years that had worn it down. Ivy clung to its exterior like persistent fingers, curling around chipped stone and cracked windows. The roof was uneven, patches of slate missing entirely, leaving jagged gaps like broken teeth. Anastasia parked in front of the overgrown garden, staring up at the house with both trepidation and wonder.

She stepped out of the car and onto the gravel driveway, her boots crunching against the stones. The air felt heavier here, colder. Anastasia shivered despite the coat she wore. Her grandmother's house. Her inheritance. She had expected something grander, something livelier—a piece of history preserved in time. But Elsmere was as much a corpse as it was a monument. She saw an older man stood in front of the door, the estate agent. "Ah, you must be Anastasia Cameron, the late Mistress Cameron's granddaughter?" Anastasia chuckled.

"The one and only" She jokingly curtseyed but soon stood up when she realised he wasn't even smiling.

"Terribly sorry for your loss, my dear. She was truly an angel on Earth." Anastasia nodded and twiddled her fingers in an attempt to not cry. "Well anyway, here are the keys. She's got good bones, just needs a lot of love" Anastasia was confused before realising he meant the manor. "Yes, don't worry she'll get fixed up as soon as humanly possible." The agent chuckled and walked away, placing his hand on her shoulder before getting into his car and driving away.

As she walked toward the heavy oak door, Anastasia noticed the paint peeling around its edges and the handle rusted with age. The brass knocker, shaped like a lion's head, seemed to glare at her as she unlocked the door. As she did, it opened with a sharp groan, swinging inward as if welcoming her—or daring her to enter. Anastasia froze, her hand still outstretched. "That's... not creepy at all," she murmured under her breath before stepping inside.

The air inside was thick with the scent of damp wood and decay, mingled faintly with the ghost of something floral—lavender, perhaps. The entrance hall stretched high above her, with vaulted ceilings that still held traces of their former grandeur. A chandelier hung from its center, its crystals coated with dust, some missing entirely. The grand staircase stood as the focal point, its once-polished banisters now dull and splintered. Anastasia ran her fingers over the wood lightly, pulling back as the surface snagged her skin.

She set her suitcase down near the wall and glanced at the faded tapestries hanging from the stairwell. Their patterns were barely discernible beneath decades of grime, but Anastasia could make out figures—a hunt, perhaps, or a battle. She turned away, unnerved by how the images seemed to watch her as she moved.

The door to the coat closet swung open suddenly, its hinges squealing sharply. Anastasia flinched and whipped around, staring at the closet. It was empty inside—only a few wooden hangers and a small pile of moth-eaten fabric lay on the floor. She swallowed hard, feeling the hairs on the back of her neck stand on end.

Taking everything in, Anastasia found herself drawn to the grand wooden staircase that dominated the entrance hall. Its mahogany banister gleamed faintly, though years of neglect had worn patches of the wood smooth. Each step groaned under her weight as she ascended, the sound echoing faintly in the cavernous space.

The staircase curved gracefully upward, splitting at a landing that overlooked the hallway below. A narrow window above the landing let in soft, filtered light, illuminating the dust motes that danced in the air like tiny spirits. Anastasia paused, leaning against the banister as she gazed down at the space she had just left. From this vantage point, the house seemed vast and unyielding, its secrets locked away in shadowed corners.

The upstairs corridor stretched endlessly, lined with doors that seemed to multiply the farther Anastasia walked. Each one was different: some were simple wooden panels, while others were elaborately carved with swirling patterns and floral motifs. Anastasia opened the first door cautiously, revealing a bedroom that had clearly once been elegant.

A four-poster bed stood in the center, its canopy sagging under the weight of dust and cobwebs. The bedding was faded but intact, the embroidered patterns barely visible. Heavy curtains hung beside the tall windows, their fabric brittle. A vanity in the corner held a cracked mirror, its surface distorted, and Anastasia swore she saw her reflection flicker as she turned away.

At the far end of the corridor, Anastasia stumbled upon an enormous set of double doors, their surface etched with intricate patterns of roses and ivy. It took both hands to push them open, and the sight beyond took her breath away.

The ballroom was vast, its ceiling soaring high above her, painted with a mural of angels and swirling clouds. Though cracked and faded, the artistry was stunning, each brushstroke still visible. Golden chandeliers hung overhead, their crystals dull but intact, catching the weak light that filtered in through arched windows.

The walls were lined with mirrors, some fractured, their silver backing peeling, creating ghostly reflections. Anastasia noticed the detailing along the baseboards—tiny carved figures of cherubs and flowers that seemed untouched by time. The floor, once polished to a gleam, was now scuffed and dusty, though the faint outlines of swirling patterns could still be seen.

In one corner of the room, a grand piano stood silent, its keys rusted. Anastasia brushed her fingers across its surface, feeling the chill of the wood. She wondered if anyone had ever danced here—if the room had once been filled with music, laughter, and the soft shuffle of feet moving in time.

Pushing open the door to the living room required effort; its hinges groaned and resisted, as though the house were reluctant to reveal more of itself. Anastasia stepped inside, her boots sinking slightly into the threadbare carpet. The room was dominated by an enormous fireplace, its ornate mantle carved with intricate patterns of flowers and curling vines.

Ashes still lay inside, untouched for years. Above the mantle hung a portrait—an aristocratic man with piercing blue eyes and sharp features, dressed in formal 18th-century attire. Anastasia tilted her head, narrowing her eyes at the painting. Was it her imagination, or did his lips seem slightly curled into a smirk? She glanced over her shoulder quickly, her pulse quickening. Something had moved—just at the edge of her vision—but the room was empty.

The furniture was a mismatched collection of ruined opulence: a chaise lounge with stuffing protruding from its seams, two armchairs with faded upholstery, and a coffee table stained with water rings and warped at the edges. Anastasia brushed her fingers across the mantle absentmindedly, recoiling as she felt something cold and wet. She glanced down at her hand—it was clean, but the sensation lingered.

The kitchen was smaller than Anastasia expected, nestled at the back of the house. A single window let in waning daylight, illuminating the cracked countertops and rusted faucets. The sink was filled with stagnant water that smelled faintly of mildew, the remnants of leaves and dirt floating on its surface. Anastasia wrinkled her nose and turned her attention to the old oak table in the center of the room, its corners chipped and its surface scarred with knife marks.

Stepping into the garden felt like walking into another world entirely—a forgotten Eden that had somehow survived the decay of time. The arches, formed from interwoven leaves and tangled vines, created natural tunnels through the garden, their emerald canopy dappling the ground below with shifting patterns of light and shadow. Anastasia paused under one such arch, her breath catching as the scent of wild roses and damp earth filled her lungs.

The trellises, once meticulously maintained, were now overrun with blooming flowers of every colour. Lavender, honeysuckle, and climbing roses had intertwined themselves across the wooden frames, spilling over the edges in an explosion of tangled beauty. Anastasia couldn't help but reach out, her fingers grazing the delicate petals of a pale pink rose.

At the heart of the garden stood an ancient stone well, its edges crumbling and softened by moss. A wrought-iron bucket rested beside it, its handle rusted but intact, as though waiting to be used. Anastasia peered cautiously into the well, but the black water inside offered no reflection—only an unsettling void.

Farther in, the garden opened up into a small clearing, where a stone bridge arched over a pond. The pond's surface was covered in moss and algae, with patches of lily pads breaking through the green film. Delicate flowers grew along the edges, their bright yellows and whites reflected faintly in the still water. Anastasia noticed the faint movement of fish beneath the surface, their flashes of silver quick and elusive.

The rose bushes were prolific, growing wildly throughout the garden in tangled clusters. Their blooms ranged from deep reds to creamy whites, filling the air with their rich fragrance. Wildflowers burst through the cracks in the stone pathways, vivid streaks of purple and yellow adding life to the worn and broken trails.

Despite its beauty, the garden carried an unsettling energy. The silence was profound, broken only by the occasional rustling of leaves as though a breeze had passed—but there was no wind. Anastasia turned sharply at one point, convinced she had seen a figure moving between the arches, but the space behind her was empty.

Anastasia stepped back into the manor, closing the heavy oak door behind her with a soft thud. The air inside felt colder than it had earlier, as though the house had exhaled all its warmth while she was outside. She rubbed her arms briskly, trying to shake off the chill that had settled over her. The garden had been beautiful, yes, but unsettling—too quiet, too alive in ways she couldn't quite explain. Now, the silence of the house pressed down on her, thick and oppressive.

She glanced toward the staircase, its grand curve leading up to the shadowed landing above. For a moment, she thought she saw movement—a flicker of something just out of sight—but when she blinked, the space was empty. Her heart quickened, but she shook her head, muttering to herself, "Get a grip, Anastasia. It's just an old house."

Her boots echoed faintly against the wooden floor as she made her way toward the parlor. She hadn't felt at home in the manor yet, and the thought of sitting in one of its dusty old chairs with a cup of tea sounded oddly comforting. The door to the parlor was slightly ajar, and she pushed it open with a creak, stepping inside.

The room was dimly lit, the late afternoon light filtering through heavy curtains that hung like sentinels on either side of the tall windows. Anastasia moved toward the center of the room, her eyes scanning the faded furniture and the ornate rug that had seen better days. The air was heavy, damp even. Ornate paintings lined the walls, staring down at her with disapproving expressions. She shivered. "What are you looking at?" she muttered, tossing the nearest portrait an unimpressed glance. "I own this place now. You can stop judging."

She clutched her jacket tightly, ignoring the cold draft that seemed to come from nowhere and everywhere all at once. "What's the point of all these fireplaces if none of them work?" she muttered. "Fancy house, useless heating." The air shifted, subtle but distinct, and Anastasia stiffened. She turned slowly toward the faint sound of footsteps echoing from the corridor. Before she could call out, a voice—low, authoritative, and deeply annoyed—pierced the silence.

"You there," it barked. "Who are you, and what, exactly, are you doing in *my* house?" Anastasia's eyes widened as a man stepped into view. He looked like he'd just walked off the cover of a historical romance novel: blond hair swept neatly to his shoulders, piercing blue eyes that glared with unmistakable disdain, and an outfit so ridiculously regal it made her wonder if she'd wandered into a costume party without an invitation. Navy coat, gold sash, polished boots, the whole look screamed important and insufferable.

"You're kidding, right?" Anastasia said flatly. The man frowned. "Do I look as though I am jesting?"

"You look as though you're auditioning for *Bridgerton*," Anastasia shot back, crossing her arms. "So why don't we cut to the part where you tell me who you actually are before this gets any weirder?" The man stepped closer, his posture impossibly stiff. "I am Prince Roland of England. This house belongs to my family." Anastasia blinked at him for a long moment before laughing sharply. "Oh, *sure*. You're a prince. In 2025. Right. You know, princes don't dress like you anymore. You're extinct." Roland's frown deepened. "I don't follow."

"Yeah, I figured," Anastasia muttered. "Listen, Mr. Prince, this house is legally mine. See." She unfurled a piece of paper from her pocket, showing the house in her name. "Miss Anastasia Cameron. That's me. I inherited it. So unless you've got documentation proving otherwise—and you don't, because you're not real—I suggest you back off."

Before Roland could respond, the room seemed to shift beneath their feet. A low hum filled the air, vibrating through the walls like distant thunder. Anastasia's breath hitched, and Roland stiffened, his hand instinctively resting on the hilt of a sword Anastasia hadn't noticed until now. "What is that?" Anastasia asked, her voice rising. Roland's grip tightened on the banister beside him. "I haven't the faintest idea."

The world spun. Golden light burst across the room, blinding Anastasia and swallowing Roland's panicked voice. When the light faded, Anastasia stumbled forward, clutching her head as she tried to make sense of her surroundings. At first, nothing seemed different but the air smelled sharper, fresher. The floorboards beneath her boots gleamed. She turned slowly, her eyes darting from the polished furniture to the vibrant curtains that replaced the faded, tattered ones she'd grown used to.

Across the room, Roland stood frozen, his earlier arrogance dissolved into confusion. His gaze flickered to the window, and without a word, he crossed the room to look outside. Anastasia hesitated before following him, her stomach twisting.

Beyond the glass, the world was impossibly different. Pristine gardens stretched across the manor's grounds, and beyond them, horse-drawn carriages rolled along cobblestone roads. Men tipped their hats to women dressed in extravagant gowns, their laughter faint but distinct. Anastasia felt her knees weaken.

"I'm back." Roland murmured, his voice distant. "This is my world." Anastasia looked at him, confused. "Back where, exactly?" Roland shared the confusion again, expecting her to say she was joking. "You really don't know? How could you not know it's 1733, have you been living underneath a boulder?" Anastasia felt the floor sway beneath her feet. Her breath hitched as panic gripped her chest. "No. No, no, no. That's—that's not possible! Time travel isn't real!" Roland's lips tightened, but there was no trace of his earlier arrogance. "It appears you have been displaced."

"I can't—" Anastasia's voice cracked. "I can't be here. I don't belong here. I—I have a life, people waiting for me, and—oh my God, how am I supposed to survive *this*?" Roland stepped toward her, his uncertainty mirrored in his gaze. "Miss Cameron, I—"

"No!" Anastasia snapped, backing away. "Don't. Don't act like this is normal. This is *insane*."

The tension between them didn't ease as the hours stretched on. Roland busied himself pacing the room, muttering about the possible consequences of Anastasia's sudden appearance. Every so often, he would glance at her, as though hoping she'd magically come up with an answer to their predicament.

"I can't stay here," Anastasia said for what felt like the hundredth time. She wrapped her arms around herself, her voice trembling. "I don't even know how to pretend to be a part of this world."

"You'll need protection," Roland said, his voice carefully measured. "Protection from what?" Anastasia snapped. "From your snooty friends? From people asking why I talk like this?"

Roland's expression darkened. "From suspicion. Strangers. Nobles. You'll draw attention the moment you step outside these walls. And in this era, attention can be dangerous." Anastasia stopped pacing, turning to him with wide, desperate eyes. "So what am I supposed to do? Hide forever?"

Roland had considered the simplest options. Keeping her within the palace walls as an honored guest? No—too many questions, too many uncertainties. Giving her a title without a binding connection? Insufficient. Easily overturned. The only choice that remained, the only choice that could solidify her presence without interference was marriage.

For her, it was protection. For him? It was freedom. Because when she left—when time corrected itself, when the world returned her to where she belonged—she would cease to exist in this kingdom. She would be declared dead, lost to tragedy, a ruler's grief bound in the memory of a woman who was no longer part of history.

He would be a grieving widower. A man whose love had been lost too soon. A ruler who could never be forced into another alliance because his heart had already been claimed, his loyalty already given, his mourning already carved into the expectations of the court.

He would never have to marry again. Never be bound by duty in the way they wanted him to be. He would be free. The thought settled in his mind, sharp but steady, curling into something that felt more like resolution than hesitation. He turned away from the window, his gaze falling to Anastasia, who had finally stopped pacing, watching him with the kind of quiet intensity that told him she knew something was coming.

Her hair was slightly tousled from hours spent unraveling possibilities, her arms crossed tightly, her lips parted just slightly, waiting. He exhaled, the weight of everything pressing against the words he was about to say. "No," Roland said slowly. He hesitated, as though weighing his next words. "We'll marry." Anastasia stared at him, her breath catching. "I'm sorry, *what?*"

"A royal union will shield you from scrutiny," Roland said, though he seemed just as uneasy as she was. "As my wife, no one would dare question your presence." She gawked at him, her voice rising. "You're suggesting we *marry?* Are you out of your mind?" Roland met her gaze with a forced calmness. "Unless you have a better idea, Miss Cameron, I suggest you accept."

Before she could process what was happening, Anastasia found herself swept into a whirlwind of preparations. Roland's staff bustled around her, adjusting her borrowed gown, muttering about protocol, and bowing every time Roland entered the room. Anastasia barely heard them. Her thoughts were a chaotic mess, bouncing between panic and disbelief.

How had her life spiraled into this? One minute she was unpacking her belongings in a slightly creepy old house, and the next she was standing at the altar in a century that wasn't even her own.

Her hands shook as she clutched the bouquet, the weight of the gown pressing down on her like a thousand unanswered questions. What was she doing? How could this possibly work? And what would happen when—or if—she returned to her time?

Roland stood beside her, his calm façade unshaken. But when their eyes met, Anastasia saw a flicker of doubt beneath his polished exterior—a tension that mirrored her own fear. The priest's voice droned on, the words blurring together. Anastasia's heart pounded in her ears as the enormity of the situation crashed over her like a wave. When it was her turn to speak, she forced herself to take a shaky breath and whisper the words that would bind her to the stranger in front of her.

"I do."

TWO

Anastasia stood frozen in the grand hall as the remnants of her whirlwind wedding echoed in her mind. The air was heavy with the scent of flowers and candles, and her borrowed gown hung uncomfortably on her frame. She barely remembered saying "I do," the words a blur amidst the chaos. Now, as the doors opened to reveal courtiers waiting to meet the newest member of the royal family, Anastasia felt her heart drop.

"I thought we agreed on *laying low*," she muttered under her breath to Roland, who stood beside her with his usual stiff posture. Roland glanced at her, his expression tight. "Believe me, this was not my idea." "Well, make it *un*-your idea!" Anastasia whispered harshly. "I am *not* ready to face a bunch of strangers who bow before breakfast!"

Before Roland could respond, a royal attendant cleared his throat loudly, signaling the courtiers to step forward. Anastasia fought the urge to back away as a line of finely dressed nobles approached, their gazes scrutinizing her with varying degrees of curiosity and suspicion. "This is going to go terribly," Anastasia muttered, plastering the most awkward smile she'd ever conjured onto her face.

Roland's attempts at keeping Anastasia hidden were immediately thwarted when the courtiers demanded introductions and whispers rippled through the castle about the hastily arranged royal wedding. The tension was palpable, and Anastasia could sense the eyes of the gathered crowd lingering on her every movement.

Roland introduced her tersely, his voice carrying a tone of barely concealed irritation. "Her Royal Highness, Princess Anastasia." Anastasia felt her stomach twist as the title landed like a boulder in the pit of her stomach. Princess Anastasia. That wasn't her. It couldn't be. When Roland's father, King George, entered the room, Anastasia straightened instinctively. The king was an imposing figure, tall and broad, with a commanding presence that made Roland look almost unassuming by comparison. His sharp eyes raked over Anastasia as he approached, his mouth set in a line that betrayed no emotion.

"So," he said, his voice heavy with authority, "this is the young woman you have taken as your wife." Anastasia fought the urge to shrink under his gaze. "Um, yes," she said, her voice cracking slightly. "It's... uh, a pleasure to meet you, Your Majesty."

"Son, a word?" He gestured toward the throne room's grand doors and Roland followed him inside, closing the doors behind them.

The air in the throne room was thick with tension, the grand chamber looming with its towering pillars and heavy crimson drapes. George sat atop the gilded throne, his fingers gripping the carved arms as Roland stood before him—emotionless, unwavering, yet entirely at the mercy of his father's wrath. "You married her?" George had growled, his voice laced with disbelief and rage.

"You have ignored every royal protocol, every tradition that has ensured this kingdom's stability for generations," George spat, his booming voice echoing against the chamber walls. "You were meant to wed the Princess of Prussia! A union carefully arranged, a match that held diplomatic value—one that is now ruined because of your reckless, selfish decision!"

Roland stood still, his expression unreadable. "I cannot undo this now," the king continued, voice climbing with fury. "A divorce would be a disgrace, a stain upon this monarchy. No king before me has been dishonoured so publicly, and I will not have my reign tainted by scandal!" Still, Roland did not react. George's anger deepened, his features twisting in frustration. "And this common girl—this stray mutt—you expect her to sit in court? To rule beside you?"

Roland's fingers twitched subtly, but he remained silent. "She is unfit," George snarled. "She lacks refinement, breeding, decorum. If you are so insistent on forcing her into this position, then she will be trained." Roland exhaled slowly, but his voice was flat. "What do you propose?" George leaned forward, his eyes gleaming with ruthless calculation. "I have ordered a wardrobe's worth of gowns to be made for her. She will dress like a princess, act like a princess, and learn to be worthy of the title she has *stolen*."

Roland nodded once, emotionless.

"Where did this wedding take place?" the king snapped. Roland responded with steady precision, as if reading off a list that did not concern him. "At St. Eustace's Church. Ordained by Father Joseph. She wore Mother's wedding dress." King George's nostrils flared, fury washing over his features. "You let her wear your mother's gown?"

Roland finally shifted, his shoulders tightening slightly. "There was no alternative." George breathed heavily, his anger momentarily clipping into something unreadable—grief, perhaps, buried beneath his relentless pride. Then, with a sharp inhale, he composed himself. "One last matter," the king said darkly. Roland waited. "Have you consummated the marriage?"

Roland barely blinked before answering. "No." King George narrowed his eyes, his lips curling in distaste. "Then I suggest you do so immediately." The command hung in the air, thick and suffocating. Roland did not react—did not flinch, did not protest. He merely gave a single curt nod. King George lifted his hand. "You are dismissed."

After the tense introduction, Anastasia was whisked away through the castle, her mind struggling to keep up with the whirlwind. Roland walked beside her, silent and brooding, while attendants murmured instructions and cleared their path. The castle was enormous, its corridors lined with gilded mirrors and tapestries so intricate they seemed alive in the flickering candlelight. Anastasia felt like she was being led deeper into an elaborate trap, each step erasing any semblance of normalcy she'd once clung to.

When they arrived at her quarters, the attendants opened the double doors with a flourish. Anastasia stepped inside hesitantly, her breath catching as she took in the sight before her. The room was magnificent—far beyond anything she had ever imagined. A canopy bed draped in silk dominated the space, its gold trim catching the light. Tall windows framed the manicured gardens below, and a plush chaise lounge sat beneath a chandelier that sparkled like starlight.

"Okay," Anastasia said, her voice shaky. "This is... ridiculous." Roland followed her inside, his gaze sweeping over the room briefly before settling on her. "It's standard," he said simply. "Standard?" Anastasia echoed, turning to him with wide eyes. "This is *absurd*. I feel like I'm trespassing in someone's dream!"
Roland didn't respond immediately. He stepped closer, his expression slightly softer but no less serious. "You'll adjust." Anastasia laughed sharply, the sound edged with panic. "Adjust? To *this?* To being a princess? To being married to someone I don't even like?" She gestured wildly at the bed, the chandelier, the embroidered curtains. "I don't know how to do this, Roland. I don't even know where to *start!*" Roland sighed, stepping into the room. "I understand this isn't ideal—"

"*Ideal?*" Anastasia cut him off, her voice rising. "This is not *normal,* Roland. You may be used to this whole royal charade, but I'm not! How am I supposed to do this without royally screwing it up?" Roland hesitated, his gaze softening slightly. "That's why I brought you here. We'll make this

34

work, Anastasia." She frowned at him, her fear and frustration bubbling beneath the surface. "Fine. Let's make this work. Where do we start?"

Moments after, Anastasia was ushered into a small room and faced with three women, her newly appointed ladies-in-waiting. Their perfect attire and studied grace highlighted Anastasia's own discomfort and sense of being ill-prepared for her new role. Roland stood by the door, looking painfully bored as the women explained their roles. Lady Margaret, the eldest, spoke firmly and without humor. "We are here to ensure that you fulfill your duties with grace and decorum, Your Highness."

Anastasia raised an eyebrow. "You're here to babysit me, is what you're saying." Lady Margaret stiffened, clearly unamused, while the youngest of the ladies, Lady Eleanor, stifled a laugh. Roland cleared his throat loudly, drawing Anastasia's attention. "I would advise against sarcasm," he said flatly. "It isn't well received here."

"Noted," Anastasia replied, though she couldn't resist rolling her eyes. Once her ladies-in-waiting had excused themselves, Roland sat across from Anastasia, his posture rigid as he began briefing her on royal etiquette. "And, of course," he added, "you must never speak out of turn or show disrespect in public." Anastasia leaned back in her chair, crossing her arms. "So, basically, be a perfectly obedient, poised doll at all times. Got it."

Roland's brow furrowed. "This is serious, Anastasia." "I know it's serious," she said quietly, her earlier sarcasm fading. "And that's what scares me." Roland's expression softened, though his words remained practical. "You won't be alone in this. I'll ensure you're prepared for whatever is required." Anastasia swallowed hard, her gaze dropping to the floor. "What if I'm not good enough?"

Roland paused, his voice gentler than before. "Then you'll fake it. That's what royals do."

The rest of the evening passed in a haze. Anastasia wandered through her quarters, her thoughts tangled and restless. The room was beautiful but cold, a gilded cage that felt more isolating than anything she'd ever known. She couldn't shake the fear gnawing at the edges of her mind: What if she failed? What if she couldn't survive this? She glanced out the window at the distant horizon, her chest tightening as she thought of the world she'd left behind.

She had done everything to stay composed today—to keep her fears from spilling over and to act like she was somewhat in control of her situation. But now, as the day settled into night, and she was left alone with her thoughts, the tightness in her chest became unbearable. Her throat burned, and her eyes stung, the tears threatening to spill over despite her best efforts to hold them back.

Anastasia paced the room, her bare feet sinking slightly into the plush carpet. The enormity of what had happened weighed heavily on her—married to a stranger, trapped in a century where she didn't belong, forced into a role she hadn't chosen. She thought about the life she had left behind. Her small but cozy apartment, her friends, the mornings where she drank coffee while the sunlight streamed through her kitchen window. And her grandmother. Her grandmother who had always been her anchor, her safe harbor, the one who sang to her when she couldn't sleep, whose gentle voice had carried her through the roughest storms.

She sank onto the edge of the bed, her hands trembling. A tear slipped down her cheek, followed by another, until the dam broke and she could no longer stop them. She buried her face in her hands and let herself cry. Her shoulders shook with each sob, and the room seemed colder as her sorrow filled it.

After a while, Anastasia's breathing slowed, though the ache in her chest remained. She leaned back against the pillows, pulling the thick, heavy covers over herself. But sleep felt impossibly far away. Her mind refused to quiet, her fear refusing to loosen its grip.

Then, faint and hesitant, she began to hum—a soft, tremulous melody that trembled in the still air. The lullaby was one her grandmother had sung to her every night as a child. The words were simple, but they carried warmth and comfort, a reminder that she was never truly alone.

Her voice cracked on the first note, but she kept singing, the sound growing stronger as the memory took hold.

"Rest your weary head, my dear, The night is calm, there's nothing to fear. Dream sweet dreams of skies so bright, Until the morning breaks the night..."

The melody carried her back to a time when she felt safe, wrapped in her grandmother's arms, free from the weight of expectations. She closed her eyes as the song continued, her voice faltering but steady enough to keep going. By the time she reached the final verse, her tears had dried, though her cheeks still burned. The song left her feeling hollow but calmer, her heartache dulled to something quieter.

As the final note drifted away, Anastasia curled up beneath the covers, her hands clutching the edge of the blanket as though it could shield her from the unfamiliar world beyond. The lullaby's warmth lingered, wrapping around her like a fragile embrace. Her breathing slowed, her exhaustion finally overtaking her, and the room faded into stillness as she drifted into uneasy sleep.

THREE

Anastasia awoke to the sound of the rustling of fabric, the low murmur of voices, and the soft clinking of porcelain against wood. Her bedchamber was already alive with motion, the servants moving efficiently, barely sparing her more than a glance before continuing their preparations.

She groaned, shifting beneath the silk sheets, not yet ready to face the day. Unfortunately, the day was already ready to face her. An older woman approached and offered a polite curtsy before announcing, "It is time to dress, Your Highness." Anastasia winced, barely holding back a sigh. Then came the corset.

She had little to no time before she suddenly found herself barely breathing. She inhaled and sucked in her stomach as the maid tied the corset up. "I am convinced this was designed as a medieval torture device," she muttered. One of the younger maids stifled a laugh, though the older maid merely continued securing the final ties. "It is tradition, Your Highness," the older maid reminded her. She exhaled, not gaining much breath back.

She stepped into the petticoat and then the skirt, feeling the warmth of the multiple layers immediately. Lastly were the shoes. Multiple pairs were lined up for her but her feet refused to fit into any of them. Eventually, they found a pair that fit and were finally done.

Anastasia had never truly appreciated the simplicity of modern clothing until she was forced into the endless nightmare that was Georgian fashion. The layers were suffocating—petticoats, chemise, stays, skirts, and an overdress so elaborate she was certain she could have built a small fort out of its fabric alone.

Breakfast was formal and suffocatingly silent, the nobles treating the meal less like an opportunity to eat and more like a test of patience and refined restraint. Anastasia stared at the pristine dishes, the lace-draped table, the quiet murmur of conversation that never rose above a certain dignified threshold. Roland sat several seats away, his expression neutral yet vaguely amused as he watched her struggle to figure out the correct utensil to use for the delicate pastries.

She made a slight mistake, reaching for the wrong knife. Roland arched a brow, barely suppressing a smirk. She caught the look, narrowed her eyes, and deliberately took a large bite, ignoring the careful, ladylike portions the others used. Roland let out a low, knowing hum, shaking his head. She considered kicking him under the table.

After breakfast, Lady Margaret, Lady Eleanor, and Lady Millicent arrived, dressed in impeccable layers of silk, lace, and ribbons, their postures perfect, their expressions unreadable yet quietly critical. Anastasia resisted the urge to sink deeper into her chair.

Lady Margaret clasped her hands before speaking. "There is much to teach you, Your Highness." Her tone was polite, but Anastasia could sense the underlying message, 'you are woefully unprepared'.

Lady Eleanor stepped forward first, explaining the proper use of titles and greetings. "When speaking to a duke, you say 'Your Grace'. To a prince, 'Your Royal Highness'. To a baron, simply 'Lord' and, of course, to the king, 'Your Majesty.'"

Anastasia tilted her head, frowning slightly. "What if I just... say their name?" Lady Millicent visibly stiffened. Lady Eleanor pressed her lips into a thin line before stating firmly, "That is not done." Anastasia sighed. "Of course not."

The ladies led Anastasia into a spacious corridor, its polished floors gleaming under the sunlight streaming through tall windows. Lady Margaret gestured for her to stand at attention. "You must move with grace, Your Highness. Each step must be measured, delicate, controlled." Anastasia hesitated before taking a step forward, her shoulders too stiff, her stride too forceful.

Lady Eleanor winced. Lady Millicent let out a quiet sigh of defeat. Lady Margaret pinched the bridge of her nose.

"You are walking as though preparing for battle." Anastasia crossed her arms. "Well, given how much effort is put into keeping women passive, I should have expected this criticism." Lady Eleanor ignored her remark, stepping forward. "Watch me," she instructed, gliding effortlessly down the corridor, her movements smooth and elegant. Anastasia sighed deeply, resigning herself to yet another lesson in restriction.

Seated in an ornate drawing room, Anastasia was handed a delicate porcelain teacup, which she quickly learned was a test of refinement.

Lady Millicent demonstrated the correct way to hold the cup—elbow slightly bent, fingers carefully placed, posture impeccable. Anastasia mimicked the motion, only to hear a soft, scandalized inhale from Lady Eleanor. "You must not lift your pinky."

Anastasia stared at her. "I beg your pardon?"

Lady Millicent sighed. "It is considered improper." Anastasia slowly lowered her pinky, muttering, "This feels ridiculous." Lady Margaret offered a pointed look. "This is court life, Your Highness. It is not meant to feel natural. It is meant to be controlled." Anastasia forced a smile, though there was little warmth behind it.

The lesson continued, an exhausting lecture on court politics, alliances, and manipulative diplomacy. Anastasia struggled immensely, the sheer weight of expectations pressing down on her.

"That's shady," she muttered under her breath after hearing about some noble's dubious dealings.

Silence.

Lady Eleanor, Lady Margaret, and Lady Millicent all stiffened immediately, their expressions horrified. Lady Eleanor blinked slowly. "That is... not a word we use." Anastasia, realizing her mistake, cleared her throat, feigning innocence. "Ah. I meant—questionable. Very questionable." Lady Margaret rubbed at her temple, clearly beginning to wonder if this was a lost cause.

Anastasia had spent the last hour attempting to walk properly, or at least attempting not to stomp around like a disgruntled soldier. The palace corridors were wide, grand, unforgiving, filled with watchful eyes and perfectly poised nobles, all expecting her to glide like an effortless vision of grace and elegance.

Unfortunately, grace was not in Anastasia's immediate skill set. And Roland knew it. She rounded a corner too quickly, nearly colliding with him where he stood, arms crossed, looking entirely too amused for his own good. "I see you've taken to charging through the palace like a bull," he remarked dryly, raising an eyebrow.

Anastasia straightened, smoothing down the layers of her gown with as much dignity as she could muster. "Oh, I deeply apologize, Your Royal Highness," she drawled, her tone thick with mock reverence, "for failing to move with the same effortless arrogance you do."

Roland chuckled under his breath, tilting his head slightly as he took in her posture. "Your posture is wrong."

"Your attitude is worse," she countered.

He smirked, unbothered. "Perhaps. But I am not the one expected to be the embodiment of refinement."

Anastasia rolled her eyes, stepping past him, only for Roland to casually fall into step beside her, continuing his assessment.

"You carry yourself too rigidly," he pointed out, ignoring her growing frustration. "A princess must move with effortless confidence, not like a woman preparing for battle."

Anastasia exhaled sharply, resisting the urge to shove him into a wall. "I feel like a decorative object shoved into a display case," she muttered. "Walking is apparently another skill I must master, as if I were a child learning to use my legs for the first time."

Roland glanced at her sidelong, expression unreadable, before offering a single piece of practical advice. "Stop thinking about how you're supposed to look," he said simply. "If you carry yourself as though you're being watched, you'll always seem uncomfortable."

Anastasia blinked at him, caught off guard by the lack of sarcasm in his voice. She expected mockery. Instead, there was a flicker of something approaching sincerity. She held his gaze for a beat, wondering if he was capable of being decent after all.

Then Roland ruined it.

"Not that it helps," he added, "but I suppose even a disaster can be improved slightly." Anastasia gasped dramatically, placing a hand over her chest. "How generous of you! Truly, what would I do without your unwavering support?" Roland snorted, shaking his head, but said nothing else.

Anastasia had never considered herself particularly antisocial—if anything, back home, she thrived in groups, adored lively debates, and found herself drawn to the energy of others. But here? Here, within the suffocating walls of Georgian court life?

Every single person grated on her nerves.

She had spent the past half-hour attempting to socialize, forced into a gathering of noble ladies, all of whom seemed perfectly content discussing embroidery, lace patterns, and the newest shipment of imported silks.

Anastasia tried to engage, she really did. But after listening to Lady Augusta drone on about the exquisite detail of French lace versus English craftsmanship, she felt her soul shriveling in protest. She shifted in her seat, resisting the urge to groan.

She shifted in her seat, resisting the urge to groan.

"How fascinating," she forced out, though her tone barely concealed her suffering. Lady Augusta beamed, oblivious. "Indeed, Your Highness!" she chirped, smoothing out the delicate folds of her gown. "One must always remember—the fabric does not simply speak of wealth, but of refinement! Our choices define us, wouldn't you say?" Anastasia blinked slowly, processing the sheer weight of nonsense that had just been spoken to her.

"I—suppose?" Lady Augusta nodded enthusiastically, launching into another lecture about the importance of knowing where silk is sourced from. Anastasia fought the urge to throw herself into the nearest fireplace.

Lady Eleanor, ever the quiet observer, eventually steered the conversation toward court rumors—which nobles were secretly feuding, who had embarrassed themselves at the last gathering, and which lord was suspected of losing a fortune to gambling.

This, at least, was more tolerable.

Anastasia leaned forward, interest flickering in her expression. "And what is the latest scandal?" Lady Eleanor glanced around before lowering her voice. "Lord Piers was seen leaving Lady Arabella's chambers at dawn." There was a quiet gasp from the group, the ladies exchanging scandalized glances. Anastasia raised an eyebrow, unimpressed.

"Dawn?" she mused. "I assumed affairs were conducted at much more dramatic hours—midnight, candlelight flickering ominously, stolen whispers down the corridor—" Lady Millicent looked deeply confused, while Lady Augusta appeared downright horrified. "Affairs should never be spoken of so lightly, Your Highness," Lady Augusta chided.

Anastasia shrugged, feigning innocence. "I was merely suggesting they add a bit of flair. If one is going to be caught sneaking out of someone's chambers, they might as well make it a story worth telling." Lady Eleanor pressed her lips together, clearly fighting amusement, but Lady Millicent looked as though she might faint from the sheer audacity of the remark.

As if conversation wasn't miserable enough, Lady Margaret soon insisted Anastasia learn the finer points of courtly dancing, ushering her toward the ballroom. She was taught the motions—how to step, glide, turn with precise control, ensuring her movements were poised, elegant, refined.

Anastasia struggled immensely.

Her natural instincts screamed for freedom—she wanted to move naturally, effortlessly, but here, everything was forced into meticulous precision. Lady Margaret corrected her at least five times before sighing deeply.

"You must follow your partner's lead, Your Highness." Anastasia huffed, crossing her arms. "What if my partner is terrible?"

Lady Margaret blinked, thrown off by the question. "That would be quite unfortunate," she admitted carefully. Anastasia smirked, tilting her head. "Then I'd much rather dance alone, wouldn't I?" The ladies exchanged bewildered glances, clearly uncertain what to do with her unfiltered logic.

After two painfully long hours, Anastasia excused herself, slipping away from the stifling gathering, desperate for fresh air, solitude, silence. She wandered the halls, her frustration buzzing beneath her skin. It wasn't just the rules, the suffocating traditions, the ridiculous expectations. It was the people.

So perfectly sculpted, so obsessed with appearances, so determined to fit their roles without question. She felt like a foreign body dropped into the middle of a performance, expected to read from a script she had never rehearsed. And no matter how much she tried, she could not play the part.

That night, Anastasia sat alone in her chambers, the fire casting warm, flickering light against the walls. She stared at her reflection in the mirror. The pinned curls. The delicate gown. The image of a princess, not a person.

Her own face felt unfamiliar, as though she was seeing someone else entirely—someone shaped by expectations, bound by duty, caught in a world that did not truly belong to her. She sighed, pressing her fingers against the polished vanity, the weight of it all settling heavily on her shoulders.

FOUR

The morning sun crept into Anastasia's quarters, warming the elaborate curtains and casting soft golden light onto the silk canopy above her bed. She blinked groggily, the heavy ache in her chest reminding her that the events of the previous day hadn't been a dream. The opulent room around her—the enormous bed, the gilded furnishings, the perfectly arranged vases of flowers—felt more suffocating than awe-inspiring.

Rolling onto her side, Anastasia stared at the distant horizon visible through the tall windows, her hands clutching the edge of the blanket like a shield. Somewhere out there was the world she belonged to—the world she understood. But for now, she was stuck in this one. A soft knock at the door disrupted her thoughts. She sat up quickly, smoothing her hair and straightening her borrowed nightgown. "Come in," she called, her voice subdued.

Lady Margaret entered first, her steps precise and her expression neutral as ever. Behind her, Lady Eleanor and Lady Beatrice followed, their hands folded politely in front of them. "Good morning, Your Highness," Margaret said, tilting her head slightly. "We have prepared your itinerary for the day. His Royal Highness awaits your presence in the drawing room to discuss royal duties."

Anastasia resisted the urge to groan. Instead, she offered a faint smile. "Thank you, Margaret. I'll be ready shortly." Anastasia found Roland pacing in the drawing room, his posture rigid as he scanned the scroll in his hand. He barely looked at her when she entered, though his expression tightened slightly at the sight of her. If the previous day had been a whirlwind of confusion, this morning was no calmer. Roland had the air of someone who was perpetually displeased, and Anastasia wasn't sure she had the energy to match his mood.

"Good morning," she said politely, keeping her voice even. Roland glanced at her, nodding curtly. "You're late." Anastasia fought the urge to roll her eyes. "I'll keep that in mind tomorrow." He ignored her reply, gesturing toward the chair across from him. "Sit. We need to discuss today's obligations."

She obeyed, settling into the stiff-backed chair as Roland began listing their responsibilities with an air of authority. His tone was brisk and matter-of-fact, as though he were instructing her on battle strategy. Anastasia tried to keep up, nodding along as he explained their first task: meeting with several dignitaries to discuss matters of trade. "After which, you are to join me in visiting the village."

"Village?" she repeated, her brow furrowing slightly. Roland looked at her, his gaze flat. "Yes. It's a public appearance." Anastasia bit her lip, her nerves rising. "And... what exactly do I do during a public appearance?" "Smile," Roland replied bluntly. "Speak to the people. Act as though you care." She raised an eyebrow, though she kept her sarcasm buried. "I'll do my best." Roland hesitated for a moment, studying her. "I assume you understand how important these appearances are?"

"I do," Anastasia said quietly, her hands folded tightly in her lap. "And I don't intend to draw any more attention to myself than I already have." Roland nodded once, seemingly satisfied, and rose from his chair. "Then we should begin."

The air hung thick with the inviting aromas of warm bread, sweet chestnuts, and the metallic scent of the blacksmith's trade. Cobblestone streets, polished smooth by countless feet, snaked through the village, flanked by vibrant stalls laden with fabrics, overflowing fruit, and unique handcrafted wares. A wave of excited anticipation rippled through the crowd as the rumble of Anastasia and Roland's carriage announced their arrival.

Anastasia swallowed her nerves as the carriage came to a halt. She barely registered Roland stepping out first, his practiced movements as effortless as breathing. When he turned, extending a hand to her, she took it without hesitation, letting him guide her down onto the cobblestone.

The murmurs in the crowd thickened. Anastasia could feel their eyes on her—their curiosity, their whispers threading through the air like invisible strings. She straightened her posture, smoothing the fabric of her gown as she forced a smile. *Don't draw any more attention to yourself than necessary. Blend in. Be gracious.*

She took a step forward, scanning the eager faces until she caught sight of a little girl clutching a small bouquet of wildflowers. Her cheeks were rosy with excitement, her dress slightly worn but clean. When their eyes met, the girl's grip tightened around the stems, as though summoning the courage to move.

"Go on, Lizzie," an older woman—her mother, perhaps—encouraged gently. The girl swallowed hard, then stepped forward hesitantly, her tiny hands trembling. "For you, Your Highness," she said in a small voice, holding out the flowers.

Anastasia's smile softened, genuine now. She crouched slightly, accepting the bouquet with careful hands. "These are beautiful," she said warmly. "Did you pick them yourself?"

Lizzie nodded quickly. "Yes, near the old bridge." Anastasia inhaled the faint, earthy scent of the blossoms. "You have a good eye for flowers, Lizzie." The girl beamed, and her mother bowed deeply. "We welcome you, Your Highness. The people are eager to see what kind of princess you will be." Anastasia's breath hitched at the words, but she forced herself to nod politely. "I hope I can serve England well."

With a slow, deliberate gait aided by a walking cane, an elderly man approached. Wrinkles etched deep into his hands hinted at a life of hard work. Despite his age, he offered Anastasia a respectful nod, his eyes studying her with quiet consideration.

"You must forgive my forwardness, Princess, but we were not expecting Prince Roland to take a wife so suddenly." Anastasia glanced at Roland, who stood beside her with his usual impassive demeanor. He wasn't offering much help.

"Yes," Anastasia said cautiously. "It was unexpected for many." The old man studied her with the wisdom of someone who had seen far too many rulers come and go. "A princess has power, you know," he murmured, almost as though testing her. "Not just in name, but in what she chooses to do for her people. If you ever find yourself with such a choice, I hope you choose kindness."

Anastasia's fingers tightened slightly around the bouquet. She wasn't sure what to say to that—wasn't sure if she had any real choice at all.

"I'll remember that," she said finally, meeting his gaze with quiet sincerity. "Thank you." The man nodded once before retreating into the crowd. Anastasia moved through to the marketplace, engaging with the vendors. She inquired about their crafts and listened to fragments of their lives, her questions revealing genuine interest. While maintaining a composed demeanor, she found herself captivated by the people's genuine openness—their laughter, their sincerity, and their welcoming attitude, which treated her visit not as a curiosity, but as a chance for connection.

A baker offered her a small roll, presenting it with reverence due to it being a recipe passed down through his lineage for three generations. She accepted, taking a bite. The flavour was an immediate revelation – profoundly rich, it seemed to melt on her tongue, prompting a soft, surprised hum of pure pleasure. Looking at the baker, her eyes alight, she declared, "You have an extraordinary gift, sir. Now I understand perfectly why this recipe has endured for years." A wide smile spread across the baker's face, chest puffing visibly with pride. "The privilege would be entirely mine," he said, "to prepare something for you at the castle one day."

"I would love that," Anastasia replied, and she meant it. A seamstress displayed bolts of patterned fabric, describing the difficulty of dyeing certain materials and how the trade had changed over the years. "Fabric carries stories," she mused as Anastasia ran her fingers over the fine linen. "Every weave, every stitch tells something of the person who wears it and the person that made it."

Anastasia thought of her wedding gown—the one she barely had time to comprehend before being thrust into ceremony. What did it say about her? That she was a stranger forced into a role she didn't understand? That she didn't belong?

"It's a beautiful craft," she said gently. By the time the visit ended, Anastasia's nerves had settled somewhat. She wasn't *comfortable*, not by any means, but something about the village—the people, their voices, their gentle encouragement—made the impossible situation feel slightly less unbearable.

As the carriage door shut behind her, she turned to Roland, whose silence had been consistent throughout the outing. "I think that went well," she offered. Roland, looking out the window, didn't immediately reply. Then, after a pause, he murmured, "It was adequate."

Anastasia stiffened, her earlier relief fading. *Adequate.* That was all it had been to him? She fought the urge to argue, instead folding her hands neatly in her lap, mirroring his posture. "Well, I suppose I'll need to do better tomorrow." Roland finally looked at her, his expression unreadable. He inclined his head slightly—a silent acknowledgment.

Anastasia turned her gaze to the streets as the carriage rolled forward, watching the people disappear into the distance. Their faces lingered in her mind—their warmth, their quiet expectations. She had no idea if she could ever become the princess they hoped she'd be. But for now, she had no choice but to try.

The morning had passed in a blur of royal obligations, rehearsed smiles, and the exhausting weight of performing a role Anastasia had never wanted. By midday, she found herself seated in the grand parlor, her mind drifting as she absentmindedly traced the rim of her teacup. The quiet was shattered by a soft, hesitant knock at the door.

Anastasia straightened, glancing up just as the door creaked open to reveal a woman. She was young, thin, and visibly exhausted. Her dark complexion was dulled by pallor, and her frail frame trembled slightly as she curtsied. Despite the effort to maintain composure, Anastasia could see the strain etched into her face.

"My lady," the woman said, her voice weak but steady. "I am Evelina. His Highness assigned me to oversee your care." Anastasia frowned. She had yet to meet many of the castle attendants, but something about this moment felt wrong, forced. Evelina was clearly unwell, yet she had been sent to serve regardless. Anastasia stood abruptly, moving toward her with quiet determination. "You're sick," she said gently, her brow furrowing. "You shouldn't be here."

Evelina hesitated, her hands twisting together anxiously. "I—I apologize, my lady. It is not my place to—"

"I don't care about places," Anastasia interrupted, her voice firm but kind. "You need rest. You're barely standing as it is." Evelina's gaze darted toward the door, panic flickering in her eyes. "If I do not serve, I will be dismissed."

Anastasia felt a sharp pang of frustration. The idea that someone could be forced to work themselves into the ground just to remain under the protection of the castle made her stomach twist.

"No," Anastasia said quietly. "I won't allow that." Evelina blinked at her, uncertainty warring with relief. "You are not serving anyone like this," Anastasia continued, gently placing a hand on Evelina's arm. "Go back to bed. Rest. I'll handle everything else."

Evelina's lips parted, a protest forming—but Anastasia was already gesturing toward the door. "Go," she urged softly. "You're under *my* care now." For a moment, Evelina hesitated. Then, as if the weight of exhaustion was finally unbearable, she nodded slowly and backed away, murmuring a quiet, breathless "Thank you, my lady."

As soon as Evelina left, Anastasia turned toward the doorway, her mind racing. Modern medicine didn't exist here—no antibiotics, no pain relievers—but there had to be something she could do. A memory surfaced—her grandmother's soothing voice, the warmth of her hands as she handed Anastasia a cup of ginger tea whenever she was sick.

Ginger.

That was something. That was a start.

Without hesitation, Anastasia turned on her heel, scanning the room until she found Lady Margaret seated near the far window, watching the exchange in silence. "Margaret," Anastasia said, urgency creeping into her tone, "I need to go to the village."

Margaret straightened, her sharp eyes flickering with suspicion. "Whatever for, Your Highness?" "For Evelina," Anastasia replied. "She needs something—anything—that will help her recover, and I don't know what resources the castle has." Margaret studied her for a long moment before standing. "You should not leave the castle without proper arrangements."

"I won't be gone long," Anastasia insisted. "I just need—" Before she could finish, a voice cut through the room like steel. "You're not going anywhere." Anastasia turned swiftly to find Roland standing in the doorway, his arms crossed, his expression severe.

Her frustration surged. "Roland, she needs medicine. I need to—"

"You *will not* leave the castle unaccompanied," Roland interrupted, his tone firm. "It isn't safe." Anastasia bristled, her hands clenching into fists. "I can take care of myself."

"You don't know this world well enough yet," Roland countered, stepping forward. "You could be recognized, followed, put into danger. I will not allow it." Anastasia glared at him. "So your solution is to do nothing?"

Roland sighed, exasperated. "Margaret will go." Margaret inclined her head. "I will personally see to the matter, Your Highness." Anastasia opened her mouth to argue again, but something about Margaret's steady demeanor reassured her. Slowly, she exhaled.

"Fine," she muttered. "Thank you. I just need ginger root" Margaret nodded and dipped into a respectful curtsey before leaving. The heavy doors shut behind Margaret, leaving the room in uneasy silence. Anastasia exhaled sharply, pressing her lips together to stifle the frustration burning in her chest.

She turned toward Roland, who remained near the doorway, arms crossed, his expression unreadable. "You didn't have to do that," she said, her voice calmer than she felt. Roland's gaze flickered slightly, but he remained firm. "I did."

"No, you didn't."

"You have no understanding of the dangers outside these walls," Roland countered, voice measured but edged with impatience. "You assume that because the people smiled at you yesterday, you are safe." Anastasia bristled. "They didn't just smile. They spoke to me. They welcomed me."

Roland scoffed. "A marketplace crowd is hardly an indication of lasting acceptance. You are still a stranger here. If anything, your presence brings curiosity—curiosity that can turn into scrutiny, or worse, if you are careless."

Anastasia forced herself to hold his gaze, refusing to shrink under his cautionary tone. "This isn't just about me," she said finally. "Evelina shouldn't have been forced to work when she was sick. And I wasn't about to stand by and let that happen."

Roland's jaw tensed at the mention of Evelina. He glanced toward the window, as if weighing his next words. "You care too much," he muttered. She let out a bitter laugh. "And you don't care enough."

Roland's eyes snapped back to her, sharp and assessing. For a moment, neither of them spoke, the weight of their differences stretching between them. Finally, Roland straightened. "Regardless, you will not leave the castle unescorted." Anastasia clenched her fists, but she swallowed the words threatening to escape. She had already drawn enough attention. A further argument would only fuel the perception that she was unruly.

"Fine," she said stiffly.

Roland nodded once, then stepped past her, leaving her alone in the vast chamber.

The rest of the afternoon passed in a haze. Anastasia went through the motions of etiquette lessons with Margaret, but the earlier confrontation lingered in her mind. As she sipped tea in the grand parlor, her eyes drifted to the heavy-bound books stacked along the far wall. She had seen them before—collections of history, records of noble bloodlines, and documentation of past rulers. If she couldn't search the village for answers, then perhaps she could start here.

When the ladies-in-waiting excused themselves for their midday rest, Anastasia slipped from her seat, crossing the parlor in quiet steps. She ran her fingers over the spines of the books, scanning the titles for anything connected to Elsmere Manor. One caught her eye. It was bound in blue leather, separating it from the shades of brown surrounding it. **'English Mythologies: A Collection of English Myths and Legends'**

She pulled it from the shelf, the leather warm beneath her fingers. Flipping through the pages, she found references to witches, demons, dragons. Nothing of any use. Suddenly, there it was. Her stomach twisted as she spotted a passage about time travel. "It is said that certain locations, touched by great emotion or sacrifice, may become bound to the fabric of time itself. A force unknown may weave these places into history, allowing them to serve as conduits between past and present."

Her breath hitched as she read on.

"A passage through time may be strengthened or controlled through binding—a ritual requiring three elements: a living soul, an object of significance, and a moment of great consequence. Once bound, the location may pull those connected to its magic forward or backward through time, allowing destiny to repeat or be rewritten."

Anastasia's pulse quickened. Was this the answer? Had Elsmere Manor been bound to time itself, forcing her displacement? Had something—someone—triggered it? Before she could read further, the door creaked open behind her.

Anastasia stiffened, heart pounding, as Roland stepped into the library, eyes immediately narrowing at the book in her hands. "A princess shouldn't read," he said evenly, though something in his tone hinted at curiosity rather than criticism. She glanced up at him, forcing her features into neutrality. "Yeah, well a prince shouldn't complain so much but here we are." Roland crossed the room, casting a glance at the book in her grip. His brows furrowed slightly, but he didn't comment.

Anastasia swallowed, closing the book as discreetly as she could. For now, she would keep this discovery to herself. Elsmere was bound to time. And somehow, she had to find a way to unbind it.

FIVE

Anastasia's visit to the village had planted a seed, one that now grew steadily, spreading through the streets like an untamed vine, threading its way into whispered conversations and lingering glances. She was no longer just a figure in the palace, a name murmured in passing. She was discussed in taverns, praised in the marketplace, debated in quiet corners, her presence sparking a rare sense of possibility among the people.

Merchants spoke of how she walked among them with ease, unguarded and unafraid, how she did not recoil from the mud-streaked streets or the coarse language of workers unloading carts. Farmers told tales of how she stopped to listen, truly listen, her expression filled with the kind of attentiveness rarely seen in figures of nobility.

Some stories grew in embellishment, becoming something larger than life. She was bold, fiery, determined, a woman who would not be tamed by tradition, who spoke her mind without caution, whose very presence felt like a defiance of centuries-old expectations. The court, of course, had taken notice.

At dinner, nobles exchanged subtle glances behind gilded goblets, their voices carefully measured, as though weighing whether her popularity was harmless intrigue or dangerous influence. Evelina, watching this shift unfold, merely found it entertaining. She leaned against the stone railing of the terrace, sipping her water as she observed Anastasia staring down at the city below.

"You are either destined to be loved or feared," she mused, swirling the opaque liquid in her goblet. "And it seems the people have chosen love." Anastasia exhaled, tapping her fingers absentmindedly against the cool stone. "I'm sure the court would rather they chose fear," she murmured. Evelina smirked. "Then the court is full of fools."

When Anastasia returned to the village days later, the change was immediate. Where before there had been curiosity tinged with hesitance, now there was genuine warmth. She walked through the bustling marketplace, her steps purposeful yet unguarded, and the people welcomed her as if she were one of their own. An elderly woman stepped forward with a bright-eyed smile, pressing a ribbon into Anastasia's palm.

"For luck, Princess," she said, voice warm with familiarity, as if she were gifting a beloved granddaughter something precious. A young baker, flour dusting his sleeves, offered her a freshly baked pastry, grinning as he insisted, "A gift, Your Highness. No coin needed. You gave me a moment of your time, I give you this in return." Anastasia's chest tightened in quiet astonishment, but before she could fully register it, a small tug at her sleeve caught her attention.

She glanced down to see a little girl, no older than five, staring up at her with wide, admiring eyes. Clutched tightly in her tiny fist was a delicate pressed flower, its petals slightly crumpled from her grip.

"You remind me of the women in stories," the girl whispered, her voice timid yet certain. "The ones who are brave." Something in Anastasia fractured at the words, not in pain, but in recognition—as if the child had unknowingly plucked a thread loose within her. She knelt down, taking the flower without hesitation, her smile soft but real. "Then I suppose I must remain brave." The girl giggled, running back to her mother, who offered Anastasia a grateful nod before disappearing into the crowd.

The warmth of the marketplace settled into Anastasia's bones, each conversation a quiet reassurance that, despite everything, perhaps she did belong somewhere after all. But then—something shifted. She caught sight of a married couple standing at a vendor's stall, discussing prices with the merchant.

Nothing seemed unusual at first. Then, as the husband reached out, placing his hand on his wife's arm—she flinched. Not noticeably. Not dramatically. But enough for Anastasia to see it. Enough for her stomach to tighten in response.

The wife's posture was rigid, her voice too quiet, too careful, as though every word she spoke had been rehearsed to perfection before leaving her lips. The husband's tone was smooth, polite, his grip firm without being overtly controlling, his gaze watchful in a way that did not seem obvious—but was undeniable nonetheless. Anastasia's heart beat uncomfortably against her ribs, instinct settling in before logic could catch up.

She stepped forward, speaking gently, trying to engage the woman directly, offering her a question—something simple, something harmless. But the wife did not fully lift her chin, only murmured a brief, restrained response, not meeting Anastasia's gaze. It was as though she was waiting for approval before allowing herself to speak freely. Evelina, standing beside her, observed the interaction with quiet intensity, her expression unreadable.

As the couple departed, Anastasia leaned toward Evelina, voice low, deliberate. "Something isn't right." Evelina continued to watch their retreating figures, her lips pressed into a thin line, eyes darker than usual. "There are things that cannot be fixed with kindness alone, Anastasia," she murmured, her tone holding a quiet weight.

Anastasia's pulse quickened, her fingers clenching slightly at her sides. She wanted to argue, to say something hopeful, certain, but the words did not come. Because Evelina was right and knowing that unsettled her far more than she cared to admit.

✳✳✳

The study was dimly lit, a low fire crackling in the hearth, sending shadows flickering against the stone walls. The scent of parchment and ink lingered in the space, mingling with the faint trace of aged whiskey from the decanter on Roland's desk.

Anastasia stood in the doorway, arms folded tightly, her jaw set with quiet frustration. She had spent the evening trying to push aside what she had seen—the woman's silent fear, the way she flinched, the quiet tension in her posture.

But she couldn't let it go.

"I met a woman today," she announced, not bothering with pleasantries, her voice holding a weight that had not settled since she left the village. Roland barely glanced up, his attention still fixed on whatever tedious document lay before him. "There are many women in this kingdom," he replied evenly, though his tone held a faint edge of curiosity despite his detached posture.

Anastasia stepped forward, not allowing him to dismiss her that easily. "She was afraid," she stated, watching for his reaction.

Roland paused—only for a fraction of a second, a breath of hesitation before he continued scribbling in his journal. "Some women are timid." Anastasia narrowed her eyes, feeling her frustration build like storm clouds tightening over the horizon.

"It wasn't timidity, Roland. It was fear." Roland exhaled quietly, finally setting down his quill as he leaned back in his chair, observing her with calculating patience. "And what do you expect *me* to do?" His tone was not mocking, but neither was it welcoming of debate.

Anastasia huffed, crossing her arms tighter. "I expect you to care." Roland's expression flickered just barely, a shift so minute it might not have been noticeable had she not been watching for it. He ran a hand through his hair, then stood, his posture as composed as ever. "It is not your place to interfere in a marriage." The words hit harder than she expected.

Not because they were cruel, but because they carried the weight of centuries-old expectations—ones she had never subscribed to. Her voice sharpened. "So I should do nothing?"

Roland held her gaze, sighing deeply, his jaw tightening before he responded. "No," he admitted at last, "You should do what you always do—create trouble and hope you survive it." Anastasia blinked once, thrown by his phrasing.

Anastasia blinked once, thrown by his phrasing. Then—she smirked despite herself, though her frustration still simmered beneath the surface.

"You say that like it's a bad thing." Roland let out a slow breath, somewhere between exasperation and amusement, as if acknowledging that this was an argument he would never win.

He studied her for a long moment, and there was something unreadable resting beneath his gaze, something restrained but present. Then, with a quiet shake of his head, he muttered, "Perhaps not entirely."

The lingering unease wrapped itself around Anastasia like an unseen thread, pulling at the corners of her mind, refusing to be ignored. The palace was silent in the early morning, the halls bathed in soft sunlight, but her thoughts were loud. She couldn't leave this alone. So, she slipped into a cloak, pulling the hood up as she navigated through the winding streets, keeping her steps light and purposeful.

The marketplace was already alive with motion—vendors shouting their prices, children weaving between stalls, the scent of fresh bread and burning tallow heavy in the air. She asked carefully, speaking in passing conversation, weaving curiosity into idle remarks.

"There was a woman I met yesterday, fair hair, quiet voice, married to—what was his name? Thomas? She seemed rather withdrawn." The merchant she spoke to hesitated, his fingers briefly tightening around the edge of his stall. "Don't know much about them," he said. "Husband's got influence. People don't ask questions." Anastasia narrowed her eyes slightly, feeling something settle—cold and sharp—beneath her ribs.

She spotted the woman near the well, standing alone for the first time, a basket balanced carefully against her hip. Anastasia approached with careful, deliberate ease, ensuring her presence wasn't intrusive or demanding.

"Good morning," she greeted, offering a smile that was warm but not overwhelming. The woman startled slightly, her hands tightening around the handle of her basket. "Your Highness," she murmured, bowing her head. Anastasia tilted her head, studying the way her posture seemed drawn inward, as if she were trying to take up as little space as possible.

"You don't have to bow," she said lightly. "I was hoping for conversation, not formalities." The woman hesitated, flicking a glance over her shoulder, her movements sharp, instinctive. Anastasia followed her gaze—but there was no one there. Still, the fear remained. "I've noticed you always seem very quiet," Anastasia continued carefully. "Is that intentional?"

The woman swallowed, adjusting the basket against her hip, her fingers twisting into the fabric of her sleeve. "It is proper for a wife to be reserved," she said finally, voice barely above a whisper. Anastasia's stomach tightened uncomfortably. "Proper—according to whom?"

Silence.

"Your husband?" The woman tensed, her fingers clutching tightly at the woven handles of her basket. And then—a sharp inhale, barely audible. She glanced around quickly, almost fearfully, scanning the nearby streets. "I must go." She turned too fast, nearly fumbling the basket as she hurried away, her steps uneven, rushed. Anastasia didn't move—only stood there, watching her retreat. And suddenly, the morning air felt much colder than it had before.

Later that evening, Anastasia paced the palace hallway, irritation buzzing beneath her skin like trapped electricity. Evelina sat on a nearby embroidered chaise, observing Anastasia. "You look like a caged animal," Evelina observed. "Perhaps the lion in you needs to rest." Anastasia huffed sharply, stopping in her tracks as she turned to face her. "She's afraid," she muttered, rubbing her temples. "I see it, feel it, and yet—"

"And yet there is nothing you can do," she finished simply. Anastasia stiffened, annoyance flaring. "That is an excuse." Evelina's smirk faded slightly, her gaze turning sharper, holding a weight that felt older than her years.

"It is a truth you refuse to acknowledge," she murmured, setting down her glass. "The power you have here is not infinite, Anastasia. You think you can tear apart generations of unspoken rules because it feels right. But do you even know what she wants?" Anastasia froze, pulse beating against her ribs.

✳✳✳

The study was quiet, illuminated only by the soft glow of candlelight, shadows flickering against the thick bookshelves lining the walls. Roland still sat at his desk, focused, expression unreadable, his posture one of effortless control.

Anastasia stepped inside, her movements slower than usual, lacking her usual sharp bite of irritation. "What happens to a woman who wishes to leave her husband?" Roland paused, fingers tightening just slightly around the edge of the parchment in front of him. His gaze lifted to hers, something cautious resting beneath it. "If she is a noble?" he asked carefully. "If she is anyone," Anastasia corrected.

Roland leaned back, crossing his arms, his jaw tensing before he responded. "She has two choices. Stay. Or leave and have nowhere to go." Anastasia's stomach twisted, cold and sharp. "And what if she has reason to fear him?" Roland's eyes darkened, but he didn't answer immediately. "Then she must have proof." Anastasia swallowed, her grip tightening at her sides.

She had wanted to help. She had wanted to fix it. But she wasn't playing with childhood dreams of heroes saving victims. This was real, and there was no easy escape. She had to find proof. No one else would.

The weight of Roland's words settled like stone in Anastasia's chest, cold and heavy. Proof was a difficult thing—not just to find, but to use. A woman could have bruises, have whispers, have fear written across her skin, and still, people would turn away. It wasn't about what was real. It was about what could be ignored. And Anastasia refused to ignore it.

She exhaled, running her fingers across the edge of the desk, as if searching for something solid—something that wouldn't slip between her fingers like smoke. "Then I'll get proof," she said simply, the conviction in her voice clearer than it had ever been before.

Roland studied her for a moment, his expression steady, unreadable. Then—a quiet sigh, a faint shake of the head, as if acknowledging that there was no stopping her now. "Do what you want," he muttered. "You always do."

The next morning, Anastasia returned to the village, this time with purpose. She didn't disguise herself, didn't try to blend into the crowds. She wanted the woman to see her. To know she was there. She found her near the church, hands folded tightly, posture drawn inward like she was trying to disappear into herself.

Anastasia approached slowly. "May I walk with you?" The woman startled slightly, looking up at her as if she wasn't sure whether she had imagined the request.

After a beat, she nodded.

They walked in silence for several moments, the village streets humming with quiet life around them, the scent of fresh pastries wafting from nearby stalls. Finally, Anastasia spoke. "I know you are afraid." The woman's breath caught, her fingers tensing against the folds of her gown. "I don't know what you mean." Anastasia tilted her head, watching her carefully. "You do."

Silence.

Then—a quick glance over her shoulder, her movements sharp, instinctive, as if expecting someone to be watching. Her lips parted slightly, as though she wanted to say something, but hesitated at the last moment. So Anastasia waited. She would not push her. She would only give her space to breathe.

Finally, a whisper, barely more than a breath. "No one would believe me." Anastasia stopped walking, turning fully toward her. "I would." The woman stared at her, something fragile flickering in her gaze, something on the edge of breaking.

Anastasia waited, standing beside her, allowing the weight of the moment to settle without force, without urgency. It was not her place to decide when someone was ready to speak their truth. It was only her place to listen. The woman exhaled slowly, her fingers twisting into the fabric of her gown.

The woman glanced at her once, fleeting, almost apologetic, before gripping her basket and stepping back. "You must not come looking for me again." And just like that—she turned, disappearing into the crowd

Anastasia stood still, watching her leave, her pulse a slow, measured rhythm beneath her ribs. She had expected resistance. But the quiet, restrained warning sat too heavy in her chest, like something carved into stone—unchangeable, final. Still—she would not let this go. Not yet.

The study was silent. Roland sat in the high-backed chair by the window, the moon

casting a faint glow across the wood-paneled walls, his fingers loosely curled around a half-empty goblet of wine. The room should have been a refuge—a space where political duties and court expectations could be set aside, if only for a moment. But his mind was restless.

Anastasia's voice lingered. "So I should do nothing?" She did not ask questions lightly. She demanded answers. She expected action. And that, that was what set her apart from the rest of them. She was stubborn, infuriating, reckless. And yet, she was right more often than anyone was willing to admit.

Roland took a slow sip of his wine, watching the city through the window, its streets illuminated only by the occasional lantern flickering in the dark. The people were talking about her now. He had heard the whispers.

A royal unlike the rest. A princess who did not shy away. A future queen, perhaps, who might actually change something. He had never cared much for speculation. But this time, he couldn't ignore the truth resting beneath it. She was doing something dangerous.

Anastasia spent the next several days thinking through every possible solution, every strategy that might lead to an answer. The problem wasn't just proving the truth, it was ensuring that once proof existed, something would actually be done about it. And that was far more difficult than she cared to admit. Still, she refused to let it go.

So, she returned to the village once more, this time with caution, with patience, searching for the woman without rushing, without alarming her. She found her seated outside her home, folding linens, her movements careful, methodical, as if she lived by routine alone.

Anastasia approached slowly, stopping just close enough to be heard, but not enough to crowd her. The woman looked up, surprise flickering across her expression, followed quickly by uncertainty. "Your Highness, you should *not* be here," she whispered.

Anastasia sat beside her without asking, smoothing her skirt as if they were old friends simply sharing a conversation. "I never listen when people say that." The woman let out a quiet breath, shaking her head. But she didn't tell her to leave. Not yet.

Anastasia kept her voice gentle but firm, not pressing, only offering space. "If I had proof," she said softly, "would you want to leave?" The woman's fingers paused, gripping the linen tighter. Silence stretched between them, thick and fragile. Finally—her voice, quiet, raw. "It wouldn't matter."

Anastasia's stomach twisted, frustration bubbling beneath her skin, though she kept it restrained. "Why?" The woman exhaled, finally meeting her gaze. "Because I have nowhere else to go." And just like that, Anastasia understood it fully. It wasn't just fear. It was entrapment.

It was the knowledge that even with proof, society would not grant her escape. She wasn't simply trapped by a cruel husband. She was trapped by the world itself.

The night air was thick with tension, a quiet stillness wrapping itself around the village streets like a held breath. Anastasia stood hidden beneath the shadow of a worn archway, her cloak wrapped tightly around her, every muscle in her body coiled with urgency. She had spent days watching, waiting, piecing together every possible moment when the woman might be alone and tonight was the night.

The door creaked open—a hesitation in the movement, a pause just long enough to betray lingering fear. The woman stepped out, her footsteps careful, measured, a small bundle clutched tightly against her chest. Anastasia stepped forward. "Come with me." The woman stiffened, her fingers curling tighter around the fabric she held.

"It's too dangerous." Anastasia lifted her chin, her voice steady. "Staying is worse." For a moment, the woman hesitated, the weight of years of silence pressing down on her. But then—a breath, a shift, a decision. She nodded and they ran.

Through winding alleyways, past dimly lit windows, feet pounding against the dirt roads as they moved faster than caution could catch them. Anastasia led her to the waiting carriage, the reins held by Evelina, who sat calmly, watching with quiet intensity. "This will not fix everything," Evelina murmured, studying the woman with knowing eyes.

"But it will give you a chance." The woman climbed inside, her hands still trembling, but her posture straighter than before.

As the carriage pulled away into the night, Anastasia exhaled, the weight of the moment settling into her bones. She had done what she could and it had been just enough

SIX

The morning air was brisk, carrying the scent of damp earth and lingering candle smoke from the castle halls. Anastasia walked with careful steps, her mind still tangled with thoughts of the book she had read the night before. If Elsmere was truly bound to time, then her presence here wasn't just an accident, it was part of something much larger. But why? And how could she undo it?

She had little time to dwell on the question. The castle moved around her in a quiet hum of activity, and today, the court luncheon loomed ahead—a test of patience, politics, and pretense.

The luncheon was as elaborate as expected. Silver trays lined the tables, the scent of roasted meats and honeyed pastries filling the chamber. Anastasia sat beside Roland, her posture stiff as Lady Eugenia's voice carried across the gathering. "Tell me, Your Highness," Eugenia purred, her voice laced with sugar-coated venom, "does your kingdom encourage its princesses to wander so freely among the commoners?"

The nobles exchanged glances, waiting for Anastasia to fumble through the conversation. She set down her goblet with quiet precision, masking the heat of irritation bubbling beneath her skin. "I was under the impression that England's royal family was meant to serve its people," she said smoothly. "How does one serve them if they never see them?"

The room hushed.

Lady Eugenia blinked, clearly startled, before forcing a delicate laugh. "How charming." Roland sighed, gripping his goblet a little too tightly. "Enough." Eugenia's expression flickered with irritation, but the conversation moved on, though Anastasia could still feel the lingering weight of their gazes.

The royal luncheon continued, the air thick with tension and barely concealed judgment. Anastasia had handled Lady Eugenia's sharp remarks with careful precision, but now, the conversation had shifted toward Henry Ashbourne, who had arrived late and thrown the carefully crafted atmosphere into mild chaos.

Henry sat across from her, a smirk playing at the corners of his lips, leaning into the conversation with effortless charm. "You must be the most talked-about woman in England," he mused, swirling the wine in his goblet. "It is rather impressive how quickly you've caused a stir."

Anastasia tilted her head, careful not to rise to his bait. "If stirring was my goal, I might have tried harder." Henry laughed, but Roland shifted beside her, his posture tense. She barely noticed him lean closer until his voice reached her ear, quiet enough that only she could hear.

"Henry is dangerous," Roland murmured, his tone just shy of warning. "Not in the way you think. He's too charming for his own good. He thrives on disrupting court balance." Anastasia glanced at him out of the corner of her eye. "And you tolerate him?"

Roland sighed, lifting his goblet but not drinking. "He's my oldest friend. That does not mean I approve of everything he does." Anastasia absorbed this, shifting slightly in her seat. She watched Henry carefully, noting the way he seemed to know exactly what to say to cause a stir.

Later that afternoon, Anastasia walked through the castle stables, seeking a moment of quiet after the exhausting display at lunch. The scent of hay and leather filled the air, the sounds of hoofbeats and soft noises of horses blending into a peaceful rhythm.

She was watching the horses when she heard an awkward shuffle behind her. She turned to see Harper, the young stablehand, standing stiffly beside a set of bridles, her hands fidgeting with the leather straps. Harper had kind eyes, though she often looked as though she was debating whether or not he should speak. Her dress was worn, her boots caked with mud, but her posture was respectful, careful, unsure.

"My lady," she said, giving a quick bow. Anastasia smiled gently. "Hello, Harper." She seemed startled that she knew her name, her ears turning slightly red. "I—uh—" She cleared her throat, seeming to reconsider whatever she had planned to say. "The Prince asked me to make sure your steed was well tended."

Anastasia glanced toward the stalls, spotting the chestnut coloured horse that pulled the royal carriage. She had grown attached to the animal, one of the few creatures in the castle that didn't watch her with suspicion. "He looks well," Anastasia said softly, reaching out to brush her fingers along the horse's mane.

Harper nodded quickly. She hesitated for a moment before glancing toward the nearby servant quarters, where Evelina was passing through, her steps slow from her lingering illness. Her gaze softened instantly. Anastasia kept her amusement to herself. "She's recovering well," she murmured.

Harper nearly dropped the bridle she had been adjusting. "I—yes. That's good." Anastasia bit back a smile, glancing at her carefully. "She's lucky to have someone looking out for her." Harper's mouth opened, then closed, then opened again, before she quickly dipped her head in a rushed bow. "I should check the horses, my lady."

Anastasia chuckled softly, shaking her head fondly before turning to Evelina, who had watched the entire exchange with barely concealed amusement.

"She's a nice girl," Anastasia said lightly. Evelina sighed, crossing her arms over her shawl. "She's... kind."

"She's clearly fond of you." Anastasia quickly noticed the animosity between the pair. "I'll... leave you two be." She giggled before hurrying off back into the castle.

Evelina turned, noticing Harper was finishing up brushing down one of the horses, her movements as methodical as ever. She was always so unshaken in her work, as though every stroke of the brush was its own quiet ritual. She lingered near the stall, watching as Harper continued her careful motions, the slow rhythm of her hands working through the animal's coat. The silence between them was comfortable, familiar, but there was something else beneath it tonight, something different.

"She means well," Evelina said after a moment, tracing her fingers absentmindedly along the edge of the stall door. Harper nodded, finally meeting her gaze. "She does." Evelina hesitated, feeling something unspoken between them, something unaddressed. The way Harper's gaze lingered just a little longer than before, the way Evelina's pulse seemed to hum beneath her skin.

"Do *you*?" Evelina asked, the words slipping out louder than she intended.

Harper's brow lifted ever so slightly, the faintest flicker of amusement curling at the edges of her lips. "Do I what?" Evelina swallowed, barely holding onto her nerve. "Mean well?" Harper's smirk grew just enough to reveal something knowing, something unreadable. "Only when necessary," she murmured. Evelina huffed out a laugh, shaking her head, but she didn't take a step back. Harper watched her for a moment longer before tapping the brush lightly against the stall's edge. "You can try, if you want." Evelina blinked. "Try what?"

Harper nodded toward the horse. "Brushing. Carefully." Evelina hesitated then reached for the brush. Harper didn't move away. Evelina hesitated as she ran her fingers over the brush's rough wooden handle, feeling its weight, the worn grooves left from years of use.

The horse exhaled, shifting its hooves slightly, and Evelina glanced up at Harper with uncertainty. "This is ridiculous," Evelina muttered. Harper only smirked. "You haven't even started yet." Evelina shot her a look but obeyed, moving the brush slowly down the animal's coat, mimicking the careful rhythm she had watched Harper perfect so many times before. She expected some kind of correction, but Harper said nothing, only nodding slightly in approval.

"You're learning," Harper murmured, folding her arms as she watched.

"I'm brushing a horse," Evelina countered. "It's not exactly the same as riding one." Harper raised an eyebrow, a glint of something unreadable flashing across her expression. Then, with effortless ease, she reached for the reins, guiding the horse forward just a step, turning to Evelina. "Then ride," Harper said simply.

Evelina stared at her like she had gone mad. "I—what?" Harper chuckled, shaking her head before grabbing Evelina's hand, pressing it lightly against the saddle. "Put your foot in the stirrup."

Evelina's pulse quickened. "I—this is a terrible idea—"

"You say that about a lot of things," Harper noted dryly. "And yet, somehow, you still end up doing them." Evelina huffed but did as she was told, slipping her foot into the stirrup, gripping the saddle with cautious fingers. Harper's hand remained firm on the reins, steadying both the horse and Evelina as she hoisted herself up.

For a moment, she sat too stiffly, holding her breath, not trusting the ground that had suddenly shifted beneath her. Harper's voice was calm, instructive. "Relax your posture." Evelina did. "Hold the reins gently, but firm enough that she knows you're guiding her."

She adjusted her grip. Harper watched her carefully, then took a deliberate step back, allowing Evelina to hold control for herself. The horse moved slightly, a slow, careful shift, and Evelina's heart nearly lodged itself in her throat, but she did not fall.

Harper smirked. "Not bad." Evelina let out a breath, gripping the reins more tightly, feeling power and uncertainty mix in equal measure. She opened her mouth to reply—to let Harper know she wasn't half as terrible as she had expected when a voice cut through the moment. "Harper." Both women turned.

Harper's father stood near the stable door, arms crossed, his expression tired but firm. He was a quiet man, but when he spoke, his words never left room for argument. "I need you to help with the new foal," he said simply.

Harper gave Evelina a wordless glance, as if sharing some secret understanding before stepping forward. "You did well," she murmured to Evelina, just soft enough that no one else would hear.

✳✳✳

Finding a bench in the gardens later in the evening, Anastasia sat quietly, running her fingers over the edge of her skirts as she considered everything that had happened that day.

It was during that moment of stillness that Henry appeared, leaning casually against a pillar, watching her with interest. He had a way of existing so effortlessly in a space, never imposing, yet somehow always commanding attention. It was an unsettling contrast to Roland's rigid formality.

"You didn't flinch today," Henry mused after a stretch of silence, tilting his head slightly. "At lunch." Anastasia let out a quiet breath. "I wanted to."

"But you didn't."

She glanced at him, brow arching slightly. "Are you impressed?" Henry chuckled, pushing off the pillar. "I would be more impressed if you had thrown your goblet at Lady Eugenia." Anastasia laughed, shaking her head. "Tempting, but I think Roland would have had an actual heart attack."

Henry smirked, stepping closer, his presence shifting subtly in a way that made Anastasia instinctively straighten. He wasn't looking at her like the nobles did, like she was something foreign, something scrutinized. He was looking at her like she was something interesting, something worth watching.

"Roland expects you to fail," Henry murmured, casually plucking a rose from the nearby bush, twirling it between his fingers. "Not because he dislikes you—but because you are *different*." Anastasia studied him carefully. "And you?"

Henry lifted the rose, considering it for a moment before sliding it onto the edge of the marble bench beside her. "I think different can be dangerous." She eyed the flower, then him. "Are you warning me or complimenting me?" Henry smiled, slow and deliberate. "A bit of both." The garden air grew heavier, charged with something quiet and uncertain. Anastasia wasn't blind—she could tell when someone was testing the waters of possibility, and Henry's gaze held something... unreadable. Amusement? Interest? Or just his usual habit of seeing what would happen if he pressed hard enough?

"I should warn you," Anastasia murmured, resting her hands on her lap. "I'm not particularly good at playing court games." Henry hummed thoughtfully. "Maybe that's what makes you interesting."

Anastasia turned toward him fully, studying him now the way he had been studying her all evening. Henry was different from Roland in every way—unrestrained, unpredictable, effortlessly charming without restraint. But charm could be dangerous, especially when it was wielded by someone who knew exactly how to use it.

She tilted her head slightly. "Are you playing one now?" Henry grinned, but there was something sharper beneath it. "I haven't decided yet." Anastasia exhaled, shaking her head. "You're impossible." Henry stepped backward, hands raised in surrender. "And yet, you're still talking to me." She rolled her eyes but couldn't quite suppress the faint smile tugging at the corner of her lips.

"I probably should go to bed now." She muttered, patting Henry's shoulder. "Of course, your highness. Goodnight" She nodded fondly and left him, walking back to the castle.

Anastasia climbed the winding staircase to her quarters, her bare feet brushing against the cold marble steps as she exhaled heavily. The castle felt quieter at night, almost eerie—too vast, too empty, too unlike home.

Home. The thought was sharp, *painful*.

She sat on the cushioned bench beside the window, staring out at the moonlit gardens, trying to summon memories of the world she had left behind. She had done her best to push away the aching nostalgia, but tonight, it was impossible to ignore. She missed the way her grandmother's voice wrapped around her like a blanket, the way she hummed softly when baking, or laughed at television dramas that she insisted weren't *that* dramatic.

She closed her eyes, trying to summon something familiar—something warm, something real. And just like that, she was eleven years old again.

✳✳✳

The toy shop smelled of aged wood and fresh paint, the shelves lined with stuffed animals, puzzles, and miniature figurines of knights and castles. Conor—still young, still uncertain of himself—walked slowly beside his grandmother, trailing his fingers across the soft fabric of plush toys. His shoes scuffed against the floor as he scanned the rows, searching for something that felt right.

"Conor, darling," his grandmother said gently, her voice laced with quiet amusement. "Pick something before the shop closes on us." He barely heard her, too focused on what he was looking for—even if he didn't know what that was yet.

And then, there it was. A blonde stuffed horse, its mane soft, its stitched black eyes round and kind. "This one," he said decisively, lifting the toy and pressing it against his chest. "I want this one." His grandmother smiled knowingly, always understanding him in ways he hadn't yet learned to understand himself.

"What's its name, then?" she asked as she carried it to the counter. Conor paused, thinking carefully. Then, with quiet confidence, he answered. "Lucky." His grandmother nodded approvingly, squeezing his shoulder. "A fitting name." Conor smiled, holding Lucky tightly as they stepped out into the cold evening air.

✳✳✳

Anastasia opened her eyes sharply, breath hitching. She sat up suddenly, the memory igniting something in her mind. If she was going to be trapped here, if she had to somehow survive this world, then she needed something—something familiar, something to remind her of who she was before all of this.

And she had an idea.

She jumped to her feet, hurriedly stepping into the hallway, her nightgown brushing against her ankles. Without hesitation, she knocked on Roland's door. Once, twice, then again, faster. The door swung open abruptly, revealing a very grumpy Roland, his shirt slightly unbuttoned, hair mussed from sleep, eyes heavy with irritation. "What?" he muttered, rubbing his face tiredly.

Anastasia ignored his tone entirely. "I need you to let Harper or her father teach me how to ride." Roland stared at her blankly, trying to process the request through his exhaustion. "It is the middle of the night," he said slowly.

"Yes, but it won't be in the morning," Anastasia shot back, unbothered by the hour. Roland inhaled sharply through his nose, as if summoning every ounce of patience he possessed. Then, with a muttered, barely comprehensible 'No', he slammed the door in her face. Anastasia blinked at the closed door, expression unreadable.

"Well," she sighed, running a hand through her hair. "That went well."

SEVEN

Roland had been avoiding Anastasia all morning. Not obviously—he was too disciplined for that. But Anastasia had spent enough time watching him carefully to know the signs. He answered her briefly, his responses short, clipped, his attention diverted elsewhere whenever she spoke.

And finally, after hours of navigating his distance, Anastasia cornered him in the hallway, blocking his path before he could disappear for another set of meetings. "Alright," she announced, hands on her hips. "What is wrong?"

Roland exhaled sharply, as if debating whether to push past her or face whatever conversation was about to unfold. "I have responsibilities, Princess," he said dryly. "Unlike you, I cannot afford time spent chasing scandal." Anastasia rolled her eyes. "If this is about yesterday's luncheon, let me remind you that you yourself said—"

"I know what I said."

She narrowed her eyes. "Then why are you acting like I've personally caused the kingdom's downfall?" Roland clenched his jaw. "You are reckless." Anastasia arched a brow, crossing her arms.

Roland huffed, rubbing his temple. "You do not belong here," he muttered under his breath. Anastasia stilled, the words sticking too deeply, too uncomfortably. Her voice was quieter when she responded.

"No," she admitted. "I don't." Roland's expression softened, though he said nothing. After a long silence, Anastasia sighed, dropping her hands from her hips.

"Well," she murmured, "since I'm apparently incapable of blending in, you might as well teach me something actually useful." Roland tilted his head slightly, studying her. "What, precisely, are you requesting?" She shrugged, feigning nonchalance. "I don't know—something that won't make me feel like I'm meant to sit in a corner and play the obedient lady."

Roland let out a slow breath, shaking his head. "If I do this, you will not complain," he warned. Anastasia grinned, lifting a playful brow. "I never complain." Roland gave her a pointed look, unimpressed.

Anastasia laughed, waving a hand. "Fine, fine. I will try."

Despite himself—despite the irritation, the frustration, the way she always found a way to get under his skin—Roland sighed and nodded. "Come with me then."

The private hall was bathed in the warm flicker of sunlight, the heavy drapes pulled back just enough to let the sun spill its golden glow onto the marble floors. The room was quiet, save for the occasional rustle of fabric as Anastasia shifted in frustration.

Roland stood before her, arms crossed, expression sharp, assessing her posture like she was some ill-trained soldier—or worse, a disobedient child.

"You walk like someone ready to engage in battle," Roland muttered, shaking his head. Anastasia arched a brow, placing a hand on her hip. "I think you mean I walk like someone with a purpose." Roland sighed deeply, his patience already thinning.

"That is not how a lady moves."

She snorted, rolling her eyes. "I was not raised to float around like a lost spirit." He gestured sharply for her to try again. Anastasia let out a slow breath, adjusting her posture as instructed—back straight, chin lifted, hands gently resting at her sides.

She took a step forward—graceful, careful—but the second step was far too forceful, her boot landing with an audible stomp. Roland pinched the bridge of his nose, clearly restraining himself from making a sharp remark. "It's not just about movement," he said. "It's about control. About presence."

Anastasia huffed, shifting uncomfortably. "Presence? The nobles already stare at me like I'm some terrifying anomaly. I hardly think I need more of it." Roland's lips twitched slightly, but he suppressed whatever amusement threatened to surface. "If they are staring, it should be because they fear your grace," he said firmly. "Not because they are questioning your place here."

Anastasia blinked, something in his tone catching her off guard. For a moment, she considered arguing. But instead, she let the words settle, testing them against her own reluctant acceptance. She straightened, adjusting herself again, taking another step—lighter this time, deliberate, poised. Roland watched, his eyes narrowed with scrutiny, but there was something else there, too.

Approval. A quiet, reluctant approval.

"I suppose that was slightly more tolerable," he murmured, but she could tell he meant it as praise. Anastasia grinned, tilting her head. "Careful, Prince. You almost sound impressed." Roland sighed heavily, shaking his head. "Do not mistake progress for victory." She laughed, the tension in the room easing, if only slightly. Perhaps royalty *could* be learned.

✳✳✳

Evelina's gasp was sharp, audible, as she clutched Anastasia's arm with sudden intensity. "By the saints above," she whispered. "Look at him." Anastasia, who had just been in the middle of detailing her latest complaints about court affairs, fell silent, her gaze locked on Henry's ridiculous, impossible perfection.

The sight was undeniable. His shirt was loosely laced at the collar, his coat hanging open, revealing just enough of the crisp fabric beneath to tease at effortless refinement. His dark hair caught the sun, a few strands falling over his forehead in a way that suggested he had just ridden through the fields but somehow still managed to look immaculate.

Evelina sucked in a sharp breath. Anastasia froze, entirely abandoning whatever thought had occupied her a moment ago.

Henry walked with easy confidence, his long strides unhurried, but commanding the space around him without effort. "Oh, come on," Anastasia grumbled under her breath, shaking her head as if to rid herself of the sight. Evelina barely blinked. "That is not a real man. That is a god mistakenly placed in mortal form."

Anastasia snapped herself out of her daze, clearing her throat. "Disgusting," Anastasia murmured, though the words lacked conviction. Henry, of course, noticed their blatant staring. With amused confidence, he grinned, tilting his head slightly as he approached. "I see you're admiring the scenery," he called, his tone dripping with playfulness. Evelina laughed, entirely unashamed. "It would be a crime not to." Anastasia huffed, crossing her arms. But before she could offer a suitably snarky response, Roland stepped onto the terrace, his usual irritated expression firmly in place.

"Oh, fantastic," Anastasia deadpanned, sighing dramatically. Roland arched a brow, clearly unimpressed. "What now?" Evelina bit her lip, struggling not to giggle, while Anastasia merely waved her hand dismissively, muttering,

"Nothing. Just lamenting life's disappointments."
Roland rolled his eyes, shaking his head as he
continued forward.

Henry, however, was thoroughly enjoying
himself. "You wound me, Princess," he said,
placing a hand over his chest in mock offense.
"Am I not pleasant company?" Anastasia snorted,
crossing her arms. "Oh, I never said you weren't
pleasant, Henry. Just... insufferably handsome,
and aware of it."

Henry grinned, amused. "A curse I bear with
great dignity, I assure you." Roland groaned,
rubbing his temple. "I cannot believe I am
standing here listening to this conversation."
Anastasia turned to him, unimpressed. "Oh, don't
pretend you aren't glaring at Henry because you
think you should be the better-looking man
here." Roland shot her a flat look, unimpressed.
"I do not care about that."

Evelina gasped theatrically. "He didn't deny
being handsome! Look how far we've come!"
Anastasia laughed, shaking her head as Roland
exhaled sharply, clearly regretting stepping onto
the terrace in the first place. Henry chuckled,
clapping Roland on the shoulder. "Let's leave
before the ladies completely tear apart our
dignity."

Roland gave Anastasia a pointed look, muttering, "I should not have to endure this." Anastasia waved him off, grinning. "And yet, you do." Henry followed Roland toward his study, tossing one last glance over his shoulder at Anastasia before disappearing around the stone archway. Evelina exhaled loudly, shaking her head. "I truly believe Henry was sculpted by the gods." Anastasia chuckled.

The study was dimly lit, the scent of parchment and faint traces of whiskey lingering in the air, mixing with the slow crackle of the fire in the hearth. Roland sat at his desk, his elbow resting against the armrest, swirling the amber liquid in his goblet. Across from him, Henry stood by the bookshelf, his fingers trailing absentmindedly over the worn spines of old tomes, his sharp gaze flickering over their titles, though he seemed far less interested in the words on the pages than in Roland himself.

"You look tired," Henry observed, his tone casual but calculated, watching Roland with faint amusement. Roland exhaled, leaning back in his chair, expression tense despite the supposed comfort of the room. "I am always tired," Roland muttered.

Henry smirked, shifting his weight slightly. "That sounds miserable." Roland shot him a pointed look, unimpressed. "You say that as if you don't already know." Henry chuckled, finally choosing a book and flipping through the pages with lazy interest. "I like to hear it from your own mouth. Makes it more entertaining."

"Where did you meet her?" Roland's fingers tensed slightly against the rim of his glass. A simple question. A dangerous one.

He exhaled slowly, careful to keep his expression neutral. "Elsmere." Henry tilted his head slightly, curiosity flickering across his features. "Elsmere?" Roland nodded, feigning boredom. "She was wandering through the grounds when I found her. Said she was lost, looking for a place to rest for the night."

Henry's lips curled into something resembling amusement. "Lost? A woman like her?" Roland shrugged, reaching for the glass but not drinking. "Not everyone knows the land well." Henry studied him—not skeptical, not entirely convinced, but not outright suspicious either.

Still, Roland could feel it—the weight behind the question, the way Henry was picking apart his words even if he didn't press further. "And you just... took her in?" Henry asked, voice light but edged with curiosity. Roland leaned back in his chair, keeping his tone even. "She intrigued me. What more can I say?"

Henry exhaled, shaking his head slightly. "You have a habit of collecting strays." Roland smirked, though there was no humor in it. "You say that like it's a flaw." Henry's gaze lingered a moment longer before he finally leaned forward, resting his elbows against the table. "Perhaps it is."

Roland huffed, but didn't refute the statement, taking a slow sip of his drink instead. Their conversation drifted in familiar ways—political pressures, court affairs, King George's latest grievances against the council. But eventually, the topic shifted to Anastasia again. "How is the little firebrand adjusting to palace life?" Henry asked, setting the book down and turning fully toward Roland. Roland sighed, running a hand through his hair before muttering, "She's... outspoken."

Henry grinned, crossing his arms. "Understatement." Roland huffed, shaking his head. "She speaks like she's lived twice the lives she should have." Henry's gaze flickered—sharp, fleeting, but revealing a glint of something hidden before he masked it.

"She is unlike anyone I've met," Henry murmured, his voice softer now, more contemplative. Roland studied him for a long moment, his brow furrowing slightly.

"You say that like you know something the rest of us don't." Henry smiled—not wide, not charming, but secretive, his golden eyes catching the dim candlelight just enough to seem unreadable. "If I did," he said smoothly, "I wouldn't tell you."

✳✳✳

The night air was crisp but pleasant, carrying the scent of damp earth and lingering candle wax from the castle corridors. Anastasia had finished a long, frustrating meeting with the queen's ladies, and the weight of expectation pressed against her ribs. So, when Henry suggested a walk outside, she agreed without hesitation.

They strolled along the garden paths, the golden glow of lanterns casting long shadows against the stone walls, and for once, there was no urgency—just idle conversation and the quiet understanding between them.

"I cannot pretend to enjoy embroidering tiny flowers onto fabric," Anastasia muttered, her arms crossed over her chest. "They made me sit for hours, Henry. Hours."

Henry chuckled, the sound warm against the cold air. "Ah, yes. The noble art of unnecessary patience. A true test of the human spirit."

Anastasia huffed, shaking her head. "If that is what makes a proper lady, I must declare myself a lost cause." Henry turned his gaze to her, a small smile tugging at his lips, something far too knowing flickering in his golden eyes.

"You were never meant to be *proper*," he murmured.

Anastasia paused in her steps, blinking up at him, something about the way he said it stirring a strange sensation in her chest. Before she could question the weight behind his words, he turned away, pointing toward the nearby fountain. "Come, I shall read your future in the waters," he declared, dramatically sweeping his arm. "I predict great and terrible things." Anastasia laughed, letting him guide her toward the fountain, allowing the moment to shift before she could dwell on it too long.

They stood by the edge, the soft ripple of water casting reflections against their faces. Henry peered into the pool, his brows furrowing in exaggerated concentration. "I see..." he paused, squinting as though uncovering a grand revelation. "Yes. There it is. A stubborn woman with wild ambitions, forever irritating those in power." Anastasia rolled her eyes. "Sounds about right. What else?"

Henry hummed thoughtfully. "A future filled with danger." Anastasia arched a brow. "Danger? How thrilling." Henry's playful demeanor shifted, just slightly—so subtly that, had Anastasia not been watching him closely, she might have missed it.

"It is," he admitted, his voice softer now. "But some dangers are unavoidable, no matter how well we try to outrun them."

Anastasia tilted her head, sensing the shift in his tone. "What are you trying to say?"

Henry grinned, masking whatever had lingered in his expression a moment before. "Nothing at all, *Your Highness*," he mused, stepping back. "Only that fate is a tricky beast. And it seems quite enamored with you." Anastasia huffed a laugh, shaking her head, but she couldn't shake the feeling that there was something Henry wasn't saying—something buried between the charm and carefully measured words.

EIGHT

The morning sunlight streamed through the castle windows, casting long shadows across the grand hall. Anastasia sat in quiet contemplation at the breakfast table, staring at the untouched plate before her. She had barely slept the night before—Roland's blunt refusal to let her learn to ride had left her restless, irritated, and feeling even more trapped than usual.

There was still so much she didn't understand—about Elsmere, about time itself, about whether or not she could ever return home. But another concern had been growing in her mind, something she couldn't shake.

The people.

She had seen glimpses of the struggle in the village, heard whispers of hardship. The way the marketplace women spoke about their days, the way the elderly man warned her about power—it wasn't just politeness or reverence. It was need. And the castle, with its extravagant luncheons and silken gowns, stood untouched by it all.

As the morning dragged on, Anastasia sat stiffly beside Roland during another political discussion in the royal council chamber. Nobles gathered around the room, speaking about trade agreements, land disputes, and court affairs, but she could barely focus. Her thoughts drifted toward the villages beyond these walls. And suddenly, she couldn't keep quiet anymore. "What is being done about the nationwide poverty?" she asked, her voice cutting through the hum of conversation.

The room stilled instantly. Several nobles exchanged glances, uncertain whether to acknowledge her comment. King George lifted an unimpressed brow. "The nationwide poverty?" Roland repeated, his tone unreadable. "The people," Anastasia clarified, sitting straighter. "The women I spoke to, the families barely surviving. What measures are in place to ensure their well-being?"

One of the advisors—a man with thinning hair and a sharp gaze—cleared his throat. "The people are sustained by their own trade and labor. They are not without structure."

"That doesn't mean they aren't struggling."

The advisor stiffened slightly, clearly not used to being challenged. "Why concern yourself with things beyond your station?" Anastasia clenched her jaw. "Shouldn't that concern everyone?" Roland sighed beside her, shifting slightly in his

chair. "We don't intervene unless necessary."
"Then what qualifies as necessary?" Anastasia
pressed.

Roland's jaw tightened, but he didn't answer.
King George leaned forward, leveling a gaze at
Anastasia. "You tread dangerously close to
matters you do not understand." The warning
was clear. Anastasia swallowed, feeling the
weight of the silence around her. She knew she
had already caused a stir at the marketplace, at
the luncheon, in nearly every room she stepped
into—but this was different.

This was questioning power itself. She held the
king's gaze for a long moment before finally
nodding. "Forgive me," she murmured, though
she did not regret her words. The conversation
shifted elsewhere, but she knew she had already
left an impression that would not be forgotten.

Later, Roland entered the drawing room, finding
Anastasia pacing near the window, her arms
crossed tightly. "You can't just ignore what's
happening outside this castle," she said without
preamble, turning to face him fully. Roland
exhaled sharply, already irritated. "We are not
ignoring it." "You're pretending it isn't bad
enough to require action."

Roland stepped forward, his stance tense. "You don't understand how these things work." Anastasia's frustration boiled over. "Then explain it to me!" Roland's jaw tightened. "It isn't as simple as distributing food or coin. We control land, law, trade—these things cannot be shifted overnight."

Anastasia clenched her fists. "So you do nothing in the meantime?" Roland's expression hardened, but something beneath it flickered—a deeper frustration, something unsaid. "You think I don't care?" he asked, voice quieter now, but no less sharp. Anastasia hesitated, thrown by the sudden shift in his tone. "I think you do nothing."

Roland closed the distance between them, his presence pressing against the space between them like a storm brewing. "You walk into this world, into *my life*, and think you understand everything," he said, voice low, controlled—but barely. "You challenge a system that has existed for centuries and expect change because you *want* it."

Anastasia refused to back down. "Because it *needs* to change." Roland's eyes darkened, but he didn't argue. "You cannot fix everything," Roland murmured finally. Anastasia inhaled deeply. "Maybe not. But I can't sit here and do nothing."

Roland watched her carefully for a long moment. Then, without another word, he turned and left.

Anastasia sat on the cushioned bench by her window, arms wrapped tightly around herself as she stared at the distant horizon. The castle, with its grand halls and gilded chandeliers, felt suffocating. She replayed Roland's words in her mind, his insistence that she couldn't fix everything. But wasn't that the point? She wasn't trying to fix *everything*. She was trying to do *something*. With a sharp exhale, she stood, determined to clear her head. The walls of the castle felt too restrictive tonight, so she decided to take a walk through the gardens.

The moon hung high in the sky as she strolled past the trimmed hedges and marble statues, the soft crunch of gravel beneath her feet soothing her frayed nerves. She was so caught in her thoughts that she almost didn't see Evelina sitting alone near the fountain, wrapped in her shawl, staring at the water with a distant expression.

Anastasia hesitated, then stepped forward. "You look lost in thought," she said gently. Evelina glanced up, surprised but not unwelcoming. "And you look troubled." Anastasia let out a quiet laugh. "That obvious?" Evelina smiled faintly, adjusting the shawl around her shoulders. "You carry frustration like a weight." Anastasia sank onto the bench beside her, staring into the rippling water. "I just don't understand how people can sit in luxury and not care about the ones struggling outside these walls."

Evelina studied her carefully before murmuring, "People only care about what benefits them." Anastasia frowned. "That's a terrible way to live."

"It is," Evelina agreed. "But it is how the world works."

Anastasia leaned back, sighing. "Do you ever think about leaving?" Evelina's expression shifted—something wistful, something longing. "All the time."

"But you stay."

Evelina gave her a knowing look. "And so do you." The words were simple, but they struck deeper than Anastasia expected. She wasn't here by choice, but wasn't she *choosing* to fight back? To challenge the way things worked? Perhaps, in some way, she was no different from Evelina—both women trapped in a system bigger than themselves, yet refusing to accept it quietly.

✻✻✻

The study was dimly lit, the morning sun barely creeping past the thick curtains framing the stone walls. King George sat in his grand chair, posture composed, watching Roland carefully as the prince stood stiffly nearby, arms crossed.

"There is a simple solution to this problem," the king murmured, swirling the wine in his goblet. Roland exhaled sharply, already irritated. "Which problem, exactly?" His father set the goblet down, folding his hands. "Your wife. She is... outspoken." Roland's jaw tightened. "She will not bend easily to court etiquette," the king continued, his tone measured but laced with underlying disapproval. "She questions too much, moves too freely. Nobles will tolerate it for only so long before they begin whispering of rebellion."

Roland gritted his teeth but said nothing. He had no patience for politics today, but ignoring his father was never an option. King George leaned back slightly. "A ball." Roland's brow furrowed. "A ball?" "A celebration," the king elaborated. "For your marriage. A grand event to ensure she is seen as belonging to court life." His lips curled slightly. "If she is surrounded by nobility, pressed in by expectation, perhaps she will settle into her role more easily." Roland scowled. "She will not settle," he muttered. King George gave him a knowing glance. "That is why you must make her." Roland hesitated, reluctant, but he knew his father's suggestion wasn't a mere request—it was an order veiled as advice.

He sighed, shoulders tense. "Fine."

Later that morning, Evelina pushed open the doors to Anastasia's quarters, her steps cautious but swift. The sunlight had spilled past the tall windows, warming the gold-trimmed furnishings, but Anastasia was still curled beneath the heavy blankets, deep in sleep. "My lady," Evelina murmured, approaching the bed carefully.

Anastasia made a sound that vaguely resembled protest, burying her face further into the pillow. Evelina hesitated only for a moment before speaking again. "His Highness requests your presence. You are to go to the village with him today." Anastasia groaned, shifting slightly but refusing to fully wake. "Why?"

"To visit the seamstress," Evelina answered patiently. "For preparations."

"Preparations for what?"

"A ball."

That caught Anastasia's attention. She blinked groggily, sitting up slightly. "A ball?" Evelina nodded. "In honour of your marriage." Anastasia squinted, trying to process this new information. Then, with a slow, tired sigh, she flopped back against the pillows, muttering into the fabric.

"This is punishment, isn't it?" Evelina smiled faintly, but she said nothing. Anastasia lay still for a beat, then finally sat up properly, rubbing her face. "Fine. I'll get ready." Evelina bowed slightly before leaving the room. Anastasia exhaled, already dreading the day ahead.

The ride to the village was quiet, the tension so thick you'd need a chainsaw to cut through it. Roland and Anastasia sat side by side in the royal carriage, the rhythmic sound of horse hooves against the cobblestone roads filling the silence between them.

Roland had barely spoken since she stepped into the carriage that morning. He had only given her a cursory glance before settling into his usual guarded posture, arms crossed, gaze fixed on the shifting scenery outside the window. Anastasia was still wrapping her head around the idea of the ball—a grand event meant to parade her existence before the nobility, meant to force her into the mold of a proper royal.

And now, here she was—traveling into the village with Roland to meet the seamstress who would outfit her for the occasion. She stared at him, waiting for him to say something—anything. But he didn't. Fine. If he wasn't going to start the conversation, she would. "So," she said, leaning back against the cushioned seat. "Are we going to pretend this isn't happening?"

Roland glanced at her briefly, then back out the window. "What exactly is 'this'?"

"Oh, I don't know," she mused. "The fact that your father is using this ball to try and make me into the perfect little noblewoman." Roland sighed sharply, not in the mood for arguments. "It is a necessary event."

"For whom?" she pressed. "The nobles who want to keep me under control? Your father, who clearly sees me as a disruption?"

Roland's jaw tightened, but he didn't answer. Anastasia scoffed, shaking her head. "You really don't see it, do you?" Roland finally turned to her, his patience wearing thin. "See what?"

"The way he manipulates you." Roland's gaze darkened. "You think you understand this world, but you don't."

"I understand enough."

"No, you understand pieces of it," he countered. "You see injustice and assume it can be unraveled like thread. That isn't the reality."

Anastasia stared at him, frustration mounting. "So you allow it to keep people in suffering because changing it would be too inconvenient?" Roland's expression flickered—a brief shift, something almost unreadable. "You think I don't care," he murmured, voice quieter now. "You assume my silence means acceptance."

"What else am I supposed to think?" she shot back.

Roland didn't respond immediately, as if considering his next words carefully. Finally, he exhaled, turning back to the window. "You keep talking about how you don't belong in this world," he said, his voice low but pointed. "So why do you fight against it as if it's your responsibility?"

Anastasia felt herself still, caught off guard. "I see no reason to sit idly by and ignore the wrongdoings of this era," she said firmly. Roland turned his head slightly, amusement flickering at the edge of his irritation. "And yet, you clearly didn't cause a stir in your own time." Anastasia clenched her jaw, hating how easily he turned her words against her.

"Maybe I see things differently now," she said stubbornly. Roland scoffed. "Then the ball should be quite the spectacle." The carriage jerked slightly, signaling their arrival in the heart of the village. Roland straightened, his posture shifting back into the controlled poise of a prince, as if he had flipped a switch, burying their tension beneath duty. Anastasia sighed, forcing herself to follow as the door swung open and they stepped out onto the bustling streets.

The seamstress's shop was nestled between the butcher and the bookbinder, its windows framed with intricate lace. Inside, bolts of fabric—deep burgundy velvets, soft blue silks, delicate ivory linens—lined the walls, stacked neatly on wooden shelves. The scent of freshly pressed cotton filled the space, mingling with the faint aroma of lavender tucked among the spools of thread.

Roland strode forward first, his presence commanding even in a humble shop. The seamstress—a middle-aged woman with sharp eyes and deft hands—curtsied swiftly before ushering them inside. "His Highness has arranged for your gown, Princess," she said smoothly, retrieving a neatly folded piece of fabric from the workbench.

Anastasia's stomach sank the moment she saw it. It was modest. Too modest. High-necked, long-sleeved, made from thick, structured material that barely allowed for movement. A far cry from the elegant gowns worn by noblewomen at court, let alone something fit for a ball meant to celebrate her.

She glanced at Roland, irritation flickering in her gaze. "This is the dress?" Roland barely spared her a glance. "It is appropriate."

"Appropriate?" Anastasia echoed, crossing her arms. "It looks like something meant for mourning." Roland exhaled sharply, clearly not interested in entertaining complaints. "You will wear it," he said flatly.

Anastasia opened her mouth to argue, but the seamstress shifted nervously, watching them carefully. She could press the matter, fight him in front of his people, but it wouldn't serve her. Instead, she bit back her protest, swallowing her pride. "Fine," she muttered. "Then we should go." Roland nodded, turning sharply toward the door. But as soon as his back was turned, Anastasia leaned close to the seamstress, her voice dropping to a whisper. "There isn't much time," she murmured, fingers brushing over a bolt of deep crimson silk. "Can you make another gown?"

The seamstress hesitated only briefly before nodding. Anastasia outlined her design quickly, describing a gown with flowing sleeves, delicate embroidery along the bodice, and a skirt that moved effortlessly when she walked. "Give it to Evelina before tonight," she instructed. The seamstress smiled knowingly, setting the fabric aside. "Of course, *banríon bán*." Anastasia blinked. "What?" The woman chuckled, gently pressing Anastasia's hand. "*Banríon bán*. White Queen. The people see you as their hope, their savior."

Something tightened in Anastasia's chest, warmth spilling through her at the words. She leaned forward, pressing a grateful kiss to the seamstress's cheek. "Thank you." Just as the moment settled, the door swung open again, and Roland appeared, impatient and expectant. "Let's go," he ordered. Anastasia stole one last glance at the seamstress, sharing a knowing wink before following Roland out the door.

The scent of fresh pastries and petrichor filled the air as Anastasia stepped onto the cobbled streets. The marketplace buzzed with quiet urgency—vendors calling out prices, children darting between stalls, weary travelers passing through with dust-covered boots. Roland wasted no time, moving toward the carriage without another word, eager to return to the castle. But just as Anastasia turned to follow him, she spotted movement out of the corner of her eye—a woman hobbling past, her arms tightly cradling a newborn baby against her chest.

The woman's clothes were thin, worn, her steps uneven as she clutched the infant closer, her features pinched with exhaustion. Roland stepped into the carriage, expecting Anastasia to follow—but she didn't. Instead, she called out gently.

"Wait."

The woman stilled, glancing up at her with tired, wary eyes. Anastasia stepped forward, lowering her voice. "Are you alright?" The woman hesitated, shifting on her feet, glancing toward Roland and the carriage as if unsure whether speaking was allowed. "I—" she started, then swallowed. "I have had to give up my food... for the baby." Anastasia felt something clench in her chest.

The woman continued, her voice thin. "My husband sold our crops to keep the cow... but now there is little left for us." Anastasia felt the weight of the moment settle—the stark difference between her life and this woman's, the vast chasm of privilege that separated them. "I'm so sorry," Anastasia whispered, shaking her head, struck by the cruelty of it all. The baby whined softly, its little hands clenching weakly. Anastasia acted quickly, her fingers reaching for the ruby necklace around her throat.

Without hesitation, she unclasped it, pressing it into the woman's palm. "Sell it," she murmured. "Get food. As much as you need." The woman's eyes widened in shock, her lips parting in disbelief. "My lady—"

"Please," Anastasia urged, squeezing her hand lightly. The woman shuddered with gratitude, blinking rapidly as tears welled in her eyes. "Thank you," she breathed. Anastasia nodded, then hurried into the carriage before Roland could question her further. The carriage lurched forward, pulling away from the village and back toward the towering castle gates.

Later that evening, as the castle settled into its usual rhythm, Anastasia made her way toward Roland's chambers, her steps quieter than usual. He was alone, standing near the hearth, the glow of the fire casting shadows against the stone walls. "I wanted to apologize," Anastasia murmured, standing at the threshold. Roland raised an eyebrow, clearly skeptical. "Apologize?"

She offered a forced, but careful smile. "For earlier. For challenging you at every turn." Roland studied her carefully, his expression unreadable. "You're not actually sorry."

"Maybe not," she admitted. "But I'm trying to make peace." Roland exhaled sharply, then nodded once. "Fine." Anastasia curtsied briefly, offering the smallest flash of amusement in her gaze before turning on her heel.

***

The knock at Anastasia's door was soft but deliberate, followed by the familiar voice of Evelina. "My lady?" Anastasia hurried across the room, excitement thrumming beneath her skin. When she pulled open the door, Evelina stood there, hands carefully cradling the folds of an exquisite gown—deep crimson silk, embroidered with delicate silver thread, the fabric shimmering under the candlelight.

"You did it," Anastasia breathed, eyes wide. "It's beautiful." Evelina offered a small smile, stepping inside. "The seamstress was swift." Anastasia couldn't contain herself—she reached forward, wrapping her arms around Evelina, pulling her into a grateful embrace. Evelina stiffened slightly, unused to such affection, but then—slowly, hesitantly—she leaned into it. "Thank you,"

Anastasia whispered. Evelina gave a small nod, voice quiet. "It suits you."

Anastasia stepped behind the divider, slipping out of her everyday dress and into the fabric that would announce her defiance tonight. The silk moved fluidly with her every motion, hugging at her waist, cascading down into an elegant skirt that barely brushed the floor. The silver embroidery caught the light, creating an almost ethereal glow. She took a steady breath, smoothing her hands over the bodice.

Then, she stepped out. Evelina gasped sharply, one hand flying to her mouth. "My lady," she whispered, eyes shining with admiration. "You look—gorgeous." Anastasia grinned, crossing the space between them in swift steps, pressing a soft kiss to Evelina's cheek. "You're very sweet," she murmured. Evelina blushed, dipping her head slightly, murmuring, "Go. They're waiting."

The palace corridors were quiet, lined with flickering torches and rich tapestries, but as Anastasia descended the grand staircase, she could already hear the murmur of voices beyond the ballroom doors. She halted before them, exhaling slowly, the weight of expectation settling onto her shoulders.

And then, the doors swung open. Gasps echoed through the ballroom, the nobles turning sharply, their expressions frozen in awe and shock. The crimson silk caught the light, draping over her frame like royalty itself, the silver embroidery glistening like scattered stars against the night sky. Anastasia held her head high, stepping forward, her presence commanding the entire room.

NINE

The ballroom was alive with murmurs, the candlelit chandeliers casting golden light against the marble floors. Anastasia stepped through the grand doors, her gown flowing elegantly, the fabric shimmering under the heavy gaze of the nobility.

The room fell into silence for just a moment—just long enough for whispers to coil through the crowd like smoke. They were watching her—every lord, every lady, every cautious court advisor. She met their eyes without faltering, without shrinking, walking with deliberate poise toward the center of the room—toward Roland, who stood rigidly beside his father's throne. The prince looked livid, his expression carefully controlled, but the subtle clench of his jaw betrayed his fury.

King George looked no better. His grip tightened around his goblet, his knuckles white. Neither of them made a scene, but the displeasure was unmistakable.

Roland's voice was low, clipped when he finally spoke. "Dance with me," he muttered. It wasn't a request. Anastasia arched her brow, but said nothing. He extended his hand. She took it, stepping onto the floor as the musicians struck up a slow, intricate melody. The crowd dispersed, forming a wide circle around them, watching as the prince and his wife moved together in careful rhythm. The first few steps were tight, controlled, but soon other couples joined, softening the intensity of the moment. Still, the weight of Roland's disapproval pressed against her, his grip firm against her waist.

"You were supposed to wear the gown I had made for you," he hissed under his breath. Anastasia smiled sweetly, tilting her head as they spun. "And I am supposed to listen to everything you say?" Roland exhaled sharply, controlling his irritation. "You're making a spectacle."

"You sound surprised." Roland tightened his hold slightly, guiding her into the next step. "You enjoy defiance too much." Anastasia leaned in closer, her voice barely above a whisper. "And you despise that you can't stop me." Roland's gaze burned, but he said nothing, only continuing the dance as the crowd watched with fascination.

After the dance, Anastasia was pulled into conversation with Henry, who smirked at her with amusement. He leaned closer, his voice smooth, teasing. "You know, I think Roland nearly combusted when he saw you enter in that gown." Anastasia smirked, taking a sip of her wine. "I was aiming for a reaction." Henry's lips curled. "And you got one. From the entire court, no less." She glanced at him, noticing the way his gaze lingered on her—not scrutinizing, not judging, but studying with something deeper.

"You make it sound as if I planned all of this," she mused. Henry tilted his head, amusement flickering in his expression. "Didn't you?" Anastasia let out a soft laugh, shaking her head. "I think you enjoy unraveling people a little too much." Henry's eyes gleamed. "Only the ones worth unraveling." She felt her stomach twist—not unpleasantly, but sharply, like the breath before a fall.

The tension between them crackled, heavier than before, charged with something unspoken—something felt rather than said. Henry's gaze traveled over her, lingering in a way that made her stomach twist. "Y'know, you look like you belong here Anastasia," he murmured, eyes gleaming. Anastasia exhaled slowly, unsure if he meant it as a compliment or a challenge. Before she could respond, Lady Eugenia materialized, her expression poised but dripping in condescension.

"My lady," Eugenia said with mock sweetness. "You've certainly captured the court's attention tonight." Anastasia smiled without warmth. "You sound pleased." Eugenia gave a soft laugh, sipping from her goblet. "Merely intrigued. You surprise me, truly. I thought you'd cower beneath all this weight." Anastasia held her gaze steadily. "Disappointing, isn't it?" Eugenia's smile faltered briefly, but she recovered quickly, her amusement turning sharper, crueler.

"I wouldn't celebrate too soon, dear," Eugenia mused. "Being adored is one thing. Being kept is another." Anastasia's jaw tightened, but she refused to let the words settle into her bones.

As the ball went on, Anastasia felt the weight of alcohol slowing her limbs, her steps uneven as she tried to walk toward Roland again. Her fingers clenched slightly at the folds of her gown, her breath hitching as the room spun for just a fraction of a second. She nearly collapsed onto the floor, her body tipping forward. Roland moved instinctively, stepping forward to catch her but Henry got there first. His hands wrapped around her waist, steady, firm, protective. Roland stiffened, his eyes flashing.

"I'll escort her to her quarters," Henry murmured, his tone both casual and possessive. Roland opened his mouth to protest, but before he could speak, his father's hand landed on his shoulder. George shook his head slowly, silencing him with a single motion. Roland clenched his jaw, but said nothing. Henry lifted Anastasia, carrying her easily, moving toward the exit as the nobles watched in stunned silence.

As murmurs threatened to spill into gossip, King George raised his goblet, addressing the crowd. "The princess has been struck by illness," he declared smoothly. "We cannot risk anyone else catching it. The help has escorted her to bed." There was no room for argument. The court nodded along.

Henry pushed open the bedroom door, stepping into the dimly lit chamber with careful precision. The candlelight flickered softly against the stone walls, casting long shadows across the space as he carried Anastasia toward the bed. She was still heavy with wine, her body languid against his chest, her breath slow, uneven.

Gently, he laid her down, fingers brushing against the silk of her gown as he adjusted the blankets, making sure she wouldn't wake shivering in the night. Her eyes fluttered open slightly, gaze hazy and distant. "I wish I'd met you in the house," she murmured. Henry frowned slightly, confused. "In the house?"

"Instead of Roland," she continued, voice softer now, more drowsy, lost in the haze of exhaustion and alcohol.

Henry paused, watching her carefully, his expression unreadable. Then, with quiet resolve, he leaned down, pressing a soft kiss to her forehead. "Sleep," he murmured. Anastasia didn't protest, her eyelids drifting shut, her body sinking into the sheets as the weight of the night finally pulled her into unconsciousness. Henry watched her for a moment longer before silently stepping out and closing the door behind him.

✳✳✳

Anastasia stood within the halls of Elsmere Manor, but the space was different, blurred, as if time itself had been stretched and distorted.

The air was heavy, and across the chamber, a woman appeared—her gown rich and dark, her presence commanding yet restrained, her delicate hands gliding across the furniture as she moved with quiet purpose. Anastasia knew her instantly, even though she had never seen her in waking life. Lucinda Cameron. The recognition struck deep, because she had—once, long ago—seen Lucinda's face in a tiny portrait framed within her grandmother's locket.

Lucinda turned slightly, as though sensing Anastasia's presence—her eyes sharp, knowing. Anastasia tried to step forward, tried to call out but the dream snapped apart, the world plunging into darkness once more.

✳✳✳

The sharp slam of the bedroom door startled Anastasia awake. Before she could properly orient herself, Roland's voice thundered across the room. "Get up," he barked. Anastasia groaned, rubbing her temple, her body still weighed down by the remnants of wine from the night before.

But Roland was relentless.

"You demean us all, Anastasia," he seethed, pacing near the window, his stance rigid with fury. Anastasia blinked sluggishly, sitting up. "What now?" Roland turned sharply, his expression storm-dark, livid. "Be quiet and listen to your husband for once." She huffed a short laugh, shaking her head. "What an inspiring lecture so early in the morning." Roland ignored her sarcasm, his teeth clenched. "Have you forgotten you're in line to be Queen?" he snapped. "Or do you simply not care?"

Anastasia met his glare with calm defiance. "You speak of royalty as if it's a leash." Roland stepped closer, towering over her now, his voice lower, sharper.

"How about, for a start, don't act like a harlot?" The words landed harshly, like a slap. Anastasia sat frozen for a beat, the insult cutting deep despite her usual resilience. Then, she exhaled slowly, smoothing a hand down the sheets. "Oh, Darling," she murmured, her voice mock-sweet, laced with venom. "If I wanted to act like a harlot, I'd hardly limit myself to your court."

Roland's jaw twitched, but before the fight could escalate, the sound of footsteps echoed down the hall. King George's voice carried from beyond the door. "We leave within the hour." Roland didn't say another word, only turned on his heel and stormed out. Anastasia sighed heavily, rubbing her eyes. So much for a peaceful morning.

The courtyard was alive with preparations, the horses saddled, bows and quivers distributed among the noblemen, laughter and boastful remarks floating through the air as the hunting party prepared to leave. Anastasia approached Roland as he adjusted the leather strap of his gloves, his expression still carved from stone.

She ignored his residual anger, instead brushing dust off his coat, straightening the folds as if performing the duty of a loving wife. Then, with a knowing smirk, she murmured just loud enough for him to hear. "Come back to me in one piece, Darling."

Roland stiffened, barely sparing her a glance. Still, he leaned forward just enough, pressing a swift, firm kiss against her lips—a performance, as much as it was an act of control. And then, without another word, he mounted his horse and rode off, joining the others as they disappeared into the woods.

The moment the hunting party was out of sight, Anastasia moved swiftly through the palace, calling upon the head housekeeper, the steward, and several senior attendants—the ones who knew the inner workings of the estate better than anyone. She listened carefully, absorbing every injustice, every overworked handmaiden, every exhausted cook, every stable hand denied adequate rest.

Then, she enacted change.

She drafted an immediate order, ensuring that every servant had at least two full days off per fortnight, a luxury unheard of before. She restructured shifts, preventing the same workers from bearing the brunt of the hardest tasks each day. She insisted on alternating duties, distributing workload evenly. She checked the servants' meal provisions, discovering that many were underfed while the court feasted lavishly. She directed extra food from the royal kitchens to be reserved for the staff, making sure no one went hungry under her rule.

Later that afternoon, Anastasia sat at her writing desk, scheming another kind of rebellion, one born of affection rather than policy. She had seen it clearly, Harper's lingering glances toward Evelina, her shy hesitations, her soft admiration, always hovering on the edge of words unspoken.

And she had seen Evelina's quiet smiles, the delicate way she looked at Harper, as if she wasn't sure she was allowed to want something more than duty. They were adorable but utterly incapable of acting on their own feelings. So, Anastasia took matters into her own hands.

With careful precision, she penned two letters. One addressed to Harper, signed under Evelina's name, requesting a meeting in the palace gardens at sunset. The other addressed to Evelina, signed under Harper's name, requesting the same meeting at the same time. Each sealed carefully, discreetly passed to the intended recipients via trusted messengers. And then, she waited.

As the sun dipped toward the horizon, Anastasia hid behind the trellis, peering out toward the fountain, watching the scene unfold. Harper stood rigidly, hands fidgeting, boots scuffing against the stone pathway. Evelina arrived hesitantly, her shawl wrapped tightly around her shoulders, her expression uncertain but quietly hopeful.

They stumbled through conversation at first, awkward, unsure until laughter spilled between them, soft, genuine. And then, Harper reached for Evelina's hand, her fingers curling around hers in quiet confidence. Anastasia grinned, satisfied, retreating just before they could catch her spying.

The evening air clung to Evelina's umber skin, crisp and heavy, the scent of earth and late-blooming roses wrapping around her like a quiet warning. She should have never come. She should have crumpled the letter, tossed it into the fire, let the words burn before they could plant themselves in her mind, before they could lead her here, to her.

Evelina stood stiffly beneath the overgrown trellis, hands wringing against the fabric of her shawl, breath shallow, uncertain. Her curly brown locks were pulled back slightly, though loose strands framed her round face, the cool air grazing over her button nose.

Harper, in contrast, was calm. **Steady.**

Harper was beside her, close but not close enough to touch, and somehow that was worse. Because Evelina could still feel the ghost of her fingertips against her skin from earlier, warm, sure, deliberate.

She stood taller than Evelina, her lean frame taut with muscle earned from years of hard work. Freckles speckled her tan skin, a constellation scattered across sharp cheekbones, trailing over the bridge of her nose. Her tweedy auburn hair, always somewhat unruly, was half tucked behind her ears, where wisps curled wildly near her jaw. When she smirked, the gap in her teeth made her look just a little more mischievous than she already was.

And now, here they were. The letter had brought them together. Had made them face something they had both been avoiding. "I shouldn't have come," Evelina whispered, barely audible. Harper exhaled sharply, tilting her head slightly as she studied her, unreadable. "But you did."

Evelina flinched. "It was a mistake." Harper huffed, crossing her arms. "You don't believe that." She wanted to argue, to deny it. Wanted to retreat into the safe numbness of pretending none of this mattered. But it did. And that was the problem. Evelina inhaled sharply, shaking her head. "People will talk."

"They already do," Harper countered, voice quiet but firm. Evelina let out a soft, bitter laugh, turning away slightly, hands trembling as she gripped the fabric of her shawl tighter. "You don't understand. This world isn't kind to women like us." Harper was silent for a moment, long enough that Evelina almost thought she had given up, almost thought she would let her run. But Harper never let anything go.

"Do you think I don't know that?" Harper finally said, voice softer now, laced with something raw. Evelina looked at her then, truly looked at her.

Harper was calm, steady, but not unaffected. There was something lingering in her expression, something careful, something Evelina wasn't sure she had ever seen from anyone before. "I know what people think," Harper murmured, gaze unwavering. "I know what they say. But I also know that I am tired of living for what other people expect."

Evelina swallowed, shaking her head. "It's not that simple." Harper's lips curled slightly, not in amusement, but in knowing. "It's never simple." Silence stretched between them, thick and suffocating. Evelina felt herself battling two halves of herself, the half that wanted to run, and the half that wanted to stay. Harper took a careful step forward. Evelina didn't move away.

"You're scared," Harper murmured. Not a question. Not an accusation. Just the truth. Evelina's breath hitched. "Of course I am."

Harper's voice remained steady. "I won't ask you to stop being afraid."

Evelina's fingers curled into the fabric of her sleeve, grounding herself in something tangible, something she could hold onto. She thought Harper would step back. Thought she would let her go, let her fall into the easy escape of pretending this had never happened. But Harper lifted a hand, hesitant and careful, giving Evelina every opportunity to step away. She didn't.

Harper let her fingers brush lightly over Evelina's wrist. A question. An offer. Not a demand. Evelina swallowed hard, her pulse loud in her ears.

Then finally, she let herself feel it. The warmth. The quiet. The terrifying, unshaken certainty that she could want this. That she could choose this. Harper inhaled, waiting. "Tell me what you want." Evelina's throat tightened. "I don't know how," she admitted, voice barely above a whisper. "You don't have to know," Harper murmured, voice softer now, quieter, more certain than Evelina had ever been in her life.

Then suddenly, Evelina leaned in, hesitant, uncertain but Harper met her halfway, her hand sliding gently to cup Evelina's cheek, her fingers pressing lightly into the softness of her skin.

Their lips touched and Evelina melted into Harper's arms. She inhaled sharply, fingers curling into Harper's jacket, grounding herself in the warmth of her body, the feeling of being held in a way that did not demand, did not force, only gave.

Harper sighed against her lips, smiling ever so slightly before deepening the kiss. And when they finally pulled away, when Evelina's head rested against Harper's chest for just a beat too long, she knew that she would never run from this again.

Evelina sat stiffly, fingers twisting in the fabric of her dress, her eyes darting toward the flickering candlelight and then away, refusing to meet Anastasia's gaze. The warmth of Harper's lips still lingered against her own, seared into the edges of her mind, leaving behind something she couldn't quite name, couldn't quite process.

"She kissed me." The words were barely a whisper, as if saying them too loudly might undo the moment entirely. Anastasia didn't react right away, didn't interrupt, didn't push, didn't pry. She simply waited. Evelina exhaled sharply, shaking her head, the weight of it all pressing against her ribs. "I don't know what to do."

Anastasia tilted her head slightly, considering. "Do you want to run from it?" Evelina swallowed, staring down at her hands. "I—" She hesitated. She had expected the answer to be yes.

She had spent her entire life avoiding things she couldn't control, things that could hurt her, things that could unravel everything she had carefully built around herself. But this wasn't something she wanted to erase. "I don't want to run." Her voice was quiet but firm.

Anastasia smiled softly, relief blooming behind her eyes. "Then don't."

Evelina huffed a weak laugh, shaking her head. "It's not that simple."

"It never is," Anastasia agreed, voice gentle, patient. "But nothing worth having ever is." Evelina swallowed, emotions thick in her throat, the vulnerability of it all threatening to consume her whole.

"I'm scared, Ana," she whispered, barely audible. "I don't know how to do this. How to let it happen." Anastasia shifted then, closing the space between them, wrapping Evelina in an embrace so certain, so unwavering that she could barely breathe. And Evelina let herself melt into it, into the comfort, into the reassurance that she didn't have to know everything right now.

"That's okay," Anastasia murmured against her hair. "You don't have to figure it all out at once." Evelina squeezed her eyes shut, her breath uneven, the weight of fear and longing tangled together inside her.

Anastasia pulled back just slightly, hands resting firmly on Evelina's shoulders, maroon eyes meeting deep brown. "You've spent your whole life afraid of what people might think," Anastasia whispered. "Isn't it time to start thinking about what you want?"

The morning mist clung to the forest, weaving through the towering oaks as the men rode through the undergrowth, their guns strapped securely against their saddles. Roland kept his pace steady, his grip firm around the reins of his stallion, but his father's presence beside him was a suffocating weight.

King George rode with calculated ease, his eyes flickering toward Roland every so often, as if measuring his restraint. "You've let her grow too bold," George finally murmured, his voice smooth but cutting. Roland exhaled sharply, already expecting this conversation. "She is outspoken," he admitted. "But that does not make her dangerous."

George's lips curled slightly, as if humored by Roland's naivety. "You are blind to what could happen if she is not kept in control."

Roland gritted his teeth but said nothing. "You know the Princess of Prussia is still unmarried," George continued, his tone laced with quiet suggestion. "The alliance could still be arranged—if, of course, there was reason enough to remove your current bride." Roland's posture stiffened immediately. "What are you saying?" he demanded, turning toward his father. George tilted his head, his expression unnervingly calm. "I am saying that there are methods—means—to ensure the future remains intact. You would do well to remember that."

Roland's blood boiled. "She is my wife," he said sharply. "And I will not stand for you speaking about her as if she is disposable."

George raised a brow, unimpressed. "You think that will be enough to protect her?" Roland's anger cracked through the air, his voice loud, seething. "She is under my protection," he snapped. "You will not threaten her again." His father was unfazed, merely watching him with mild amusement, but as Roland's fury escalated, his horse sensed the tension—rearing up violently, its hooves thrashing against the dirt. Before Roland could calm it, the force knocked him off, sending him crashing into the forest floor.

Roland's vision blurred slightly from the impact, but he remained conscious as Henry swiftly dismounted, stepping toward him. George barely spared his son a glance before addressing Henry. "Carry him back," he ordered. "Make sure he is seen to properly." Henry hesitated for only a moment, then nodded, gripping Roland under the arms and hoisting him onto his own horse. Roland grumbled in protest, but Henry ignored him, riding swiftly toward the palace.

The castle loomed in the distance as the riders approached, the guards stepping aside as Henry led his injured prince through the grand entryway. Anastasia was already waiting, rushing forward the moment she spotted them. "What happened?" she asked quickly, reaching to steady Roland as Henry began to dismount. "He fell," Henry muttered, swinging down smoothly. "Hard."

Roland huffed, irritated. "I didn't fall. The horse bucked." Henry rolled his eyes. "Same result." Anastasia shook her head, dismissing their bickering. "I've got him from here." Henry studied her for a beat, then nodded, stepping back.

Roland grumbled under his breath as Anastasia guided him inside, leading him to his chambers, where she swiftly fetched a pot of warm water and a cloth.

She dabbed the wound gently, her fingers steady despite his occasional complaints. "You're terrible at sitting still," she muttered, pressing the cloth against his temple. Roland hissed slightly, exhaling through his nose. "You're terrible at following rules," he countered. Anastasia smirked, dipping the cloth back into the water. "Then I suppose we're even."

Roland watched her carefully, his anger quieting into something softer, his gaze lingering too long on her face. The silence stretched between them—charged, uncertain, fragile. Anastasia paused, the cloth hovering near his cheek, her breath hitching slightly as their proximity grew too close, too intimate. Roland's gaze flickered, the space between them vanishing by inches—

Until the door swung open abruptly, Evelina's voice piercing the moment. "My lady," she said quickly. "The King has returned. He wishes to speak with you in private." Anastasia snapped back into focus, straightening immediately. Roland's jaw clenched, his expression darkening once more.

Anastasia exhaled, placing the cloth aside. "Then I suppose I shouldn't keep him waiting," she murmured.

The throne room was cold, imposing, the towering pillars casting long shadows against the stone floor. Anastasia stood before King George, her hands folded neatly in front of her, her posture carefully measured—controlled, deliberate. The king sat on his throne, watching her with calculated scrutiny, his expression stern, unimpressed. "You will need to adjust, Princess," he began smoothly. "Your presence in this court is... unrefined."

Anastasia held her tongue, resisting the urge to retort. George continued, his tone dangerously even. "A princess must be poised. Dutiful. Elegant in silence." The message was clear. Less thinking. Less speaking. Less being herself.

She forced a polite nod, keeping her wit buried beneath practiced restraint. George watched her for a moment before leaning forward slightly, his fingers tapping against the carved armrest. "You enjoy meddling," he observed. "Perhaps too much." Anastasia did not falter, but she could feel the weight of the conversation shifting—from correction to something else. Something heavier.

"Do you believe you have power here?" he asked casually. Anastasia chose her words carefully, her voice soft but firm. "I am the wife of your son, Your Majesty." George tilted his head, amusement flickering at the edge of his irritation. "Yes. And yet..." he exhaled slowly, feigning thoughtfulness. "It would not be difficult to replace you."

Anastasia's blood ran cold, but she remained composed, masking the sharpness of her reaction beneath quiet calculation. He was threatening her. Indirectly, deliberately. She lifted her chin slightly, a deliberate gesture—not defiant enough to be disrespectful, but just enough to show she wasn't frightened.

"With all due respect, Your Majesty," she murmured, her voice layered in faux sweetness, "I imagine it would be far more difficult to explain why your heir's first wife mysteriously vanished."

George's eyes darkened, but his expression remained composed. "You assume I play fair," he mused. "You assume I don't know how to play at all," Anastasia countered, still controlled, still careful, but no longer pretending to be meek. The king's gaze lingered, sharp as a blade. Then, he waved a dismissive hand. "You are dismissed." Anastasia curtsied smoothly, turning sharply on her heel and leaving without hesitation.

She rushed down the corridor, her pulse hammering as she pushed open Roland's door, stepping inside without waiting for permission. Roland looked up instantly, his expression tight. "What did he say?" he demanded. Anastasia exhaled sharply, pushing her hair back. "He told me I was unfit. That I needed to adjust." Roland rolled his eyes, clearly expecting that part. Then she paused, choosing her words carefully.

"He implied I could be replaced." Roland stilled, his grip tightening around the armrest of his chair. For a moment, he looked ready to storm out—ready to march into the throne room and unleash hell. But the instant he tried to stand, pain flared in his ribs, forcing him back down with a sharp inhale.

"Damn it," he muttered, exhaling through gritted teeth. Anastasia stepped forward, placing a firm hand on his shoulder, guiding him back into the seat. "You're injured, Roland," she said softly but firmly. "And I can handle myself." Roland's jaw clenched, frustration evident, but he didn't argue.

She adjusted the cloth against his wound, careful, methodical, deliberate. After a beat of silence, he finally spoke. "Thank you," he murmured. Anastasia paused, surprised by the sincerity in his tone.

Then, just as quickly as the moment came, Roland blinked, straightened his posture, and hardened his expression once more—slipping back into formality, into duty, into the emotionless facade that protected him. She shook her head, amused but unimpressed. "Ah," she muttered. "There he is again." Roland didn't respond, only watched her carefully as she gathered herself and stood.

The sunlight filtered softly through the grand windows, casting a warm glow against the polished floors as Anastasia stood near a mirror, carefully adjusting the folds of her gown. A knock at the door pulled her attention, and when she turned, Evelina stood at the threshold, her cheeks flushed with excitement. "My lady," Evelina murmured, her fingers twisting together, almost as if she were trying to suppress a grin.

Anastasia arched a brow, feigning innocence. "You look particularly bright today. Something to share?" Evelina shifted on her feet, then exhaled quickly, her voice brimming with quiet giddiness. "I kissed Harper."

Anastasia's eyes widened dramatically, gasping as if she had just heard the most scandalous confession in history. "You kissed him?" she echoed, pressing a hand to her chest. "Evelina, how could you keep such a momentous event from me? I am absolutely devastated I wasn't present."

Evelina laughed, shaking her head, her amusement shifting into knowing mischief. "You planned this," she accused lightly. Anastasia blinked, feigning confusion. "Whatever do you mean?"

Evelina held up the letter she had received, tapping a finger against the page. "I know your handwriting." Anastasia froze for a fraction of a second, then burst into laughter, her secret betrayed. Evelina smiled fondly, stepping forward and wrapping her arms around Anastasia in a quick, grateful hug. "Thank you," Evelina whispered. Anastasia hesitated only briefly, then hugged back, warmth spreading through her. When Evelina finally pulled away, her eyes still gleamed with happiness, and she rushed off, disappearing down the corridor, leaving Anastasia grinning to herself.

She turned back into the room, still smiling. Only to hear Roland chuckle from his seat near the fireplace. "You really cannot stay out of anything, can you?" he mused, leaning back against the armrest, his amusement clear despite the lingering pain in his ribs.

Anastasia rolled her eyes, but she couldn't quite suppress the satisfied smirk that lingered on her lips. "No," she admitted smoothly. "And I never will." Roland shook his head, muttering something under his breath, but his laughter didn't fade.

TEN

The stable smelled of hay and fresh leather, the golden afternoon light filtering through the cracks in the wooden beams overhead. Anastasia trailed her fingers along the stable walls, her mousey brown curls tumbling messily over her shoulders, when Roland's voice cut through the quiet.

"Still want to learn how to ride a horse?" She turned sharply, brushing stray strands of hair away from her freckled face, her eyes narrowing in suspicion. Roland stood near the gate, his arms folded across his chest, his usual air of irritation replaced by something unreadable. The sunlight skimmed over the golden strands of his hair, his posture rigid but notably less combative than usual.

She studied him carefully. "You're offering to teach me?" Roland exhaled heavily, as if regretting his words already. "Consider it repayment. You helped me after the fall."Anastasia grinned, stepping forward. "Ah. So you do acknowledge that I saved your life." Roland rolled his eyes, grabbing the reins of his stallion. "Get over here before I change my mind."

Anastasia walked over to Roland, her gaze sweeping across the stalls—until her breath hitched slightly. There, standing calmly, his ears flicking at the sounds around him, was a blonde stallion, his golden coat glimmering under the streaks of afternoon light. There, standing calmly, his ears flicking at the sounds around him, was a blonde stallion, his golden coat glimmering under the streaks of afternoon light.

She froze.

Her fingers instinctively reached out, brushing over the horse's mane, feeling the familiar texture beneath her touch. *Lucky*. It was absurd, really—the way her mind immediately latched onto the memory of her childhood toy, the stuffed horse she had once held tightly against her chest in that tiny toy shop, the one her grandmother had bought for her without hesitation.

The sensation swelled too quickly, catching her off guard, emotion pressing at the back of her throat. Her eyes stung, threatening to spill before she could stop them. Roland noticed immediately, his brows knitting together. "What's wrong?" he asked, his voice steady but laced with curiosity. Anastasia cleared her throat, blinking rapidly, brushing the wetness from her eyes before the moment could stretch too far.

160

"Nothing," she muttered. "Just... he reminds me of something."

Roland tilted his head slightly, observing her with mild skepticism. "Something or someone?" She exhaled lightly, sidestepping his question. "Both, maybe." Roland didn't push further. Instead, he patted the horse's side, nodding toward Anastasia. "This is Dogberry," he introduced. "Named after Shakespeare's fool." Anastasia arched a brow, amused despite herself. "A fool?" Roland smirked, glancing at the stallion. "He's not the brightest creature, but he's loyal."

Anastasia pressed a hand against Dogberry's nose, her expression softening instantly. "Well, hello, my darling," she murmured, her voice dipping into a playful, affectionate tone, the way one might speak to a beloved pet. Dogberry snorted lightly, his ears flicking in curiosity. Anastasia grinned, scratching gently beneath his mane.

"I bet you're the sweetest boy, huh?" she cooed. "You're just misunderstood. Unlike a certain prince, I suspect." Roland rolled his eyes, muttering something under his breath, but Anastasia ignored him entirely, too focused on stroking Dogberry's mane, whispering small praises into his ear like he was some pampered lapdog. Roland watched her for a beat, amused.

"You realize he's a horse," he pointed out. Anastasia didn't even glance at him, just smirked. "You say that like it's supposed to matter."

The moment Anastasia mounted Dogberry, she knew it was going to be a disaster. Roland stood beside her, steadying the reins, but she could already feel the lack of control, the unfamiliarity of the movement beneath her. "This feels... terrifying," she muttered.

Roland smirked, adjusting the strap near her boot. "For someone who talks endlessly, you are surprisingly afraid of simple things." Anastasia huffed, gripping the reins tightly. "Simple things? This is an enormous animal with the power to throw me across the yard." Roland stepped back, giving her a pointed glance. "Only if you keep holding the reins like you're trying to strangle it."

She loosened her grip—barely—but enough for the stallion to shift comfortably beneath her. Roland watched carefully, then nodded. "Now, move forward." She hesitated. "Like... now?" Roland raised a brow, unimpressed. "Unless you'd like to sit there forever."

Anastasia muttered something under her breath, then pressed gently against Dogberry's sides—and the moment it began to walk, she let out a small yelp. Roland snorted, shaking his head. "You are ridiculous." Anastasia glared at him, but when she steadied herself a second time, her movements were less clumsy, more natural.

After several minutes, Anastasia felt herself ease into the rhythm, Dogberry moving smoothly beneath her, her body adjusting to the movement in a way she hadn't expected. Roland walked beside her, observing quietly, his brown eyes glinting with faint approval. "You're picking it up faster than I thought," he muttered.

Anastasia grinned, flashing him a triumphant look. "You doubted me." Roland exhaled, rubbing his temple. "Of course I doubted you. You scream when a door swings open too fast."

They continued deeper into the woods, the air thick with the scent of damp earth, pine, and the lingering sweetness of wildflowers. Birds trilled from the canopy, the sound mingling with the soft crunch of hooves against dirt.

"This place is beautiful," Anastasia murmured, running a hand across Dogberry's mane. Roland watched her for a moment, then nodded. "It's peaceful." The silence between them was comfortable, no longer weighed by the tension that had ruled their early days together.

Anastasia tilted her head slightly, eyeing him from the corner of her vision. "Do you come here often?" Roland exhaled through his nose, shifting

in his saddle. "Not as much as I used to."
Anastasia arched a brow, sensing something
unspoken beneath his words. "Used to?" Roland's
jaw tightened slightly, but after a brief pause, he
spoke. "My mother used to ride here," he
admitted. "It was her escape from court."
Anastasia stilled, sensing the weight of the
memory.

She didn't press further—but she understood.
Instead, she leaned down, stroking Dogberry's
neck, offering a quiet distraction. Roland
watched her, his eyes trailing the way she
handled the reins now—far more naturally, far
less hesitant.

"You've improved," he muttered. Anastasia
smirked, sitting straighter. "You sound shocked."
Roland gave her a pointed look. "I am." She
laughed, shaking her head.

Then she winced, remembering her previous
dream. She knew she had to tell Roland. He was
the only one that might have known Lucinda. "I
have to tell you something. Something that might
sound weird but you just have to have an open
mind, okay?" Roland looked confused but
nodded in response. Anastasia took a breath, "I
had a dream last night. It wasn't much but an
ancestor of mine, Lucinda, was stood in the
manor. She looked at me like- like she saw me. I

know it sounds crazy but it *must* mean something, Roland."

His face showed how puzzled he felt, but then his eyes softened. "Okay. I believe you. If you feel it may mean something more, I shall follow your intuition Anastasia." Anastasia smiled, feeling relieved that he actually backed her on something.

Roland sat astride his own horse beside her, watching with barely concealed amusement, his arms folded across his chest. "You're gripping the reins like they're going to save your life," he pointed out, smirking. "Relax your hands. Let him feel your direction, not your panic." Anastasia huffed, rolling her shoulders. "Easy for you to say. You were practically born on one of these."

"And yet you claim people in your time don't use horses at all?" Roland raised a brow, guiding his horse to circle hers at a slow, steady pace. "What do you travel in? Walking everywhere seems terribly inefficient."

She laughed under her breath, shaking her head. "We have cars. Machines that run on gas—or electricity—that can take us anywhere faster than a horse ever could." Roland blinked at her, unimpressed. "You expect me to believe there is a way to move without hooves touching the ground?"

She grinned. "Oh, much more than that. We have airplanes—metal birds that can fly across entire oceans in hours." Roland exhaled sharply, shaking his head as if trying to absorb something too absurd to be true. "You're either a terrible liar or the future is madness."

"Probably both." Anastasia smirked, loosening her grip slightly, letting Dogweed take a few unhurried steps forward. Her body stiffened as he moved, but she forced herself to stay steady. Roland watched her carefully before speaking again, his tone quieter now. "Tell me more."

She glanced at him, then at the horizon stretching endlessly before them. "Everything is different. Everything is faster. We don't grow our own food the way you do—most people buy it, already prepared, wrapped in plastic. Cities are enormous, filled with towering buildings made of glass and steel, lights blinking from every corner." She sighed, a wistful smile tugging at her lips. "There are places where you can get coffee at any time of day. Music plays from tiny devices you carry in your pocket. You can talk to someone on the other side of the world without ever leaving your house."

Roland listened intently, something unreadable flickering across his expression. "And yet you miss things."

Anastasia inhaled, nodding. "I miss the quiet. The simplicity. The way the stars feel closer here, the way the world feels... untouched." She glanced at him, forcing a small smile. "And I miss home. But not in the way I expected."

Roland tilted his head slightly. "What do you mean?" She hesitated, shifting against the saddle, meeting his gaze with quiet honesty. "I miss the people. My friends, my family. But when I think of home now—" Her breath hitched, voice soft, hesitant. "I think of here. I think of you."

Roland's posture straightened, the teasing edge in his eyes fading into something else—something deeper, something warmer. "You are the strangest thing that has ever happened to me, Anastasia." She let out a breathless laugh, shaking her head. "Tell me about it."

The gardens were alive with colour, the roses in full bloom, their petals brushing softly against the breeze, filling the air with their delicate fragrance. Anastasia walked beside Evelina, her hands folded loosely behind her back, trailing her fingers against the hedges as they wandered along the cobbled pathway.

"You look different," Anastasia mused, her lips curling into a smirk. Evelina tilted her head, amusement flickering in her dark eyes. "Different how?"

"Like someone who kissed a certain stable hand in the gardens."

Evelina giggled, shaking her head. "You are insufferable." Anastasia laughed, nudging her gently. "Admit it. You're happy." Evelina exhaled softly, her expression shifting. "I am." Anastasia smiled, but something in her chest twisted—a quiet longing, something unspoken.

"I wish I had a Harper," she murmured absently. Evelina raised an eyebrow, giving her a knowing glance. "You have Roland." Anastasia forced a breathy laugh, feigning mock admiration, clasping her hands to her chest dramatically.

"Oh, yes," she sighed. "How lucky I am to have a prince who constantly reminds me how inconvenient I am." Evelina rolled her eyes, but she studied Anastasia carefully, as if searching for something beneath the humor. Anastasia looked away, letting her gaze drift toward the treetops, the afternoon light filtering through the leaves.

It wasn't just Roland. It was... everything. The truth was, she had never truly felt in love—not in this time, nor in her own. She had admired people, had been drawn to them, but the feeling—the deep, all-consuming love people spoke about—had never settled in her bones. And now, standing in a time that wasn't hers, among people who barely understood her, she wondered if she ever would.

The pair continued to walk through the gardens when they heard footsteps behind them. They quickened their pace but the footsteps kept pace with them until Lord Percival appeared beside them. "Your Highness, Miss Elizabeth. How are you fine ladies this morn?" Anastasia cleared her throat, visibly uncomfortable. "It's Evelina, sire." Evelina meekly said, her eyes looking anywhere but Lord Percival. "Ah, Elizabeth, Evelina. An honest mistake." He said, a grin growing on his beet red face. "Now, forgive me for being crude but Miss Anastasia you truly have a good taste in servants. She is simply delectable." Anastasia nodded, trying to answer him without entertaining his conversation. She placed one hand on Evelina's back, trying to be prepared for any direction he may go.

"Not going to answer? Hmm, just as well that I only need your servant to help me... unburden myself. Her mulatto skin makes no difference to me, never you mind." Anastasia had no words, she froze in place. "Eva, run!" She yelled, pushing Evelina forward. Evelina sprinted into the closest door she could and when she was safe, Anastasia turned to run as well. However, her efforts were in vain as Lord Percival had grabbed her arm and kept her in place.

"Please. Just let me go." She pleaded but he seemed to have no reaction. "Never mind, you'll just have to do. I prefer a smaller woman but a wench is a wench." He started to lift her skirt, despite Anastasia's attempts at fighting him off. "Help! Someone please, help me!" She screamed but Lord Percival shoved a handkerchief in her mouth and continued lowering his britches.

"No one will help a *bitch* like you. Not with your diseased views." Anastasia sobbed and still tried to scream but minimal noise escaped the small gaps of her mouth that the cloth didn't cover. Just when all hope seemed lost, Roland ran out from the same door Evelina had run into. She had gone to get him.

Roland sprinted over to Anastasia's aid and punched Lord Percival in the nose, sending him reeling. Lord Percival stood up, blood dripping from his nostrils, and swung at Roland. Roland blocked the blow and countered with a powerful punch that knocked Lord Percival unconscious.

Anastasia, still shaken and traumatized, fell into Roland's arms. She refused to speak and only cried, her body trembling with fear. Roland carried her to her quarters, ensuring she was safe and secure. He sat with her, holding her and stroking her hair, trying to calm her down.

✳✳✳

The morning sunlight filtered softly through the curtains, casting a hazy glow across the chamber, but Anastasia had barely moved from where Roland had placed her the night before. Her body felt heavy, drained, as though every ounce of her energy had seeped away into the silence of the room.

The echoes of yesterday's horror lingered in her mind, looping in a cycle she couldn't break. She had no words. No strength. Just the quiet sound of her own breathing, her own mind racing beneath a mask of exhaustion. Then, a gentle knock tapped at the door.

The door creaked open, and Evelina stepped inside first, her careful hands balancing a tray of breakfast—a plate of warm bread, soft fruit, and tea steeped perfectly. Roland followed behind her, his movements stiff, one hand gripping a bouquet of roses, their petals a soft, delicate shade of blush pink. Neither of them spoke immediately. Evelina set the tray down gently beside the bed, watching Anastasia carefully. Roland lingered near the doorway, his grip tightening slightly around the stems of the flowers, as if unsure what to say or do.

"You need to eat," Evelina murmured, her voice soft, careful, not pushing—just guiding. Anastasia blinked sluggishly, staring at the tray but making no move toward it. Roland stepped forward, clearing his throat. "I brought these," he muttered, awkward but sincere, setting the bouquet beside her.

Anastasia exhaled slowly, her fingers tracing the smooth fabric of the blanket beneath her. After a long beat, she finally reached forward, plucking one of the roses from the bouquet. Evelina and Roland exchanged a glance, the tension in the room deep but fragile, settling into something unspoken—something that neither of them quite knew how to fix. But for now, they were there.

The curtains billowed softly as Evelina sat carefully at the edge of Anastasia's bed, her expression guarded but deeply concerned. "I should have stayed," Evelina murmured, her voice tight with guilt. Anastasia shifted slightly, reaching forward and taking Evelina's hand in hers, squeezing it gently.

"You did the right thing," she whispered. "You got help." Evelina exhaled shakily, but she nodded, her fingers tightening around Anastasia's. "I was scared," she admitted. Anastasia nodded, understanding without needing to say more. "You need fresh air," Roland announced flatly, crossing the space with ease. Anastasia arched her brow, unimpressed with his abruptness. "Do I?"

Roland exhaled sharply, shaking his head. "Evelina thinks so. I think so." He paused, studying her. "You cannot just sit here forever, Angel." Anastasia blinked, caught off guard. "Angel?" she echoed, a smirk curling onto her lips. "Are you feeling alright?"

Roland rolled his eyes, but he didn't take the remark back—if anything, he liked seeing her grin again, even if it was brief. "If calling you that gets you outside," he muttered, "then I'll tolerate the consequences."

Anastasia laughed softly, shaking her head. "How generous of you." Roland watched her for a beat, waiting. Finally, she sighed, stretching slightly, feigning deep reluctance. "Fine," she relented. "I'll go." Roland nodded, stepping back toward the door. "Good." Anastasia stood slowly, smoothing the wrinkles from her gown. As she passed him, she tilted her head slightly, amusement flickering in her green eyes.

"I didn't take you for a man of affectionate nicknames," she mused. Roland huffed a laugh, shaking his head. "Don't get used to it." She grinned, but said nothing more, walking past him and out the door toward the gardens. Roland followed, his steps steady beside hers.

The gardens were alive with the scent of roses, their petals stretching toward the sunlight. Anastasia walked slowly, her skirts brushing against the cobbled path, her fingers trailing lightly against the hedge-lined walls. Evelina walked beside her, her steps graceful, her eyes darting occasionally toward Anastasia, checking on her without words.

Roland followed a few paces behind, his presence subtle but constant, as if ensuring she wouldn't disappear. "You seem happier today," Evelina observed, tucking a stray curl behind her ear. Anastasia smirked. "I have no choice. My husband insisted I leave the cave."

Evelina laughed, then sighed. "I was worried about you," she admitted. Anastasia exhaled slowly, kicking a stray pebble with the toe of her boot. "I was worried about me too." The words hung between them, quiet but sincere. But Evelina, ever lighthearted, quickly steered the conversation elsewhere. "Harper asked if he could see me again," she confessed, her cheeks dusting with pink.

Anastasia smiled, feeling some of the heaviness lift ever so slightly. "That stable boy is utterly taken with you," she teased. Evelina rolled her eyes, but the happiness in them remained.

Anastasia lifted her face toward the sky, inhaling deeply, as if trying to absorb the peace the gardens offered. "You seem calmer," Evelina noted beside her, her voice gentle but observant. Anastasia exhaled slowly, letting her fingers skim the rough bark of a nearby oak tree. "Momentarily," she admitted, offering Evelina a small smile. "This place makes it easier to forget, even if just for a little while." Evelina nodded, adjusting her shawl around her shoulders.

For a brief moment, she allowed herself to breathe—to exist outside the confines of fear. But then—rushed footsteps sounded behind her, sharp against the cobbled stone. The world tilted. Her breath hitched violently in her chest.

The memory ripped through her like a blade. She whirled around, eyes wide, and the sound tore from her lips before she could stop it—

"No!" Her voice cracked, raw and sharp, her body trembling as sobs broke through the barricade of her composure. Evelina gasped, stepping toward her, but before she could reach Anastasia, Roland was already there.

Roland caught her instantly, arms wrapping around her with fierce determination, pulling her close, solid, steady, grounding. Anastasia shook violently, her hands clutching at his coat, gripping onto something tangible—something real in a moment where everything felt like drowning.

Roland pressed a firm hand against her back, his voice low, unwavering. "You're safe," he murmured. "You're safe. No one will hurt you." Her body pressed against his chest, her sobs muffling against the fabric, but Roland didn't flinch, didn't pull away, didn't hesitate. "I'll always protect you," he promised, his voice quieter now, steadier, as if willing her heartbeat to slow.

She inhaled shakily, her breath uneven. Roland held her for as long as she needed, his grip strong but careful, no urgency—just unwavering presence.

The evening came quietly, the palace settling into its usual rhythm. Anastasia sat by her bedside, brushing her fingers over the cool silk sheets when she noticed something left beside her table.

A silver dagger.

Unembellished. Simple. Yet undeniably meant for her. There was no note, no explanation. But Roland's message was clear. *For protection.* *Anastasia* picked it up slowly, tracing her fingers along the hilt, feeling the cool metal press into her skin. He had left it deliberately, without words—because Roland did not waste them when they were unnecessary.

Her jaw tightened, memories flashing through her mind in sharp waves, unrelenting. Without thinking, she gripped the dagger tightly, her breath quickening, and swung—a fierce, desperate slash into the air. She imagined Percival standing there, his smug, predatory gaze fixed on her, his arrogance poisoning the air.

She swung again, faster, harder, her heart pounding violently against her ribs. She wanted him to feel powerless, just as she had. She wanted to erase his existence with every movement. But then—the dagger slipped from her grasp, clattering loudly against the floor. Her breath hitched, and suddenly, the fury cracked, leaving behind only exhaustion. Anastasia stared down at the dagger, realization settling over her. She had no idea how to use it.

Without wasting another second, she grabbed the dagger, shoved it into her corset, and marched toward Roland's quarters, determined. The corridors were quiet, the flickering torches casting shadows along the stone walls as she paced through the winding halls.

She reached his door, knocking firmly once, twice—then pushing it open without waiting for permission. But the room was empty. Anastasia exhaled sharply, frustration bubbling under her skin. She had come here to thank him—to ask him to teach her, to show her how to wield the weapon he had placed into her hands. And yet, he was nowhere to be found. She stepped inside anyway, her fingers brushing against the edge of his desk, her thoughts spiraling, unsettled.

The ride to Lord Percival's estate was brisk, the wind whipping against Roland's coat, but he barely noticed. His focus was sharp, his anger coiling tightly in his chest, fueling the powerful strides of his stallion as it tore across the dirt road.

By the time the grand manor loomed into view, Roland's grip had tightened around the reins, his knuckles white, his breathing measured but dangerously calm. The guards at the entrance hesitated, but as soon as they saw the murderous look in his eyes, they stepped aside without question.

Roland dismounted swiftly, barely giving his horse a second glance before storming inside, his boots echoing against the marble floors, his presence a force that demanded immediate attention.

The servants whispered hurriedly among themselves, stepping back as he marched toward the study, his movements precise, unwavering, entirely deliberate. And then—he threw open the doors, the heavy wood slamming against the walls, rattling the shelves and sending a sharp jolt through the quiet air.

Percival sat leisurely in a grand armchair, swirling a goblet of wine, his expression utterly composed—mocking, even. Roland did not hesitate. With a swift, furious motion, he grabbed Percival by the collar and slammed him back against the bookshelf, the glasses clattering wildly against the surface, the wood groaning under the sudden impact.

Percival choked out a breath, shock flickering across his features before he forced himself to smirk. "My, my," he drawled, shifting slightly despite Roland's crushing grip. "Has marriage softened you, Prince?" Roland's jaw clenched, his brown eyes dark with fury. "If you ever touch my wife again," he growled, his voice dangerously low, "you won't live to see another sunrise."

Percival let out a strained chuckle, feigning amusement even as Roland pressed him harder against the wood. "You act as though you can dictate everything within these walls," Percival muttered. "She—" Roland cut him off instantly, shoving him back another inch, knocking over a small stack of books with the sheer force.

"She is the princess," Roland snarled, his voice razor-sharp, his grip unrelenting. "You will treat her as such or you will find yourself cast out of this country entirely."

Percival's expression darkened, his amusement dripping away, replaced now with something colder. Roland finally released him, shoving him roughly away, watching as Percival stumbled forward, gripping the desk for balance. "You're making a mistake," Percival muttered, straightening himself, wiping at his collar, attempting to salvage whatever scraps of dignity remained.

Roland stepped back, but his presence did not waver. "No," he corrected, his voice quiet but lethal. "You did." His stare lingered for a moment longer—a warning, a promise, a statement of absolute finality. Then, without another word,

Roland turned sharply on his heel, his boots echoing with finality against the polished floors as he strode out of the study, leaving Percival in stunned silence.

ELEVEN

The palace felt smaller than before, as though its towering walls had closed in around Anastasia, pressing against her from all sides.

She tried everything to push the lingering trauma away, long walks beneath the sprawling oaks in the courtyard, the cool morning air biting against her skin, the scent of damp earth and distant blooms wrapping around her like a whisper of something familiar.

She spent hours wandering the grand halls, avoiding corridors where she knew Lord Percival's shadow might linger, tracing the edges of gold-lined tapestries with absent fingers, trying to lose herself in history rather than memory.

She let Evelina drag her into distractions, into conversations about courtly affairs, about trivial gossip, about whatever nonsense the nobles whispered about behind closed doors. She laughed at Evelina's sharp remarks, her well-crafted observations, but the laughter felt borrowed like something she had stolen for the sake of pretending.

None of it worked.

She was jumpy, restless, flinching at the echo of footsteps, at the sudden creak of a door swinging open behind her.

Her muscles locked tight every time she heard his name, every time she imagined him sitting in court, comfortable, untouched, breathing the same air she did. She refused to attend court meetings.

When summoned, she sent word that she would not be present, her refusal clear, unwavering. She would not sit in the same room as him. She would not grant him the satisfaction of knowing she could withstand his presence.

No one pressed her. Not yet. But the silence was growing louder.

It was late when Roland found her.

She barely noticed his entrance, too consumed by the sight of herself in the gilded mirror before her, a woman who should have been fearless, unshaken, but instead looked like something fractured, something struggling to piece itself back together.

Her posture was rigid, her fingers curled against the vanity, her shoulders tight with exhaustion she refused to acknowledge. Roland lingered in the doorway, watching her with the kind of patience that felt like waiting rather than mere observation. "You are avoiding court."

Anastasia's grip tightened on the edge of the vanity, the polished wood cool beneath her fingertips. She exhaled slowly, shaking her head. "Brilliant observation," she muttered, her voice thick with sarcasm. "What gave it away?"

Roland didn't rise to her sharp tone, only studied her, quiet, assessing, as if weighing the correct response. "You cannot hide forever." The words settled too heavily in the space between them, pressing against her ribs, curling beneath her skin. She whipped around to face him, her eyes dark with frustration, with something raw and unrelenting.

"Why have you done nothing?" Roland's expression remained unreadable, but she saw the way he exhaled slowly, as if preparing himself. "Nothing?" he echoed, voice calm, controlled. "Yes, nothing," she snapped, stepping closer. "You have not spoken to your father. You have not spoken to him. You let him sit there, in court, among men who will never know—"

Her voice cracked slightly, the weight of unspoken words catching at her throat. She forced the bitterness down, refusing to let it show. Roland was silent. Too silent. Anastasia clenched her fists, her pulse beating sharply in her temples.

"I should not have to fight this alone," she spat, her voice shaking with rage, exhaustion, the unbearable weight of it all. Roland's jaw tightened, his gaze flickering just slightly before he responded. "You are not alone." The words fell flat, hollow in the dim candlelight. Anastasia laughed sharply, humorless, bitter.

"You say that like it means something." Anastasia snapped. The anger burned through her, sharp, untamed, consuming the air between them. She yelled, swore, called him every name she could think of, throwing words like daggers, demanding to know why he had done nothing, why he had let this happen.

Roland stood there, unmoving, his gaze steady, unreadable, letting her tear through the silence between them with brutal honesty. He did not interrupt. Did not try to calm her or contain her. He let her burn through every ounce of anger, let her crack beneath the weight of unspoken resentment, let her unravel the bitterness clawing at her chest.

And when she finally faltered, her breathing ragged, her hands shaking, Roland stepped forward slightly, his voice low but firm. "I have already confronted him." Anastasia froze, her breath catching in her throat.

The words hit her like something unforgiving, something sharp lodging itself deep beneath her ribs. Then, a sharp inhale, a narrowing of her gaze, betrayal lacing her voice. "Then why didn't you tell me?" Roland didn't answer.

Didn't justify himself, didn't attempt to mend the wound he had just created. And that, that was worse than anything. Anastasia exhaled sharply, biting back the overwhelming ache pushing at her chest, her next words quiet, but edged with ice.

"Coward."

Roland did not flinch. Did not defend himself. Did not break beneath the weight of her accusation. Only held her gaze, silent. The walls of the palace felt too close, the air too thick, as Anastasia found herself wandering without purpose, avoiding the places where her mind could fall too deep into memory, into pain, into everything she was trying so desperately to silence.

Her feet carried her toward the lower halls, past the kitchens, where the scent of burnt sugar and aged herbs lingered in the air, where the warmth

of the ovens never quite faded, even late into the
night.

She stopped outside a small wooden door, the
edges worn with time, the frame uneven, as if it
had been repaired more than once. Evelina's
room. Anastasia hesitated, her hand hovering
near the door, doubt pressing against her chest.
This was not something she could take back. But
then—her fingers curled into a fist, knocking
twice before she could talk herself out of it.

There was a pause, then footsteps, and the door
swung open to reveal Evelina, half-dressed for
sleep, her hair loose, her brows furrowed in sharp
confusion. "If this is about whatever disaster
you've caused today," Evelina sighed, "I'd rather
sleep." Anastasia didn't laugh.

Didn't offer any of her usual sarcastic remarks.
Instead, she simply stood there, silent, her hands
tight at her sides, her face drawn, pale, uncertain
in a way Evelina had never seen before.

Evelina's posture straightened slightly, sensing
the change. "What happened?" she asked, her
voice losing its sharpness, softening just enough.

Anastasia opened her mouth, then shut it.
Because how did she say it? How did she force
the words out, make them real? She shook her
head, stepping inside without asking, closing the

door behind her, sealing herself in the small, dimly lit space Evelina called home. "I shouldn't be here."

Evelina frowned, arms crossed, watching her carefully. "Well, that's obvious. You belong upstairs in your golden palace." Anastasia exhaled sharply. "No. I mean—I shouldn't be here. In this time." Evelina blinked, her expression unreadable, before she let out a small, humorless laugh. "What?"

Anastasia pressed her palms against her temples, her breath uneven, her heartbeat loud against her ribs. "I came from the future."

Silence. Thick. Sharp. Heavy.

Evelina's lips parted slightly, as if ready to argue, then stopped—but not because she believed her. Because she saw the way Anastasia's shoulders curved inward, the way her fingers trembled, the way her voice had lost all its usual fire. Anastasia let out a bitter, broken laugh, shaking her head.

"I married Roland because I had no choice. It was survival. And now—now I have to live in a world that nearly killed me." The words fell hard between them, like dropped stone, like something that could not be undone.

And then, the tears came. She didn't want to cry here, in this tiny room, in front of Evelina, in front of someone she wasn't sure would understand, believe, or help. But she couldn't stop it.

Her breath hitched, her chest tight, raw, breaking apart, as exhaustion—months, weeks, years of exhaustion—finally pushed her over the edge. Evelina sat heavily on the edge of her bed, rubbing her temple. "You expect me to believe that?" Anastasia flinched.

"I—"

"That you're some poor lost soul from the future? And what? You just woke up in this world one day and thought, 'ah, yes, I'd love to be miserable in history'?"

Anastasia clenched her fists. "I did not ask for this!" The words came out too loud, too sharp, but Evelina did not pull away from them. Instead, she exhaled slowly, watching her closely. "You truly believe this." Not a question. A statement.

Anastasia forced herself to breathe, forced herself to steady her voice, to push past the panic clawing at her chest. "I don't care if you believe me," she whispered, her voice raw. "But I needed someone to know." Evelina sat there for a long time, watching her.

Then—she sighed, rubbing her forehead, shaking her head slightly as if she were already regretting whatever she was about to say next. "Fine." Anastasia blinked. "Fine?"

Evelina leveled her with a pointed look, her tone dry. "You are clearly one tragic breath away from losing your mind entirely. If believing you keeps you from hurling yourself out the palace window, then fine. I believe you Anastasia" Anastasia let out a soft, broken sound, pressing her fingers against her eyelids, as if trying to contain the emotion threatening to spill over again.

✳✳✳

The evening air was sharp, cutting through the palace corridors like something alive. Anastasia walked with purpose, each step echoing against the marble floors, her breath controlled, even though the fire burning beneath her ribs threatened to consume her entirely.

Roland refused to speak to the king so she would do it herself.

She reached the ornate doors of the throne room, her heartbeat loud in her ears, the weight of the moment pressing against her like a tightened grip around her throat. The guards at the entrance shifted slightly, exchanging uncertain glances as she approached.

"Announce me," she ordered, her voice steady, unwavering. One of them hesitated. "The king is not expecting—"

"Announce me," she repeated, cutting him off, her tone leaving no room for refusal.

The air was thick, charged with something almost tangible, a weight pressing against Anastasia's chest as she stood in the center of the throne room, surrounded by nobles who watched her with wide eyes, hushed whispers, expressions ranging from shock to barely concealed disdain.

She had never been more aware of the rules she had just shattered. A woman did not march into court unannounced. A woman did not demand the removal of a nobleman, much less one with influence. But Anastasia had never cared for rules. And she would not begin now.

King George narrowed his gaze at her approach, his posture remaining perfectly composed, yet there was no mistaking the careful weight in his expression. "What is the meaning of this?" Anastasia stopped a few feet from the throne, straightened her shoulders, and spoke without hesitation. "Lord Percival must be removed from court." Gasps rippled through the room, whispers breaking out in hushed voices, the nobles exchanging glances of alarm.

King George's gaze hardened, his fingers curling slightly around the armrests of his throne, his posture that of a ruler accustomed to obedience, not disruption. "You dare make such a demand?" His voice was calm, yet laced with something sharp, something warning. Anastasia did not flinch, did not falter. She lifted her chin, her voice unwavering.

"I do."

There was a sharp, hushed ripple through the court, murmurs exchanged between lords and ladies, some watching with fascination, others outraged by her audacity. And finally, Lord Percival himself stood. The movement was slow, deliberate, a calculated display of control, as he adjusted the folds of his dark blue coat, his expression carefully arranged into something unreadable.

"Your Highness," he said smoothly, the words coated in the kind of false politeness that sent chills down her spine. "I fail to understand your reasoning behind such a grave accusation."

Anastasia turned her head sharply, meeting his gaze with nothing but unwavering fire. "You are a danger to this court," she stated plainly, letting each word settle into the room like a blade pressing against the air between them. "And I will not stand by while you remain seated among honorable men who do not realize what you truly are."

Lord Percival smiled. The kind of smile that was not real, was not warm but rather was something carved from careful cruelty.

"Are you certain, Princess?" he murmured, tilting his head just slightly, like a predator toying with prey. Roland stepped forward then, his voice clipped, sharp, a warning in itself. "She does not need certainty, Percival. She is right." The court gasped.

Because Roland never spoke out of turn, never defied order without calculation, and now—he had sided with her, publicly, against a man the king had long tolerated.

King George leaned forward slowly, exhaling, before speaking with something far quieter, deadlier, beneath his voice. "You have become a source of disruption, Lord Percival." The words were final, but Percival did not react, did not shift, did not let even a flicker of discomfort cross his features.

Because men like him did not show weakness, not even in loss. King George continued, his tone firm, authoritative. "You are hereby stripped of your title and dismissed from court."

Gasps erupted across the chamber, some nobles standing from their seats in stunned silence, others turning to exchange hurried whispers. Anastasia's breath hitched, her pulse racing—not in fear, but in victory.

Lord Percival exhaled quietly, adjusting his cuffs, before stepping toward her just slightly, lowering his voice until only she could hear. "You believe yourself safe now," he murmured, his tone almost amused, almost casual, but beneath it—something unspoken, something edged with warning.

Anastasia did not move. Did not break eye contact. Did not let his words settle into fear. Instead, she smiled.

"You believe you still hold power," she murmured back, voice steady, unwavering. "You are mistaken." He studied her—for just a moment, for just a fraction too long, before nodding ever so slightly, and turning toward the exit.

The grand doors shut with a hollow echo, the murmurs of court settling in the absence of Lord Percival's presence. Anastasia stood tall, shoulders squared, refusing to let her lingering anger dull the satisfaction of his departure. The evening had been tense, the whispering vipers of nobility circling, waiting for a moment of weakness.

King George watched her, his expression unreadable beneath the golden glow of the chandelier. Though the ballroom remained alive with quiet conversations and clinking goblets, this moment belonged to them alone. The air between them was thick, tense.

Anastasia lifted her chin slightly, stepping forward, voice measured. "Thank you, Your Majesty." George exhaled slowly, swirling the deep red wine in his goblet, eyes flicking over her as though assessing an opponent rather than accepting gratitude. "Do not mistake my actions for generosity, girl." His tone was sharp—cutting in the way only seasoned rulers could manage. Anastasia stiffened but did not falter. "Lord Percival was a disgrace. I only sought to uphold the dignity of—"

"Of this court?" George scoffed, setting his goblet down with deliberate precision, the sound sharp against polished marble. "You think you understand court politics? You believe a single request makes you powerful enough to alter its course?" Her jaw tightened, but she forced herself to maintain control. "I understand enough to know that his presence was an insult."

George studied her for a long moment, then shook his head, the faintest hint of amusement curling at the edges of his lips, not warmth, but something cold. Calculated. "You misunderstand, Princess. I did not abide by your request because I agreed with it. I did it because I refused to let you embarrass me."

George leaned back slightly, his gaze sharp and unrelenting. "You have been granted a position you did not earn, a title bestowed upon you by the naïve affections of my son. And while Roland may tolerate your impulsiveness, I will not." Anastasia's fingers curled slightly into her gown, hidden beneath layers of silk, forcing herself to stay composed. "I am only trying to do what is right."

George let out a quiet, humorless laugh. "Right? And what do you know of what is right? The world does not bend to righteousness, girl, it bends to power. And you? You have none of your own." Silence settled between them, thick and suffocating. Anastasia inhaled, steadying herself before speaking. "You underestimate me."

George's lips curved, just slightly. "No, *Princess*. I see you clearly." And with that, he turned, stepping away, leaving her standing there, alone, but unbroken.

✳✳✳

Anastasia found Roland alone in his private study, the glow of the fire casting long shadows across the walls, his posture relaxed yet sharp, always controlled, always guarded. She hesitated for only a moment, just long enough to acknowledge how rare these moments between them truly were, before stepping inside, closing the door behind her.

Roland glanced up, sensing her presence, but said nothing. Anastasia exhaled slowly, pressing her fingers against the edges of a nearby desk, grounding herself before speaking. "I wanted to apologize." Roland raised a brow, leaning back in his chair slightly, waiting. "For earlier," she clarified, meeting his gaze. "For—everything. I was angry, I was unfair, and I took it out on you when I should have—"

Roland cut her off with a simple shake of his head, his voice quiet but firm. "You have nothing to apologize for." Anastasia blinked, her lips parting slightly, expecting resistance, expecting irritation—expecting anything but understanding.

Roland watched her carefully, his expression unreadable at first, but then—a flicker of something softer, something distant, something real. "You were right to say something today," he murmured, his tone lacking its usual sharpness. "You made my father listen when no one else dared. That wasn't me. That was you."

Anastasia let out a quiet breath, the weight of the moment settling somewhere deep in her ribs. "Still," she muttered, crossing her arms. "I appreciate that you spoke up, even if I wish you had done it sooner."

Roland huffed a quiet laugh, shaking his head. "You say that as though I ever stood a chance of stopping you." Anastasia smirked slightly, a ghost of the confidence that had carried her through the day returning, but only just.

Then—she hesitated. Because the next words were heavier, dangerous. Because the next words were something she had never meant to say to him—not yet, maybe not ever—but suddenly, holding them inside felt impossible. She swallowed, shifted, exhaled.

"I told Evelina the truth."

Roland stilled completely, his expression unreadable, his breath measured. She waited for the anger, waited for the irritation, the accusations, the sharp demand of why she would possibly risk revealing something so unthinkable. But it never came. Instead, Roland exhaled slowly, studying her with careful patience, before leaning forward slightly, resting his forearms against the desk. "You needed someone to know."

Anastasia felt something fracture in her chest—not painfully, but gently, like the weight of unspoken loneliness finally breaking apart. She nodded, barely, slowly, not trusting herself to speak. Roland tilted his head slightly, observing her, before adding—not unkindly, not critically, "Did she believe you?"

Anastasia laughed under her breath, shaking her head. "Not at first." Roland smirked faintly, his expression carrying just enough knowing amusement to remind her why she often wanted to shove him into walls. "That surprises no one." She rolled her eyes but felt lighter than before, felt less alone than before.

TWELVE

Anastasia was done wallowing, done sitting in silence, nursing wounds that refused to heal with time alone. She needed a distraction, something grand, something untamed, something that reminded her she was still alive. And so, she stormed into Roland's study, the silk hem of her gown sweeping against the polished floor, her determined steps echoing against the stone walls.

Roland barely looked up from the pile of documents before him. "Absolutely not." Anastasia gasped dramatically, clasping her hands together as though delivering the most tragic monologue of her life. "Roland, I have suffered immensely. Would you deny me a moment of joy after all I have endured?"

Roland exhaled sharply, rubbing his temple, as if already regretting his own existence. Anastasia waited, unwavering, patient only because she knew she had already won. Finally, after a long beat, he muttered, "Fine. But do not make me regret it." Anastasia grinned victoriously, tilting her chin up. "I make no promises."

Roland shook his head, running a hand through his hair, letting out a quiet huff of amusement. "Of course you don't."

The village streets buzzed with life, the scent of fresh bread and roasted chestnuts lingering in the cool air, merchants calling their prices, the occasional laughter of children weaving between carts and stalls. Anastasia had grown accustomed to the shifting energy of the town, the way people paused in their work to greet her, how conversations naturally drifted toward her arrival.

She and Roland moved through the marketplace, gathering supplies for the gala: candles, imported silks, fine spices for the feast, gold-dipped embroidery for the banners that would hang across the palace halls. A young man, no older than nineteen, standing beside his mother, the town's seamstress, his hands clasped behind his back, eyes wide with admiration so pure it was almost amusing.

He hesitated only briefly before speaking, voice laced with wonder. "A true princess," he murmured, as though speaking some great truth that had been waiting to be acknowledged. "So kind, so beautiful, so—"

Roland, watching with a smirk that promised trouble, interrupted smoothly. "Careful, boy, or she'll start believing she is divine." Anastasia gasped, turning sharply, shooting Roland an unamused glare. The young man flushed slightly, fumbling with his words, but Anastasia simply turned back to him, amused by his enthusiasm.

"Ignore him," she said lightly, picking up a spool of ribbon from a nearby table, testing the fabric between her fingers. "He enjoys ruining my moments of adoration." Roland huffed a quiet chuckle, shaking his head. But the boy still watched her, his gaze lingering with something close to reverence, as if trying to memorize every detail of her presence before she disappeared back into the world of nobility, far from his reach. And Anastasia, for once, let herself enjoy the attention.

Later, Anastasia spotted the young man alone by the well, his posture stiff, his hands locked tightly together, watching the movements of another villager—a farmer bundling straw nearby. There was something in his gaze, a quiet longing pressed tightly beneath restraint, something unspoken curled against his ribs.

Anastasia approached, sitting beside him without invitation, resting her arms against her knees, letting the silence stretch without force, without urgency. She followed his gaze. Watched the farmer—his careful hands, the way his sleeves were rolled to his elbows, the ease of his strength as he worked.

Then, as though she were commenting on nothing of particular importance, she mused. "He's cute, right?" The young man froze, his breath hitching, his eyes darting sharply around the square, scanning the nearby streets as if expecting someone to hear, as if expecting someone to condemn him for the mere thought of it.

"Do not say such things," he whispered, voice quick, urgent, heart hammering beneath his ribs. "It is not proper."

Anastasia tilted her head slightly, watching his reaction with careful patience before lowering her voice. "But you think so?"

"Yes."

She let the word linger, let it fill the space between them, unchallenged. He exhaled sharply, shaking his head, gaze dropping to his hands, fingers curling against his own palms, gripping tightly. "But it is wrong."

Anastasia shifted, turning toward him fully, watching the way his muscles tensed, the way his shoulders stiffened against the weight of shame that had been pressed into him for far too long. "No, it isn't." His fingers twitched, tightening further, his chest rising and falling too quickly, too unevenly, refusing to meet her gaze. "The church would say otherwise."

There was a quiet pain in his voice, something that had been ingrained into him, carved into his bones before he had ever had a chance to choose what was right or wrong for himself. Anastasia felt anger rise—not at him, but at the world that had made him believe this lie, at the hands that had shaped him into someone afraid of his own heart.

So she reached out, grasping his hand, squeezing gently. "You deserve happiness," she murmured, her tone firm but soft, unwavering. He did not meet her gaze. But she saw the smallest unraveling in his shoulders, the faintest relief in his exhale.

Anastasia burst into the tailor's shop, the bell above the door jangling loudly, startling a few of the customers inside. Roland stood near the counter, still engaged in conversation with the town seamstress, his posture effortlessly composed, his expression calm as if nothing in the world could ever shake him.

Anastasia, still breathless from her wild dash across the village, threw up a hand. "Don't ask," she declared. "But I am inviting the entire village to the gala." She expected resistance—expected a frustrated sigh, a lecture on proper etiquette, some long-winded remark about how nobles and commoners did not mix in such settings.

Instead, Roland barely glanced up before muttering, "Fine." She stared at him, stunned. "Fine? Just like that?" Roland finally looked at her fully, arching a brow. "Yes."

Then, as if she had not just upended centuries of tradition, he simply returned to his conversation, utterly unbothered. Anastasia narrowed her eyes, suspicious. He was never this agreeable. But instead of pushing, instead of questioning, she accepted the victory, turned on her heel, and rushed back toward the well.

The young man was still seated where she had left him, his fingers tightly wound together, his body rigid, his expression set in quiet uncertainty. She didn't hesitate. "Ask him." His head snapped up, panic flickering across his face. "I can't." Anastasia huffed, dropping onto the seat beside him, her voice playful but firm. "Yes, you can. Ask him to the gala."

He fidgeted, glancing toward the farmer, watching him as he continued tying bundles of straw, his muscles flexing with each careful motion. "What if he refuses?" he whispered. "What if—?"

Anastasia grabbed his hands, squeezing them gently, grounding him. "What if he doesn't?" The young man exhaled sharply, doubt still pressed tight against his ribs, but there was something fragile, something new, in his expression now.

A moment passed. Then another. And then, he stood. Slowly, hesitantly, he walked toward the farmer, each step carrying the weight of possibility. Anastasia watched closely, her pulse steady as the farmer turned to him, blinking in surprise. And then, the farmer smiled, nodding once. The young man sucked in a breath, his entire frame relaxing in a way Anastasia had never seen before. She didn't say anything—just smiled to herself, satisfied.

The palace came alive. Gold-draped tables, candles flickering in ornate holders, live musicians tuning delicate strings, preparing their instruments. The halls hummed with energy, servants rushing about with trays, court officials watching the transformation with mild fascination and lingering skepticism. And, most importantly, the doors were open.

The entire village was welcomed, nobles and commoners alike mixing in hesitant curiosity, unsure of how the evening would unfold.

206

Anastasia floated between conversations, laughing, drinking, letting herself enjoy the night in a way she hadn't in far too long. Then she spotted him. The young man stood near the entrance, his hands tight at his sides, his posture set with nervous anticipation.

His eyes scanned the room restlessly, searching. Anastasia stepped beside him, nudging him gently. "Relax. He'll be here." A moment later, the farmer stepped inside, his clothes simple but carefully arranged, his gaze scanning the room until he found who he was looking for.

"Do not let fear steal your night."

The young man exhaled sharply, biting his lip, his fingers twitching slightly at his sides. "It is not fear," he murmured, but Anastasia could hear it there, woven beneath his voice. "Then prove it," she challenged, tilting her head toward the space where the musicians had begun to play a slow, elegant melody, couples stepping into movement across the ballroom floor.

The young man hesitated, watching the farmer, watching the way he glanced toward the dancers, how his fingers tapped lightly against his wrist as if considering joining. Then, Anastasia took his hand, squeezed it once, firmly.

"Go." He swallowed, then stepped forward, each movement careful but determined. When he reached the farmer, he stood still for a moment, waiting, searching his expression for any trace of hesitation, any trace of rejection.

But instead the farmer smiled and without a word, he held out his hand. The young man stared at it, eyes wide, uncertain but then, slowly, carefully, he reached forward, taking it. Together, they stepped onto the ballroom floor. Anastasia watched them, watched the way the tension in the young man's shoulders faded with each passing second, watched the way the farmer held him gently.

Evelina had spent the evening avoiding the inevitable, keeping herself tucked behind conversation, behind obligation, behind anything that kept her from facing her. But she had invited her and Harper had come.

Evelina found her in the gardens, standing near the stone fountain, the soft light from the ballroom casting shadows over her auburn curls. She looked breathtaking, freckles dappled against her olive skin, her blue eyes scanning the night like she might find answers there.

Evelina swallowed hard, fingers clutching at the fabric of her gown as she stepped forward. Harper turned before she could speak, her gaze locking onto Evelina's, unreadable. Silence stretched between them, heavy and uncertain. "I..." Evelina hesitated, shifting on her feet, breath uneven. "I know I've been avoiding you."

Harper let out a slow exhale, crossing her arms. "You have." Evelina winced but nodded, forcing herself to look at her, to truly face her. "I was afraid." Harper tilted her head slightly, waiting. "Of what?" Evelina inhaled deeply, steadying herself. "Of how much I love you." Harper froze, blinking rapidly, as if she hadn't expected the words as if she hadn't believed Evelina could ever say them out loud.

She took a determined step forward, gripping Harper's hands between her own, not letting her slip away, not this time. "I love you," Evelina whispered, voice trembling but true. "I love you so much it terrifies me. Because you—you make me feel like I can be more than what this world expects me to be. You make me want to fight for something that I've spent my entire life pretending I didn't want."

Harper swallowed hard, her fingers tightening around Evelina's own. Evelina pushed on, her words pouring out, unshaken, unstoppable. "You taught me to listen to myself, to my heart, to everything I tried to silence. And I don't want to silence it anymore. I don't want to hide, Harper. I want this. I want us." Harper inhaled sharply, her blue eyes searching Evelina's face, looking for doubt, for hesitation. There was none.

Evelina saw movement behind her, the ballroom, alive with celebration. She caught sight of two men, their figures twirling in the middle of the dance floor, laughing, carefree, unbothered by the weight of expectation.

And for the first time, Evelina felt like she could take on the world. She turned back to Harper, eyes gleaming, heart pounding. She held out her hand. Harper hesitated but only for a moment. Then she took it.

And Evelina didn't wait, she dragged Harper quickly toward the ballroom, through the golden glow of the chandeliers, past startled nobles, toward the center of the dance floor where the two men swayed, lost in their own happiness. Harper let out a startled laugh, but she followed, she always followed. And then, they danced. Together. In front of everyone. And this time, Evelina wasn't afraid.

Anastasia stood near the edge of the dance floor, watching as the two men and now Evelina and Harper all swayed gracefully together, their movements careful, measured, yet undeniably tender. The sight filled her with warmth, a quiet victory in a world that so often sought to keep love confined to narrow rules.

But not everyone in the room shared her sentiment. She heard the murmuring before she saw the men responsible. Two noblemen, graying, stiff-backed, draped in the colors of old wealth, stood near the edge of the ballroom, eyes narrowed as they whispered between themselves, their expressions twisted with quiet disapproval. "Disgraceful," one muttered. "A display unfit for the court."

"The prince allows this?" the other scoffed, shaking his head. "It will not be long before his reign is questioned, if he insists on entertaining such... indulgences." Anastasia's breath hitched, anger curling hot beneath her ribs. She took a step forward, ready to speak,ready to tear into them with all the grace and ferocity the moment deserved.

But Roland was faster, he had heard them too. He moved with effortless precision, stepping between them before they even noticed, his stature commanding, his presence cutting through their quiet mutterings like a blade. "Is there a problem?" His voice was calm, measured, but laced with something unmistakable, a warning. The noblemen stiffened, exchanging uncertain glances. One cleared his throat, straightening his posture. "Your Highness, forgive us. We merely—"

"Were speaking ill of two guests in my home." Roland's tone did not waver, his gaze sharp as steel. "You seem mistaken in believing your opinions hold weight here." The older man frowned, shifting his feet slightly, as if searching for a way out. "Surely you understand, Your Highness, that certain traditions must be upheld—"

"Traditions?" Roland echoed, his expression remaining unreadable. "Do you believe tradition is what makes a ruler strong? That clinging to outdated expectations will serve this kingdom? That love, of any kind, should be dictated by men who fear change?"

The noblemen faltered, their gazes darting between Roland and the couples twirling across the dance floor. They had no answer. Roland inhaled slowly, tilting his head slightly, his next words steady but final. "You are in my court. My home. And you will show respect to every person in it."

Neither of them spoke, they didn't dare oppose the prince. Roland turned away from them, his glass in hand, the reflection of the fine wine catching the flickering candlelight as he surveyed the room, the nobles, the dignitaries, the wary eyes of those who still whispered behind gilded fans.

Anastasia stood beside him, regal in her own right, her presence a defiance, a victory, a reminder that the future belonged to those who dared to claim it. Roland exhaled, lifting his glass higher before his voice rang through the air, strong and unwavering.

"I have seen battles, victories, the weight of ruling, and the blood of betrayal. But tonight, I celebrate something far greater. Tonight, I raise my glass in honor of my wife."

A murmur rippled through the crowd, soft and curious. Anastasia lifted her chin slightly, watching him, waiting. "She is not a woman born into this court, not someone shaped by its traditions or confined by its expectations. And yet—" His gaze flickered toward her, warmth bleeding into his sharp expression. "She has commanded its attention, earned its respect, and proven herself to be more than any title bestowed upon her."

Some in the audience stiffened, exchanging glances, but Roland continued, his voice steady, laced with quiet challenge. "There are those who believe strength comes from lineage, from convention, from holding firm to the past. But strength, true strength, lies in those who build their own path, who stand against the tide, who dare to redefine what is worthy."

A few nobles shifted uncomfortably, their previous murmurs of judgment now ringing hollow beneath his words.

"And so, tonight, I honor not only my wife but every soul within this ballroom who has chosen love over fear, who has chosen happiness over expectation."

The two men whom Anastasia had helped earlier stood near the back, now watching the prince with quiet awe, as if they hadn't quite believed he would say it, would acknowledge them, would shield them with his words before an entire court.

Roland turned his attention back to the crowd, a knowing smile tugging at the edges of his lips. "If there are any among you who question such love, I can only offer you my sincerest condolences. For it is not them who have lost something tonight, it is you."

The room was silent, applause scattered across the guests. The musicians began again and everyone continued as they were before, as if he hadn't said anything.

Later in the evening, Roland stood at the edge of the ballroom, arms crossed, watching the festivities unfold with a mix of exhaustion and amusement. Anastasia twirled in front of him, gown flowing as she gestured toward the crowd. Evelina sat on the nearby steps, smirking as she sipped wine, clearly entertained.

"Look at it, Roland! If I do say so myself, I've mastered this whole princess thing." Roland chuckled, knowing if he even attempted to disagree that Anastasia wouldn't shy away from yelling at him in front of the crowds.

"Yes. I will undoubtedly regret allowing it." He avowed, taking a sip of wine from his goblet. "Ah, but see, you already allowed it. So the regret is meaningless now." Evelina remarked as she glided over to the couple.

Roland let out a sigh, rubbing his temple as if trying to ward off the headache that was sure to follow. "You two are insufferable."

Anastasia gasped dramatically, placing a hand over her chest as if he had wounded her deeply. "Insufferable? Roland, I have just made history! Commoners and nobles drinking together, laughing together, an elegant display of progress!"

Roland did not look impressed. "An elegant display of reckless indulgence." Evelina smirked at Anastasia before saying, "He's upset because he hates fun." Roland huffed, shaking his head slightly. "I hate disorder. There is a difference."

Anastasia grinned, spinning once for emphasis before teasing, "And yet, the world keeps spinning, Roland. You may fight it, but joy finds a way." Roland exhaled sharply, shaking his head in defeat. "I hate you both." Evelina raised her goblet in mock celebration. "To mutual suffering."

Lady Eugenia approached Anastasia near the ballroom entrance, her posture stiff, her lips pursed with disapproval. Anastasia barely concealed her irritation, turning to face her with forced patience.

"You truly insist on turning this palace into a place of recklessness?" Lady Eugenia asked, her voice cutting, sharp as steel. Anastasia tilted her head slightly, smiling but there was nothing soft about it. "Ah. Lady Eugenia. You must be thrilled to witness history in motion."

Lady Eugenia scoffed, her gaze sweeping across the room, lingering with pointed disdain on the villagers mingling with the nobles. "History? A princess lowering herself to entertain peasants?" Anastasia's smile did not falter, but there was fire behind it now. "No, dear lady. A princess reminding everyone that the world does not belong solely to those born into titles."

Lady Eugenia narrowed her eyes, her posture stiffening further. "You will undo centuries of structure with this foolishness." Anastasia took a step closer, lowering her voice but making sure it was just as sharp. "Perhaps structure is the very thing suffocating progress."

Lady Eugenia inhaled sharply, as if trying to steady herself. "You are reckless, Anastasia. And recklessness breeds disaster."

Anastasia's smirk widened, slow, deliberate. "And yet, disaster is often followed by revolution." Lady Eugenia exhaled harshly, shaking her head before walking away, clearly unwilling to engage further. Anastasia watched her go, satisfied.

✳✳✳

Roland sat in his study, the firelight flickering against the stone walls, shadows stretching along the room's edges. He barely looked up when Henry entered, though he immediately sensed the shift in the air, the way Henry lingered in the doorway before stepping forward.

"You let her do it," Henry remarked, crossing the room with casual ease, though there was weight behind his words. Roland exhaled, leaning forward slightly, resting his forearms on his desk. "She was going to do it regardless." Henry chuckled, shaking his head slightly. "You could have stopped her."

Roland lifted an eyebrow. "Do you know her at all?" Henry smirked, leaning against the edge of the desk. "Fair enough," he admitted. He paused for a moment before adding, more seriously, "But she is changing things, Roland. And I do not think you mind as much as you pretend to."

Roland was silent at first, his jaw tightening slightly, though not in frustration. He exhaled, shaking his head. "I admire her resolve," he admitted after a moment. "But admiration and recklessness are not the same."

Henry smiled knowingly. "You may admire her more than you let on." Roland smirked faintly, shaking his head once. "That is irrelevant." Henry did not press further, but his expression carried amusement nonetheless.

THIRTEEN

The town sat nestled between rolling hills, its cobbled streets lined with lanterns, their flames casting eerie gold glows against twisting shadows. October air clung to the buildings, crisp and restless, filled with scents of burning wood, spiced cider, and damp autumn leaves.

Roland, ever the reluctant participant, rode beside Anastasia as they entered the square, the voices of merchants and festival-goers mingling in waves of excitement.

The Halloween Parade was the town's most beloved tradition—a celebration of history, folklore, and spirits said to roam when the veil between worlds was thinnest. Anastasia pulled her cloak tighter, watching costumed children rush past, their laughter shrill with delight.

"See, this is what you need, Roland. A night of revelry. Of wonder. Of—"

"Of nonsense," Roland cut in, adjusting his gloves, his gaze sharp as he scanned the crowd. She rolled her eyes and looped her arm through his, pulling him forward. "Not everything needs a purpose. Just look around—ghosts, witches, spirits. Tell me this doesn't make your heart stir even slightly."

Roland eyed a boy wearing a handmade ghost mask, then the group of young girls dressed as will-o'-the-wisps, their scarlet fabric fluttering unnaturally in the wind. He let out a small sigh.

"Fine. The charm is undeniable. But the weather is turning." Indeed, the skies had begun to darken unnaturally, clouds rolling in like ink spreading across parchment, swirling in slow, deliberate patterns. Still, the parade continued.

The parade swelled, drums thrumming in deep, hypnotic beats as figures in elaborate masks wove through the streets. Fire-dancers sent rings of flame spiraling into the air, shadows flickering against worn brick walls.

Anastasia caught sight of a small tent nestled between two alleyways, its entrance covered in deep violet fabric, illuminated faintly from within. A sign hung crookedly above the doorway:

Fortunes.

Something about it made her pause. Roland noticed her hesitation and exhaled sharply. "Don't." She turned to him, tilting her head. "Don't what?"

"Don't entertain their nonsense," he muttered, already irritated. "These people prey on fools

looking for meaning where there is none."
Anastasia smirked, stepping toward the entrance.
"Luckily, I specialize in nonsense."

Roland groaned as he followed her inside. The
space was small, draped in dark velvet, filled with
the scent of burning incense and something
herbal—dried sage and lavender mixed into the
air. A woman sat behind a low wooden table, her
fingers adorned with rings, a candle flickering at
her elbow. She lifted her gaze, and Anastasia felt
the shift in the air immediately—like something
tightening around her throat.

"You carry two worlds inside you," the woman
murmured, her voice melodic, rolling through the
quiet space like water. "One lost. One unknown."
Roland's entire body went rigid. Anastasia
blinked. "Excuse me?" The woman gestured
toward the table. "Sit." Against her better
judgment, Anastasia did.

"There is a name that lingers in your path," the
woman continued, brushing her fingers across a
spread of cards. "A name tied to time itself." A
chill crept up Anastasia's spine. "Lucinda." The
woman smiled—slow, deliberate, as though she
had been expecting the answer. Roland pushed
off the wall abruptly, shaking his head. "Enough.
We're leaving."

"She has been here before," the woman continued, ignoring him. "In a storm." Anastasia's breath hitched. "What do you mean, 'been here before'?" The woman tilted her head. "You already know." Outside, the thunder growled again, deeper this time, as if something was listening.

Anastasia barely had time to process the fortune before the sky cracked open above the town. Lightning ripped through the heavens, its light flashing against the rooftops, followed by a deep, guttural growl of thunder that rattled the windows.

Gasps rippled through the crowd as vendors scrambled to cover their stalls. The smell of wet stone and electricity thickened, the wind twisting violently. A parade-goer, his coat whipping against his legs, ran past, shouting to the organizers. "It's coming in fast! We need to clear the streets!" And just like that, the festival collapsed into chaos.

Anastasia grabbed Roland's arm as the rain began to pelt them with force, the cobbled streets slickening underfoot. Merchants hauled their carts away, mothers gathered panicked children, and all around, doors slammed as people fled indoors. "We're not making it home tonight,"

Roland muttered, already scanning the streets. "The roads will flood."

They stumbled into a warm, dimly lit tavern, breathless and drenched from the storm. The scent of aged oak, burning tallow, and damp wool filled the room, as clusters of townsfolk huddled around the massive stone hearth, exchanging uneasy whispers. Roland removed his cloak, shaking off the rain before turning to Anastasia. "We'll wait here until morning."

She nodded, tucking loose strands of hair behind her ear, trying to rid herself of the lingering chill that had settled deep in her ribs. A woman served them steaming mugs of cider, the spiced liquid heating Anastasia's fingertips as she curled her hands around the cup. The storm outside continued its wild assault, wind howling against the windows.

She sat down, sipping the hot cider. The sound of rainfall rattled the tavern roof. As she took a breath, her mind started to wander to one stormy night when she was younger.

Conor tugged at his grandmother's skirt, getting impatient. "Now, now sweetheart. Granny's almost finished your hot chocolate. Go sit on the sofa for me, okay?" Conor nodded with an innocent smile and waddled over to the large sofa and pulled himself up onto the cushions. He wiggled his feet and patted his knees, unable to contain his excitement.

His grandmother hobbled into the small room, placing the mug on the coffee table in front of the sofa. "Now then, it's hot so just wait a second sweetie." Moments later, he took a long sip of the sweet beverage. The warmth was like pure comfort, like drinking a hug.

Conor took a deep breath, feeling nothing but content. The warm room, the childlike joy of a hot chocolate, the love from his grandmother. It was heaven on Earth. He knew he wouldn't be at his grandmother's house much longer so he made sure to make the most of every moment. His grandmother was the only one who truly made him feel content. The only one who made him feel happy.

The town had settled uneasily beneath the storm, its lantern-lit streets now slick with rain, casting fractured reflections against the cobblestones. The festival's laughter had long faded, replaced by low murmurs and the hurried steps of those seeking shelter.

Anastasia stood beneath the wooden eaves of the tavern, staring into the turbulent night, watching as lightning split the heavens in jagged bursts. The air was thick with the scent of soaked earth and burning candle wax, and despite the warmth of the tavern behind her, she felt an unnatural chill coil down her spine.

Roland stepped beside her, his presence solid, grounding, but his gaze remained unreadable. "Storms like these pass quickly." She hummed, pulling her damp cloak tighter around her, eyes lingering on the way the shadows stretched unnaturally across the rain-slick streets. "Or they linger longer than expected."

Later that night, restless in the candlelit tavern, Anastasia found herself wandering through the narrow streets, drawn toward the small chapel near the square. Inside, rows of wax-dripped votives flickered, illuminating worn wooden pews and an altar long softened by time.

She ran her fingers along the stone walls, tracing the grooves where history had settled into place. And then she saw it—a carving, faint but deliberate, hidden marked into the back of one of the pews.

L.C. + E.A.

Her breath hitched. The letters, though weathered, still stood boldly, untouched by decay. She knew it had to be Lucinda but she was clueless of who E.A could be. Below it, almost too faded to notice, was another marking. A date.

1723

Anastasia's pulse quickened. That was the year that Lucinda had disappeared. Had someone tried to remember her? Or had this been a warning? She turned, suddenly aware of how the candles burned lower, their flames flickering against the damp air as if struggling to hold themselves upright. Outside, the wind howled too sharply, rattling the stained-glass windows.

Returning to the tavern, Anastasia noticed the alleyway beside the inn, its entrance cast in shadows, the rain pooling between uneven stones. And then, she saw a figure. A woman, standing too still, her long coat brushing against the ground, her hair loose beneath the storm's restless winds. Anastasia's breath caught. For a fleeting second, she swore the woman had silver strands woven through her dark hair, a ghost of a resemblance to a name she could not say aloud.

She stepped forward, the instinctive pull stronger than reason, heart hammering against her ribs.

But before she could cross the threshold—the woman disappeared, vanishing into the rain as though she had never been there at all.

Inside the tavern, the fire burned low, casting long shadows that stretched lazily across the walls. The voices of weary travelers and locals murmured beneath the crackle of embers, filling the space with a restless quiet.

Anastasia sat across from Roland, her hands wrapped around a ceramic mug, the heat bleeding into her fingertips. "I saw someone." Anastasia spat out, unable to keep it to herself for a second longer. Roland lifted his gaze from his drink, slow and unreadable. "Where?" She hesitated, fingers tracing the rim of her cup. "Outside. In the alleyway. A woman." Roland exhaled softly, his brow furrowing, as if considering whether to entertain the thought.

"And then?" he asked. Anastasia shook her head. "She was gone. Like she was never there at all." She expected him to dismiss it—to say it was a trick of the light, a figment of storm-drenched imagination. But he didn't. Instead, Roland leaned back, studying her, his jaw tightening ever so slightly. "You're unsettled."

She huffed a quiet breath. "Wouldn't you be?" Roland set his cup down deliberately, his fingers tapping lightly against the worn wooden table.

"The storm rattled the town. People see things when the world is restless." She shook her head. "This wasn't just something imagined." Roland didn't argue. He didn't brush her off. That alone made her stomach tighten.

She hesitated before speaking again, voice quieter now. "And at the chapel... I found initials carved into one of the pews." Roland's eyes flickered briefly with interest. "Whose initials?" She swallowed. "L.C. + E.A." For a moment, Roland said nothing. Then, he blinked once, slow, deliberate. "A lover's mark, perhaps." He didn't recognize the initials, neither of them did. So once again, they were at a loss.

By dawn, the storm had passed, leaving behind pools of rainwater that reflected the softened light of morning. The world smelled fresh—earthy, damp, laced with the scent of bread baking from the market stalls.

Anastasia stretched her arms, stepping into the street with Roland beside her. Though they had barely spoken since the night before, the tension between them had faded into something quieter, unspoken but acknowledged.

The town, bustling once again, welcomed them with the calls of vendors preparing their wares, the chatter of mothers pulling children along by the wrist, and the rhythmic clatter of wooden cart wheels rolling across uneven stone.

Near the blacksmith's shop, a group of raggedly dressed children chased each other through the streets, their laughter sharp and carefree, their small boots splashing through leftover puddles. Anastasia smiled watching them, feeling a rare sense of ease.

"You were right," she murmured. "Storms don't last forever." Roland, who had remained observant but distant, sighed, though there was no bite in his tone this time. "I have been right about many things." She rolled her eyes, but before she could craft a retort, something unexpected happened.

One of the children, a boy no older than seven, tripped as he turned too sharply, landing hard against the stone. The other children paused in surprise, waiting for him to cry, to complain. Before Anastasia could step forward to help, Roland did. His movements were calm, effortless, as if he had done this before, kneeling beside the boy, brushing damp curls away from his forehead, inspecting the scraped skin of his palms.

"Stand up," Roland said, voice steady but not unkind. "If you stay down, the others will think you've lost." The boy sniffed, his expression torn between pain and admiration, and after a long pause, he stood.

Roland handed him a small piece of cloth from his sleeve, a subtle gesture meant to clean the wound, though the boy likely would not use it. The other children grinned, approving, and without another word, they resumed their game twisting through the alleys, chasing imaginary monsters. Anastasia watched, something strange tugging at her chest. "You don't like children," she mused aloud.

Roland did not look at her. "I understand them." She tilted her head. "You were never like them, though." This time, he glanced at her, the corner of his mouth twitching, an almost-smile. "No. But I would have liked to be."

FOURTEEN

The grand hall was heavy with the scent of ink and parchment, the council members seated around the long table, their expressions wary yet intrigued as they awaited the discussion to begin. King George sat at the head, his presence commanding the room without effort, his cold gaze sweeping over his advisors.

Anastasia sat beside Roland, her hands folded neatly in her lap, but her mind already turning, the words ready to spill the moment she was given the opportunity. The conversation shifted toward alliances through marriage, the nobles murmuring about future prospects, political benefits, and the necessity of ensuring control through unions.

And that was when Anastasia spoke.

"You treat marriage like a business contract," she announced, her voice clear, unwavering. "Tell me, when did a woman's future become currency for men to trade?" The room fell silent, the air thick with unspoken shock.

Several nobles exchanged glances, others shifted uncomfortably in their seats. King George arched a brow, clearly unimpressed. "Marriage has always been a matter of duty," he stated coolly. "It is tradition." Anastasia leaned forward slightly, her green eyes bright with defiance.

"Tradition or control?" she countered. "There is a difference, Your Majesty." A murmur rippled through the room, some nobles whispering sharply to one another, others looking outright scandalized. Roland exhaled heavily, running a hand through his hair before finally speaking.

"She is not entirely wrong," he muttered, though his voice was begrudging, reluctant. Anastasia snapped her attention toward him, surprised. King George's jaw tightened but he said nothing, only watched Roland carefully, measuring his response. The discussion continued, but the unease in the air remained.

After the meeting, Anastasia approached Roland as they strode through the halls, her fingers lightly tracing the folds of her gown, her mind still reeling from the tension in court. "I have to ask you a question," she said casually. Roland did not stop walking, his posture rigid, unreadable.

"What is it, Angel?" Anastasia arched her brow. She slowed her steps, turning toward him fully, her voice more serious now. "Can you teach me how to use the dagger?" Roland studied her, his brown eyes searching her expression for a long moment. Then, after a beat, he nodded once.

"Come," he muttered, turning toward her quarters.

The candlelight flickered against the walls as Roland stepped inside Anastasia's chambers, closing the door behind them. "Give me the dagger," he instructed. Anastasia removed it from her belt, handing it to him carefully. Roland weighed it in his hand, turning the blade over, assessing its balance before stepping forward.

"Watch closely," he murmured. He demonstrated with ease—fluid movements, precise flicks of the wrist, controlled strength behind each stroke. Then, without hesitation, he passed it back to her.

"Now, you." Anastasia gripped the dagger, adjusting her stance, then swung—clumsy, uncoordinated, too slow. Roland sighed, shaking his head. "You're going to get yourself killed holding it like that." Anastasia huffed, irritated. "Well, clearly, that's why I'm asking for help." Roland stepped forward, positioning himself directly behind her, his presence towering, commanding but controlled.

"Here," he murmured, gripping her wrists gently. His hands guided her arms, adjusting her posture, leading her through the motion with quiet precision. The world felt smaller for a moment, the proximity charged, unspoken, delicate. Anastasia's breath hitched slightly, awareness creeping in—not fear, but something else entirely.

Roland felt it too, though he said nothing. The moment stretched—held still, fragile in its silence. Then Anastasia broke it, clearing her throat. "Thank you," she murmured, stepping forward and turning toward him. Roland blinked once, his expression neutral, unreadable, before he finally nodded. Without another word, he turned and left, closing the door behind him.

Roland found Anastasia near the eastern wing, leaning against the stone archway, watching the afternoon sun stretch lazily across the horizon. He approached without hesitation, his presence steady yet unspoken, until Anastasia finally acknowledged him with a glance.

"I assume you came here for a reason," she mused, pushing off the wall. Roland exhaled through his nose, crossing his arms. "You wanted change. You spoke about it in court. The lower districts have been restless." Anastasia tilted her head, curiosity flickering in her green eyes. "And?" Roland studied her for a beat, then finally said, "Come with me." Anastasia grinned, feigning mock surprise. "An invitation? From my ever-brooding husband?" Roland rolled his eyes, already regretting his decision. "If you don't want to go—"

"Oh, no, no," Anastasia interrupted, smirking as she stepped beside him. "You've piqued my interest." He sighed heavily, turning toward the palace gates.

The streets were alive with murmurs, the air thick with the scent of earth, sweat, and the distant perfume of baked bread from small market stalls. Anastasia walked with quiet determination, watching as women gathered near the well, their voices layered in frustration, worry, exhaustion. She heard it instantly—the grievances, the suffering.

A widow begging for protection from debt collectors. A mother struggling to feed her children after her husband's wage was docked without cause. A young woman forced into marriage because there were no other options available to her.

Anastasia's jaw tightened, the pulse in her wrists thrumming with restless energy. "These women need change," she told Roland, her voice firm, her breath hitching in restrained frustration. Roland watched her, silent, listening. "And you have the power to start it."

Roland nodded and placed a hand on Anastasia's back, gently pushing her toward the pub in front of them. "I have an informant that'll tell us just what needs to be done in the village."

The pub was dimly lit, the scent of spiced ale and burning candle wax settling heavily in the air. Roland and Anastasia stood near the counter, their presence drawing quiet glances from the patrons, but the barmaid—a woman with tired eyes and a streak of soot across her sleeve—was quick to approach.

She curtsied briefly, but wasted no time before speaking. "The people are restless," she admitted, her voice hushed but firm. "The crops suffered in the last frost. The taxes are too high. Our children go hungry." Roland exhaled sharply, crossing his arms. "The council claims the villages are stable." The barmaid scoffed, wiping her hands along the hem of her apron.

"The council claims a great many things," she muttered. Anastasia pressed a hand lightly against the counter, her green eyes searching the barmaid's face, studying the exhaustion etched deep into her features. "There is something else," Anastasia murmured. "Something more than just hunger." The barmaid hesitated, then exhaled heavily, her fingers instinctively brushing over her stomach—the motion subtle, but telling.

"I am with child," she admitted.

Anastasia's breath hitched slightly, but she said nothing—just listened. "I do not know if I will be able to keep the baby alive once it's born," the barmaid confessed. "There is no food. No medicine. No means to care for an infant while working long hours." Roland's brow furrowed, his posture shifting. "The father—"

"He is a nobleman," the barmaid cut in sharply, her tone curled with bitterness, her fingers tightening against the wooden counter. Roland stilled, his expression unreadable.

The barmaid laughed dryly, but there was no humor in it. "He erased me from memory the second he found out I carried his child," she spat. "As if I never existed." Anastasia's stomach twisted violently, nausea curling in the back of her throat. She had a suspicion that Lord Percival was the man she spoke of. She didn't want to say it aloud.

Roland was silent for a moment, then without hesitation, he reached for the pouch attached to his belt, undoing the clasp and handing it to the barmaid. She hesitated, her fingers brushing over the smooth leather, her brow furrowing. "What is this?" she murmured.

Roland's jaw tightened slightly, but his voice remained level. "A newborn baby's weight worth of gold." Anastasia blinked, surprised, watching as the barmaid gasped softly, her eyes widening as she weighed the pouch in her palm.

Roland met her gaze evenly. "More will be done," he assured her. "But until the king can be moved on this, this will have to do—for you, for the village." The barmaid stared at him, her lips parting in silent disbelief, before she stepped forward and hugged them both—firm, grateful, deeply relieved. Anastasia closed her eyes briefly, allowing the warmth of the gesture to settle before stepping back.

And just as she opened her mouth to speak a chair scraped violently against the floor. Then shouting, then chaos.

A riot ignited like a wildfire, fists swinging, tables overturning, the pressure that had been building for weeks, months, years—erupting into violence. Roland was quick, grabbing Anastasia's arm and pulling her toward the exit, his voice low and sharp.

"You'll take what you're given!" the noble barked, slamming his hand onto the table. "Or starve like the rest of your kind!" A man lunged forward, grabbing the noble by his collar, shouting something incoherent but furious, his face red with years of pent-up rage.

Then, a fist swung, connecting with the peasant's jaw, sending him stumbling backward. Another man intervened, pushing the noble aside, shouting, "We're done begging for scraps from our *masters!*"

Shouts tangled into a singular roar of frustration, voices demanding change, demanding justice, demanding something more than silence. Roland reacted instantly, grabbing Anastasia's wrist.

"We need to leave, Angel" he muttered. Anastasia struggled slightly against his grip, watching as people shouted, argued, fought, demanded change in a language only the desperate understood—rage and destruction. "This is what happens when people are ignored," she hissed, but Roland did not loosen his hold. "We are royals," he reminded her. "If anyone sees us here, they'll twist the story. They'll say we caused this."

Anastasia opened her mouth to argue, but then, a voice cut through the riot, sharp and mocking. A drunken bar patron, slouched over his ale, watching her with lazy amusement. "Look at her," he laughed loudly, his words slurred but cruel. The others barely paid attention, too engrossed in the chaos—except Anastasia. "She's more a man than her husband," the drunk jeered, smacking his goblet against the wooden table, liquid splashing across the surface.

Anastasia froze, her breath catching sharply. Roland did not react, barely acknowledging it—to him, it was just another insult thrown carelessly in a drunken haze. But to Anastasia, it was like a knife buried deep. Years of fighting to be seen as a woman, years of rejection, years of struggling to be respected, to be acknowledged, to be understood.

And in a single careless sentence, it was dismissed like a joke. Her fingers trembled slightly, her pulse hammering behind her ribs. Roland finally noticed her shift, his brows furrowing as he studied her expression. "Angel?" She snapped herself out of it, blinking rapidly, forcing herself to move, to breathe, to push the words down. "I— I need to leave," she muttered quickly. Roland nodded, no further questions—just action.

The castle was quiet when they returned, the lingering echoes of the riot still settled deep in Anastasia's bones, rattling her mind, curling under her skin. Roland had walked beside her the entire way—silent, steady, watchful. But now, as they stood in the dim glow of her chambers, the weight of the evening felt unbearable.

"You've been quiet," Roland finally said, breaking the silence as he leaned against the doorway. Anastasia tensed slightly, fingers curling against the edge of the desk. "The words you heard," she murmured, her voice tight, guarded, "they meant something to me." Roland tilted his head, his brown eyes narrowing slightly in thought. "It was just a drunken insult." Anastasia swallowed, exhaling a slow, shaky breath.

"It was more than that," she admitted. Her fingers toyed with the fabric of her sleeves, grounding herself before finally telling him her truth. "I am trans." Roland stilled, his expression unreadable—not cruel, not dismissive, just... processing.

Anastasia saw the flicker of confusion, but she didn't let it stop her. She continued like a river finally breaking free of the dam. "I was not born with the name Anastasia. I was given another, one that did not belong to me, one that did not feel like mine. I was born a boy but I knew that wasn't who I was meant to be." Roland said nothing and just listened. And she kept talking—her voice gaining strength.

"My parents never accepted me. They refused to see me for who I was, as if their rejection alone could change reality." Roland listened, his jaw tightening slightly, but not in anger—just quiet understanding. "My grandmother was the only one who believed me. She raised me, protected me, loved me when no one else would."

She let out a shaky laugh, not out of humor, but exhaustion. "I fought for this. I fought for the right to be seen, to be acknowledged, to exist as myself. And now—here, in this place, in this time—it's like I have to prove it all over again." Her voice cracked slightly, the weight thick, unbearable.

Roland was silent. For a moment, Anastasia felt her stomach twist, panic settling in. Would he reject her? Would he look at her differently now?

Then, without hesitation Roland stepped forward and kissed her. When he pulled away, his voice was quiet but firm, as if the words he spoke carried absolute certainty. "You are a woman, Angel. I'm not sure if I understand how you managed to change *everything* but I believe you." His gaze held hers, unwavering. "You are the most well-known woman in England, in fact."

Anastasia's heart raced as she felt the weight of Roland's gaze upon her. The fire crackled in the hearth, casting a warm glow over the worn wooden floors and the heavy velvet curtains that hung at the windows. The air was thick with tension as the two of them stood there, the chemistry between them palpable.

Her mind was a whirl of thoughts and emotions as she kissed him back. She knew that it was a bad idea – that she should resist the temptation and maintain her dignity. But the validation and respect that Roland had shown her had temporarily clouded her judgment. She wanted him, and she couldn't deny herself any longer.

As they broke apart, Anastasia could see the desire in Roland's eyes. He reached for her again, pulling her close and wrapping his arms around her waist. She could feel the heat of his body against hers, the roughness of his clothing against her soft silk dress.

Without a second thought, she kissed him again, harder this time. She could feel the tension in his muscles as he held her, the way his hands roamed over her body. She let out a soft moan as he trailed kisses down her neck, his lips leaving a trail of fire in their wake.

Before she knew it, they were moving towards the bed, their bodies entwined as they stumbled across the room. Anastasia's heart raced with anticipation as Roland gently laid her down on the soft mattress, his body covering hers as he continued to kiss her.

Roland's hands began to work at the lace of Anastasia's corset and skirt, slowly undoing them with expert precision. Once the dress was open,

Roland slid it off Anastasia's shoulders, letting it pool at her feet. She stood before him in her undergarments, feeling more vulnerable than she ever had before. But Roland's gaze was anything but critical. He looked at her with pure desire, and Anastasia felt herself blossom under his gaze.

Roland's hands roamed over Anastasia's body, caressing her skin. She responded in kind, her own hands exploring the muscled planes of his chest. "You're a feast for the eyes, Angel," he growls, his hands gripping her hips possessively. He kisses her belly, dipping his tongue into her navel, then moving lower.

Wrapping his arms around her waist, Roland lifts Anastasia slightly before lowering her back down onto him, filling her completely. He groans, his face contorting with pleasure as he begins to move his hips upward, the bed creaking beneath them. "Anastasia..."

The early morning light filtered softly through the sheer curtains, casting long streaks of gold against the stone walls. Anastasia lay curled beneath the sheets, her body warm, her mind restless. Beside her, Roland sat upright, his back pressed against the headboard, his gaze fixed on the ceiling—lost in thought, conflicted, silent.

Neither of them spoke at first. The truth of last night lingered between them, unspoken but heavy. Finally, Anastasia exhaled slowly, shifting slightly beneath the covers.

"This can't work," she murmured, breaking the silence. Roland's jaw tightened, but he did not argue. "I know," he muttered. Anastasia turned her head to face him, her green eyes searching his expression, reading every flicker of emotion he tried to mask. "This was bound to end before it even started," she admitted, her voice softer now, not bitter—but resigned.

Roland ran a hand through his messy blond hair, letting out a slow breath, his posture rigid but his features conflicted. "You will leave," he said, and it was not a question. It was a fact.

Anastasia nodded, her fingers tightening slightly against the sheets. "I don't belong here," she whispered. "Not forever." Roland finally turned his gaze toward her, studying her, his brown eyes dark with thought. "And yet—" he paused, shifting slightly, voice lower now, as if admitting something even he didn't fully understand. "And yet, I don't know if I want you to go."

Anastasia's breath hitched, a soft ache blooming in her chest. She smiled faintly, but it was sad—not the playful smirk she had always worn, but something softer, almost regretful. "I don't know if I want to go either," she admitted. "But I have to." Roland watched her for a long moment, then let out a quiet, humorless laugh.

"Leave it to you to make me care about something impossible, Angel."

Anastasia snorted, shaking her head. "If it makes you feel any better, I do that a lot." Roland shook his head, then reached forward, brushing a stray curl from her forehead before pulling away again, retreating. "This changes nothing," he murmured, but his tone wasn't sharp—it was layered, careful, filled with unspoken meaning. Anastasia nodded, swallowing. "I know."

The silence between them stretched, no longer tense, just lingering.

FIFTEEN

The palace guard stood stiffly at the entrance to Roland's study, his expression unreadable but his presence alone signaling urgency. Roland barely glanced up from his letters. "Speak." The guard hesitated. "Elsmere Manor has been breached, Your Highness."

Anastasia, seated across the room, felt the words settle deep in her chest like stones dropping into water. Roland's movements slowed, but his tone remained impassive. "When?" There was a pause. "We don't know exactly, my lord. It's been... a while."

Silence stretched between them. Someone had entered the manor, disturbed something, searched for something—and no one had noticed until now. Roland exhaled sharply, the grip on his quill tightening. "And why am I only hearing of this now?" The guard cleared his throat. "It was found by accident. A patrol passing by noticed the damage. No one could say how long ago it happened."

Anastasia exchanged a glance with Roland, a shared unease settling into the air. Roland finally stood, rolling his shoulders, his expression shifting to something colder, sharper. "Prepare the horses. We leave at first light."

The journey was long, the roads still damp from the storm, leaving behind treacherous patches of mud beneath the hooves of their horses. Roland was silent, his grip firm on the reins, his thoughts somewhere far away.

Anastasia stole glances at him now and then, watching the way his jaw remained locked in quiet frustration, the way his posture carried a tension he refused to acknowledge. She didn't speak, not yet. She already knew what silence meant for him.

By the time they arrived, Elsmere Manor stood before them, grand, still, untouched for too long. The scent of aged paper, lingering dust, and damp wood filled the halls. For a place meant to hold presence, it felt abandoned, like it had been waiting for someone to return, someone to remember it existed. The damage was subtle at first glance, but it became unmistakable the farther they walked.

A grand portrait above the fireplace had been removed, its frame leaning haphazardly against the wall, the space behind it exposing a hidden compartment, its contents missing. Drawers left open, documents misplaced, books knocked from shelves, a broken window leading into the south wing. Someone had been here. Someone had been searching.

Roland stiffened beside Anastasia, his sharp gaze scanning the room, his fingers curling into a tight fist. "Someone searched here. Not just for valuables, but for something specific." Anastasia moved toward the desk, where papers lay in disarray, scattered like fallen leaves, some crumpled, others torn at the edges, as if they had been rifled through with urgency.

She picked up a letter, her stomach twisting at the sight of the broken wax seal. "Whoever did this... knew exactly where to look." Roland's jaw tightened. "Or they had help." She frowned, turning toward him. "You think someone from the inside allowed this to happen?"

Roland didn't answer immediately, his gaze locked onto the shattered window near the far wall, where the wind stirred the curtains sluggishly, letting in the sharp scent of damp leaves and distant rain. "The staff would have reported intruders," he finally said, voice measured. "Unless they were told not to." Anastasia swallowed, unease creeping into her bones.

They followed the mess deeper into the manor, past abandoned corridors until they reached the library—its shelves towering, its books untouched for years or they *had* been. Several volumes had been pulled from the shelves, left open on tables, ink-stained pages scrawled with faded notes. Anastasia moved toward one, brushing dust from its surface, revealing the title beneath.

A Study on Temporal Anomalies.

Her throat went dry. Roland, standing beside her, eyed the book carefully before reaching for another lying on its spine—this one older, the leather cover cracked, its edges worn. "Whoever did this was looking for something tied to time," he muttered.

She hesitated. "You believe that?" Roland exhaled sharply, placing the book down with deliberate care. "I don't believe in coincidences. And neither should you." The fire in the hearth crackled softly behind them, casting long shadows against the floorboards, stretching out the uncertainty in their thoughts.

The air that evening was cool, carrying the scent of damp stone and autumn winds. Anastasia leaned against the cold balcony railing, her thoughts circling like vultures. Roland approached, his presence steady but guarded, his usual restraint resting heavily between them. "Being a ruler is suffocating," he admitted. She blinked, startled by the honesty. "That's not something I expected you to say so easily."

He let out a quiet, humorless laugh, shaking his head. "People assume it's power. Influence. Control. But mostly, it's obligation. A constant demand to be more than you are, even when you don't know who that is." She studied him—the tension in his shoulders, the exhaustion he rarely let slip. "I get that," she murmured. Roland glanced at her, waiting for her to explain.

"In my time, people think the world has moved forward. That it's easier to exist as yourself," she admitted, voice softer now. "And maybe, for some, it has. But it never felt simple. Every room I stepped into, every introduction, every glance—there was always a question beneath it. Always uncertainty. A demand to prove who I was, even when I had nothing left to prove."

Roland didn't interrupt, didn't dismiss. He only listened—which, she realized, was more than most ever did.

"You process things differently," he murmured after a long pause. She turned slightly, arching an eyebrow. "Is that an observation or a complaint?" The corner of his mouth twitched, a rare flicker of amusement, but it faded quickly. "It's an observation."

She hummed, tilting her gaze back to the horizon, where the mist curled low along the treetops. "I analyze first. Feel later." Roland exhaled, slow and measured. "Then we are opposites." She studied him, something deeper threading between the conversation now. "You feel first?" His jaw tensed. "I react first." Another pause stretched between them—not uncomfortable, but heavy with quiet understanding.

"And this?" She gestured vaguely to the manor, the break-in, the scattered evidence of someone searching for things they were never meant to find. "What does this make you feel?" Roland's fingers curled slightly against the fabric of his sleeves, as if restraining something. "It makes me wonder what comes next." She swallowed. "You're always thinking ahead?"

His gaze flickered toward her, sharp but contemplative. "In court, you either think ahead, or you fall behind." Her pulse thrummed beneath her ribs, the implication settling before he said what she knew was coming next.

"Not everyone in court wants you here."

The words fell between them—not cruel, not even a warning, just the truth spoken plainly. Anastasia let out a slow breath. "I know." And for the first time, Roland didn't look away.

The warmth of the manor's candlelight did little to chase away the weight of their conversation. As they walked through the halls, Roland's steps were steadier than Anastasia's, his gaze fixed ahead, locked in thought. Anastasia, however, was uneasy in a way she couldn't quite name. The knowledge that she was not truly wanted in court was something she had long suspected—but hearing it aloud, from Roland of all people, made it real. Made it *dangerous*.

The road stretched before them in long, winding paths, the last remnants of the storm clinging to the horizon in distant streaks of fading gray. Anastasia rode beside Roland, the quiet of the evening settling between them like an unspoken thought, neither oppressive nor comforting—just there.

Every time the horse's hooves met damp earth, she felt the weight of the manor still lingering behind her, pulling at her thoughts, making her wonder what exactly had been disturbed. Roland was tense but not restless, his grip firm on the reins, his gaze locked ahead as if dissecting every step forward.

By the time they arrived, the castle had slipped into its usual rhythm, the halls alive with murmured conversations, the glow of lanterns casting golden hues against the stonework. Anastasia was tired, not from the journey, but from the heavy swirl of unanswered questions tightening around her thoughts. Evelina met her near the palace kitchens, her arms crossed, an expression somewhere between amusement and concern.

"You look like you heard something unpleasant," Evelina murmured, leaning against the stone archway, inspecting Anastasia with keen interest. Anastasia let out a breath, rubbing at her temples. "More like something I already knew, but didn't want to hear."

Evelina's gaze flickered knowingly. "Let me guess. Roland finally told you the truth about how many people wish you weren't here?"

Anastasia blinked. "You knew?"

"Please." Evelina snorted, crossing her arms. "I'm a handmaiden. I hear conversations when no one realizes I'm there." Anastasia felt something tighten in her stomach. Evelina studied her for a long moment before sighing, shaking her head. "You'll never be one of them. And that's the problem."

Anastasia swallowed. "I don't need to be one of them." Evelina's smirk was thin, humorless. "Maybe not. But they need to believe that you belong here, or they will make sure that you don't."

Later, Anastasia found herself wandering past Roland's study, the door slightly ajar, allowing the faint glow of lantern light to slip through. She hadn't expected to find him still awake. inside, Roland stood near the window, his silhouette sharp against the flickering hearth, a glass of untouched wine resting at his fingertips. For a man who rarely showed uncertainty, he looked... unsettled. She didn't announce herself immediately—just watched. He caught her staring before she could step back. "You're still awake."

She huffed softly, stepping inside. "So are you." Roland exhaled, setting the glass down, dragging a hand through his hair. "I expected court life would become difficult. I did not expect this." Anastasia tilted her head. "The break-in?" He shook his head. "You." She blinked, caught off guard by the bluntness. "Me?"

Roland looked at her properly now, his gaze steady but tinged with something unreadable. "You make them question things they have never questioned before." She swallowed. "Is that bad?" Roland didn't answer immediately but his silence told her enough.

The room was bathed in bronze light, as if trapped between day and dusk, the kind of glow that felt like it did not belong to any real time at all. Lucinda sat by a window, her silver-streaked hair tumbling over her shoulder, her expression soft but tense, caught between caution and something deeper.

Across from her, a man stood—but his face was blurred, indistinct, just beyond the grasp of clarity, like trying to recall a memory that was never truly yours. Yet, despite the absence of his features, the presence of him was undeniable. Lucinda laughed—quietly, but with warmth, the kind of laughter that didn't belong to someone reckless, but rather someone who had long learned what it meant to guard happiness carefully.

He reached for her hand, and she let him—fingers brushing, hesitating, then entwining with certainty. Their closeness was not rushed, not stolen, but something carefully built—the kind of bond that had defied something. Something forbidden, something fragile.

Then, a whisper, not from Lucinda, not from the man, but from somewhere deeper in the dream itself. "She was not meant to love him. But she did anyway." The words curled like smoke, slipping into Anastasia's thoughts, settling into the space between reason and fate.

The dream shifted, softened at the edges, unraveling like torn silk, pulling away from Anastasia before she could reach farther. And then darkness. She awoke breathless, shaken, and certain that Lucinda's fate was not only hers to discover, but hers to understand.

The palace had already begun to stir, the early morning smelling of damp stone, fresh bread baking in the kitchens, and the lingering scent of rain from the previous day. Anastasia barely slept. Her dreams had been restless—Lucinda's laughter, blurred whispers of a name she couldn't quite grasp, the empty halls of Elsmere Manor still stretching out in her thoughts. She shook the exhaustion from her limbs, blinking against the early sunlight as she stepped onto the cool stone floors.

The great dining hall was quiet. Too quiet. Roland sat across from her, his posture stiff, composed as ever. But something was different. His movements were precise—slicing into his fruit without pause, sipping his tea as if doing so would allow him to ignore the weight of the previous night.

Anastasia watched him, resting her chin against her hand, studying the tightness in his jaw, the way his brows furrowed ever so slightly. "You're quiet." Roland didn't look up. "I am always quiet." She huffed softly. "Not like this."

He finally set down his fork, his gaze sharp when it met hers. "There are too many things to consider. I have no time to waste on unnecessary conversations." She raised an eyebrow. "Is that what I am? Unnecessary?" A flicker of something unreadable crossed his face—gone as quickly as it came. "No."

As Anastasia wandered through the corridors later, passing through grand halls lined with tapestries older than kingdoms, she overheard a quiet conversation. Two noblewomen, adorned in silk, their jewelry catching the morning light as they whispered near the grand staircase. Their voices were low but sharp.

"She does not belong here." "I heard she intends to integrate herself permanently. Can you imagine the scandal?" Anastasia felt their glances before she actually saw them. She kept walking, calm, measured, controlled but the weight of their words settled in the back of her mind, curdling beneath her skin like spoiled wine.

She could feel their gazes trailing after her, the way their whispers curled around her like smoke—thin, creeping, meant to smother. But instead of responding, instead of acknowledging them, she walked past—head high, unbothered, unworried. She would let them wonder if she had heard.

The courtyard was alive with movement—knights sparring, the clash of steel against steel ringing through the crisp air, the scent of sweat and earth mixing beneath the midday sun.

Anastasia found Roland near the edge of the sparring grounds, his blade flashing in smooth arcs, movements sharp but controlled, every strike precise. He had always been skilled, effortlessly powerful in his technique, but today—there was an aggression beneath his strikes, a tension barely concealed.

The knight sparring against him stumbled slightly, Roland's blow landing harder than necessary, and for a brief moment, Anastasia saw something raw flicker in his gaze—something unresolved. When the match ended, sweat lining his brow, he turned toward her, as if sensing her presence before actually seeing her. She tilted her head. "You're fighting harder than usual." He wiped his brow with the back of his hand, breathing steady despite the exertion. "Would you prefer I fight less?"

She smirked. "Just making an observation." Roland approached, resting his sword against the rack, folding his arms. "People are talking."

"People always talk."

"They talk about you." Anastasia exhaled, rolling her shoulders. "Do they truly believe I will disrupt their world?" Roland's gaze held hers, steady, direct, serious. "Yes," he said simply. Not cruelly. Not with mockery. Just fact. She swallowed but didn't look away. "Do you?" Roland's jaw tightened slightly, his fingers curling ever so slightly against his sleeves. "I think you already have."

SIXTEEN

Genevieve.

Her name slipped through the palace halls like incense—slow, curling, deliberate, carrying traces of history that could never quite be washed away. The whispers came first—servants exchanging hushed words, nobles tilting their heads in knowing acknowledgment.

She had been gone for years, tied to a marriage that had taken her far from court, far from the power she once wielded with an effortless grace. But now, she was back. And though her husband's death had granted her freedom, there was something about her return that did not feel like grief—it felt like purpose.

Anastasia heard the murmurs before she saw her. The words slipped through doorways, across tables, from courtiers who still remembered the way Roland had once looked at Genevieve before duty had decided otherwise.

The great hall was bustling with movement when Genevieve entered, dressed in deep emerald silk, her posture unshaken, powerful in its precision. She didn't simply walk into the space, she commanded it. The rich fabric of her gown caught the light, pooling at her feet like smoke curling from a dying flame, her auburn hair carefully pinned with gold accents, deliberate yet seemingly effortless.

She carried herself like someone who had already won whatever battle she had decided to fight, even if no one else had realized it yet. And when her gaze finally found Anastasia, there was no hesitation. No flicker of surprise, no moment of brief assessment—just a slow, deliberate smile.

Anastasia saw the shift the moment Genevieve's presence settled—how people paused, how conversations faltered for a fraction of a second, how even Roland's gaze flickered as she approached. But Genevieve was looking at her. And her smile seemed to be not meant for pleasantries, it was meant for something sharper.

A challenge.

Roland approached, not hesitant, but guarded, as though he was already prepared for whatever game Genevieve was ready to play. Genevieve, however, was effortless. She greeted him with familiarity, touching his arm just a second too long, the gesture carefully placed, deliberately timed. "It has been too long, Roland."

Her voice was smooth, carrying the exact amount of weight necessary to remind everyone listening that she had once had a place by his side. Roland nodded, his response measured. "You are welcome, Genevieve." Nothing more. No indulgence. No acknowledgment of whatever memories she was attempting to stir.

Genevieve's smile did not waver but it did shift—just barely—as if recognizing that her efforts would not be so easily met. She turned her attention to Anastasia then—assessing, curious, entertained. "And you must be Lady Anastasia."

Anastasia inclined her head slightly, refusing to break eye contact. "I must be." Genevieve laughed—not loudly, not unkindly, but with the exact amount of amusement required to make Anastasia wonder if she was laughing at her or with her.

Genevieve moved through the hall like a woman who knew exactly where she stood—exactly who she needed to speak with, exactly how much interest she needed to feign. As she did, Evelina stepped beside Anastasia, watching the scene unfold with mild fascination.

"You're about to witness the great battle of courtly charm and manipulation." Anastasia let out a breath, glancing at Evelina. "Who's winning?" Evelina tapped her chin thoughtfully, lips curling. "Hard to say. She is playing the long game."

Anastasia shifted her gaze back to Genevieve, watching how she placed herself at just the right distance from Roland, not too close, but not far enough to be ignored. "And what game am I playing?" Anastasia murmured. Evelina smirked. "Oh, my dear? You are the enemy."

Genevieve played the role flawlessly. She was polite, poised, charming—never rude, never hostile, always speaking as though her words carried hidden meanings waiting to be unraveled. She did not push too hard, did not demand Roland's attention outright. Instead, she wove the past into conversation. Little reminders. Small memories. Moments Anastasia was not meant to be a part of, but was forced to hear anyway.

"Do you remember the summer in Brighton? The festival?" she asked casually over dinner, a delicate sip of wine between words. "The fire-dancers? The wager?" Roland did not entertain her nostalgia.

But she did not need him to. The mention was enough. And as Genevieve spoke, her gaze flickered to Anastasia—not obviously, not sharply, but just enough for Anastasia to understand that her presence was the interference.

The terrace was quiet, save for the gentle flicker of lantern light and the distant hum of conversation from the great hall. The stone railing beneath Anastasia's fingertips was cool, the evening breeze teasing loose strands of her hair.

Henry stood beside her, his posture relaxed, his expression amused, and, if she wasn't imagining it, just the slightest bit indulgent.

He had a way of looking at people that was too knowing, too sharp, as if he always found something worth entertaining in the spaces between conversations. Tonight, Anastasia had the distinct feeling that she was the entertainment.

"You've been watching her," Henry murmured, tilting his head toward the hall where Genevieve still held court with the nobles. "Genevieve, I mean." Anastasia exhaled through her nose, eyes narrowing slightly. "Would you prefer I pretend not to?"

Henry's lips curled, something like satisfaction flickering through his expression. "No, I prefer honesty. Even when it makes things... complicated."

There was something deliberate about his tone, something that made her stomach twist—not uncomfortably, but with interest. "Complicated isn't always a bad thing." Henry hummed, leaning against the railing, fingers brushing the worn stone. "No, I don't suppose it is."

Anastasia turned her attention back toward the hall, watching Genevieve—the way she moved, the way she settled into conversations as if they had been designed for her. "Tell me," she murmured, letting the words slip between them like stray embers. "What was Roland like with her?" Henry chuckled, deep and quiet, shaking his head. "Ah. That's what you want to know."

"I'm curious," she admitted, shifting to face him more fully, fingers trailing absently along the carved edges of the railing. "That's hardly a crime." Henry glanced at her, sharp but warm. "No, but it is dangerous. Curiosity often leads to answers people don't want."

She arched an eyebrow. "Do I look like someone afraid of answers?" Henry exhaled, something like appreciation flickering through his gaze. "No. You look like someone who will pull at every thread until the entire tapestry comes undone."

There was a short pause, then he spoke. "It wasn't love." The words were simple, spoken without embellishment, without dramatic flair. "Roland and Genevieve, I mean. Whatever they had—it wasn't something fragile or soft. It was calculated. Deliberate. A game played in shadows, behind closed doors, beneath the watchful gaze of a court that never truly forgets anything."

Anastasia listened, absorbing the weight of his words, the quiet certainty beneath them. Henry exhaled. "Roland cared for her. That much was clear. But love? No, I don't think he allowed himself that."

Anastasia considered that. Considered what it meant, what it said about Roland and the way he carried himself now, so carefully measured, so restrained. "And Genevieve?" she asked. "What did she want?" Henry's gaze flickered, not distant, but calculating. "Genevieve never wanted a crown."

That surprised Anastasia. She had expected ambition, had expected the same hunger she had seen in the glances of noblewomen eager to carve out a place beside power. But Genevieve had clearly not returned for a throne. Then why? Henry leaned closer, his voice dipping just enough to send a strange thrill through her spine.

"She wanted Roland but only when it was inconvenient." Anastasia blinked, her lips parting slightly.

Henry smirked, watching her reaction with something dangerously close to amusement. "He was the one thing she could never fully possess. And that, I imagine, made him far more interesting than he would have been otherwise." Anastasia laughed, not because it was funny, but because it was maddeningly true.

Henry tilted his head, studying her now—not idly, not teasing, but deliberately. "You ask a lot of questions." Anastasia held his gaze, refusing to let the moment slip between them without claiming it first. "And you like answering them." Henry's smirk deepened, something like approval flickering through his expression.

"Do I?" She exhaled, tilting her chin up slightly. "You haven't told me to stop." His gaze flickered toward her lips—just briefly, just enough for her to catch it before it was gone. "No, I suppose I haven't."

✳✳✳

The room was dim, illuminated only by the flickering glow of a lantern set near the far wall. The night air slipped through the window, cool against her skin, but Anastasia barely noticed. She had expected to feel amused by Genevieve's presence, maybe even indifferent. Instead, she was restless.

She sat on the edge of the bed, fingers grazing the embroidered quilt beneath her, mind tangled in thoughts she didn't want to entertain but couldn't seem to abandon. It wasn't jealousy—not exactly. But it was something sharp, something uncomfortable, a sensation buried beneath layers she had yet to fully unravel.

Genevieve had moved too easily through the palace, had slipped back into its rhythms as though she had never left. She was calculated. Beautiful. Dangerous in the way only women who knew exactly what power felt like could be.

And Roland had been with her. Had touched her, had laughed with her, had at some point wanted her. Anastasia swallowed, shaking the thought away, but the feeling remained, lingering, curling into the spaces between certainty and doubt.

She closed her eyes, trying to push away Genevieve, trying to replace the weight in her chest with something else. And then, she remembered him.

Joey.

The first boy she had ever truly loved.

She had barely come out when she met him—still figuring out herself, still unsure of how the world would shift beneath her after stepping into the truth of who she was. But Joey hadn't cared about the weight of expectations or the struggles of identity. He was reckless, magnetic, the kind of boy people warned you about but secretly wanted anyway.

He had been the classic bad boy—leather jacket, cigarette tucked behind his ear, sharp smirk that made everything feel like a dare. And she had wanted every moment of him.

There had been late-night drives with the windows down, music blaring, Joey tapping his fingers against the steering wheel in rhythm with whatever song filled the empty space between them.

There had been sneaking into theaters after hours, sitting in the empty rows, laughing too loudly at bad films, stealing popcorn from the concession counter as if they were characters in some cliché teen romance.

There had been kisses against the back wall of a café, hands grasping fabric, Joey whispering stupid, reckless things against her lips like he would never get tired of her. She had loved him fearlessly. Had believed, naively, that he would be hers.

But then, he left for Esme. The new girl at college, the one with the effortless charm, the one who seemed to step into Joey's world like she had always belonged there.

Anastasia had never truly known heartbreak until then. It wasn't just that Joey had chosen someone else, it was that he had never even warned her it was coming.

One day, he was hers. The next, he was Esme's. She had cried in her grandmother's kitchen, eyes burning, breath shaky, feeling foolish for believing in permanence.

Her grandmother had watched her break, had let her grieve, had wiped her tears with quiet understanding.

And then, she told her a story about Edward. He had been her grandmother's first love—too charming, too intense, a man with a rogue smile and a dangerous ability to make someone feel like they were the center of the universe. But that intensity had turned suffocating.

Edward was clingy, obsessive, never satisfied with simply loving—he had needed possession, needed control, needed Anastasia's grandmother to be something fragile in his hands. She had loved him—deeply, foolishly, desperately.

But she had also left him. Because love should never demand pieces of yourself that you aren't willing to lose. Anastasia had clung to that lesson, had let it reshape the way she understood love, the way she understood heartbreak. And now, she wondered if Genevieve was Roland's Edward or her Esme.

SEVENTEEN

It began quietly, unobtrusively, as if it were nothing at all. Genevieve did not demand Roland's time—she simply made herself present.

She joined his morning rides, guiding her horse beside his, her laughter slipping through the crisp morning air like mist curling over the fields. She stepped onto the training grounds, lifting a fencing sword with the ease of someone who remembers every movement, every strike, every moment she had once spent beside him.

"You still favor your right side too much," she commented, lunging forward, matching his movements with sharp precision. Roland blocks her attack, his grip steady, but the words settle—a quiet familiarity between them, a knowledge shared only through experience. She had spoken of times past, of jokes that once made sense between them. Never pulling him into nostalgia outright but leaving enough of it lingering for him to think about later.

Genevieve did not strike outright—there had been no cruelty, no open dismissal of Anastasia's place in court. Instead, she planted seeds.

Subtle observations, woven effortlessly into conversation, each one gentle, thoughtful—yet undeniably sharp beneath the surface. "It must be exhausting for her, always trying to adjust to a world she does not understand."

Roland had not responded—but later, he had watched Anastasia in the council chamber, watched her pause before speaking, watched the quiet uncertainty she tried so desperately to hide.

And for just a moment—he had wondered. "There is a softness in her, but softness can be dangerous in court." Roland had known this to be true. He had seen the cost of softness, the way it could turn into weakness if wielded without careful restraint.

Genevieve had not lied. She had simply stated what Roland already knew but had never wanted to admit. "I wonder if she ever misses where she came from. How tragic it would be, to always feel displaced." Roland had never asked Anastasia this—never questioned if she felt like she truly belonged. Now, he wondered why he hadn't.

Roland did not question himself often. It was not in his nature—his decisions were measured, his thoughts precise, his judgment something he prided himself on. But Genevieve's words, small, subtle, always placed at just the right moment—had begun to shift something in him. Anastasia was struggling.

She was sharp, intelligent, resilient—but court life had not been kind to her. Roland had seen it in her hesitations, in the frustration that flickered in her gaze when nobles spoke in circles, when expectations suffocated.

And now for the first time, he wondered. Genevieve was not wrong and that unsettled him more than anything. Genevieve had stepped beside him—silent for a moment, letting the quiet settle before speaking.

"She is drowning, you know."

Roland had inhaled slowly, steadying himself, measuring his response before he had let it leave his lips. "Anastasia is adjusting." Genevieve had smiled, tilting her head slightly, as if amused by his restraint. "Adjusting to what?"

Roland had not answered. She had exhaled, her voice softer now, calculated. "You cannot teach someone to thrive in court if they do not understand its rhythm. You know that." She had let the words linger, had let the silence stretch between them—until the seed had been planted deeply enough to grow.

The garden was silent except for the faint rustling of leaves, the lantern light flickering in golden pools against the damp stone pathways. Anastasia stood with her fingers clenched around the railing, her breath shallow, her thoughts twisted into something she couldn't quite untangle.

Genevieve was everywhere, woven into the palace, into conversations, into the space Roland once filled beside her without question. And now? Now, Roland hesitated. He considered things he never had before. He listened to Genevieve's words like they held truth.

Evelina stepped beside her, arms crossed, expression sharp with awareness. "She's not just here for Roland, she's here to unravel you." Anastasia let out a slow breath, measured and controlled, but inside something cracked. She turned toward Evelina, forcing a scoff, forcing something that resembled detachment.

"That's dramatic."

Evelina huffed, arching an eyebrow. "Do you honestly think she's wasting her time reminiscing about festivals and fencing matches for fun?"

Anastasia shifted, her grip tightening on the railing, the cold metal grounding her. "She's playing a game." Evelina tilted her head. "You think she wants to win him?" Anastasia hesitated. "I don't know."

And that was the truth—Genevieve never demanded Roland outright, never pushed too far, but she lingered in just the right spaces, crafted just the right conversations, placed just the right doubts.

Evelina sighed, shaking her head. "She doesn't need to win him, Anastasia. She just needs to make sure you lose." The words settled, heavy and sharp, cutting deeper than Anastasia expected. She swallowed, staring down at her fingers. "I don't know how to fight her."

Evelina studied her, then exhaled. "You don't fight her with words. You fight her by not letting her dictate your place here."

Anastasia met her gaze, searching for something—a plan, a solution, some kind of certainty that she wasn't already slipping too far. Evelina smirked, though it held no humor. "You're asking the wrong question." Anastasia frowned. "What should I be asking?" Evelina leaned in slightly. "Not how do I fight her? But how do I remind Roland that I don't need to?"

The last few days had been a test of patience, of restraint, of fighting against the urge to demand answers Roland no longer seemed willing to give. Henry had noticed.

She had found him standing by the terrace that afternoon, the sky stretched in soft golds and deep blues, the sun lingering before giving itself to dusk. He had leaned against the railing, arms folded, watching her carefully—not with pity, not with amusement, but with the look of someone who saw exactly what she was trying to hide.

"You need to leave for a bit," he said. Anastasia scoffed, adjusting the sleeve of her gown. "It's not that simple." Henry arched an eyebrow. "Of course it is. You step outside. You breathe. You remember that the world is bigger than this palace and bigger than whatever game Genevieve is playing."

Anastasia shook her head, exhaustion curling into her voice. "And you assume a ride through the woods will fix everything?" Henry smirked. "No. But it'll remind you that she hasn't won yet." The words settled in the space between them, heavy, cutting through her frustration more effectively than she wanted to admit.

She glanced at him, wary. "Roland wouldn't approve." Henry chuckled, tilting his head. "That's why we aren't telling him." Before she could respond, a voice cut through the quiet. "You're telling me now."

Evelina stepped forward, arms crossed, expression unreadable but undeniably sharp. "His Highness already ordered that I go with Anastasia wherever she goes if he isn't there. So, if you're taking her, I'm coming too."

Henry exhaled dramatically. "I was hoping for a peaceful escape, not a chaperone." Evelina grinned, stepping beside Anastasia. "Then you shouldn't have picked the princess to go with you."

Anastasia let out a breath, shifting her gaze between them. The tension inside the palace had felt suffocating, dragging her deeper and deeper beneath unspoken rules and weighted expectations. Maybe Henry was right. Maybe she did need to breathe.

"Fine," she said.

"Let's go."

The forest had been alive with the scent of dirt and pine, the evening air crisp as Anastasia let herself breathe beyond the palace walls. Henry had brought her here to clear her head, to shake Genevieve's presence from her thoughts like dust off an old book.

And Evelina, ever loyal, ever sharp—had come along at Roland's request, his voice lingering in her mind before they left. "If I am not with her, you go. No exceptions."

The cabin had been small, aged, leaning slightly to one side as if the years had pressed too heavily against it.

Inside, dust curled from the floorboards, caught in the low glow of lantern light, the scent of old wood settling deep into the air. Henry had kicked the door open easily, the rusted hinges groaning, his usual smirk pulling at the edges of his mouth.

"Not exactly a palace, but it'll do."

Anastasia had rolled her eyes, stepping inside, trailing her fingers along the walls, feeling the chill of untouched space. Evelina had examined the place with one sweeping glance, crossing her arms.

"I assume this is where you bring women when you need privacy."

Henry had scoffed. "Please. If I wanted privacy, I wouldn't pick a place where the wind threatens to knock it down." Anastasia had smiled, just barely, shaking off the lingering weight of Genevieve, of Roland's quiet distance.

And then, the door slammed. The wind rushed against the walls, sharp and sudden, the force pushing the wooden frame inward—pressing, pressing, until the hinges snapped inward. Henry had lunged for the door, pulling at the handle. Nothing.

Anastasia had frowned, stepping beside him, trying to shove it forward. Still nothing. Evelina had sighed dramatically, tapping the floor with her boot. "Congratulations. We're stuck in the middle of nowhere. How romantic." Henry had groaned, pressing his forehead against the door. "This wasn't part of the plan."

EIGHTEEN

Henry found a plank of wood that hadn't started to rot and began to rub it against the wooden table standing in the corner of the small room. Eventually, sparks emerged and he tossed the plank into the fireplace.

The fire crackled weakly, its orange embers licking at the damp wood but never fully devouring it, as if reluctant to burn. The shadows stretched too tall, too thin, crawling up the cabin walls like fingers grasping at something unseen.

Evelina sat closest to the flames, her expression sharp, distrustful. She rubbed her arms, the chill settling into her skin. "I hate how this place feels." Henry reclined on the wooden bench, flashing a smirk that didn't quite reach his eyes. "It's just old, Evelina."

His voice was light, casual, almost too casual. Evelina raised an eyebrow, flicking a glance toward the ceiling where dust swirled, catching the fire's flickering light.

"And that's supposed to comfort me?"

Henry chuckled, "fair enough." He sat down on one of the chairs beside the table, the seat barely withstanding the weight of a grown man on it.

Anastasia chuckled at the sight, it was like a bear sitting on a potty.

The silence pressed against them, thick and unmoving, suffocating in its weight.. Henry stretched his legs out, leaning back against the creaky bench, flashing a grin. "Since we're stuck here, let's entertain ourselves. We tell stories, we pass the time, and no one loses their mind."

Evelina huffed, adjusting her cloak. "How very sentimental of you. What are we doing? Tragic childhoods? Lost loves? Crimes unpunished?" Henry chuckled. "Whichever makes the best tale." Anastasia crossed her arms, watching him carefully. "Fine. Start." Henry's smirk widened. "You want my childhood story? Oh, it's a masterpiece of good fortune and wasted opportunity."

"I grew up surrounded by wealth—gold in the halls, tutors who never raised their voices, expectations stacked high enough to suffocate." He spoke smoothly, his voice like warm honey, great banquets, grand celebrations, endless luxuries.

"I never wanted for anything. Never struggled, never fought for my place. It was simply there." Evelina scoffed. "Must have been miserable, being adored for existing." Henry laughed. "Some would think so. But that wasn't the worst of it."

His voice shifted just slightly, his rhythm faltering, his usual confidence dipping into something quieter.

"My parents weren't around much. Important matters, politics, traveling. All the things that kept them busy. I barely knew them."

Anastasia frowned, catching the faint edge of hesitation. "That doesn't sound perfect." Henry recovered quickly, flashing a grin. "It was good enough." Evelina narrowed her eyes, tapping her fingers against the floorboards. "Funny. When someone says good enough, they usually mean not good at all." Henry ignored her comment, shifting the conversation with an easy shrug.

"Your turn."

Anastasia leaned back against the wall, exhaling slowly. "You want a story of mistakes? Here's mine." Henry gestured for her to continue. "I'm ready for heartbreak and regret. Impress me." She smirked, shaking her head. "His name was Joey. My first love."

Evelina raised an eyebrow, intrigued. "What happened?" Anastasia sighed, running a hand through her hair. "Everything you would expect. He was wild, reckless, and magnetic. The kind of person you love without thinking. And that's what I did. I didn't think."

Henry chuckled. "Ah, dangerous. Go on." Anastasia stared into the fire, watching the embers pulse. "I thought the world stopped when we were together. I thought he was my future. And then, one day, he left."

Evelina frowned. "Just like that?" Anastasia nodded. "For someone else. Esme." Henry tilted his head slightly. "And what did you do?" Anastasia forced a smile. "I survived."

Her voice was steady, but beneath the surface—a wound that had never quite healed.

"My grandmother told me a story then. About Edward—the man who thought love meant possession, that passion was supposed to chain someone to your side." Evelina hummed, thoughtful. "And what did she say about him?" Anastasia smirked. "That she left him. Because love should not demand pieces of yourself you aren't willing to lose."

Evelina leaned back against the wooden bench, stretching her legs out and exhaling slowly. The firelight flickered unevenly across her face, making the shadows dance strangely across her sharp features.

"Fine. I'll tell you something real." Henry smirked. "Finally, some honesty." Evelina rolled her eyes. "Don't push your luck." She watched the flames twist, the embers pulsing deep orange before continuing.

"I grew up in the Labouant estate. Not as a noble. Not even as a favored guest. My mother was a servant there—one of many, lost in the endless halls, in the kitchens filled with thick smoke and the scent of roasting meat. She scrubbed floors, poured wine, cleaned after people who didn't bother to learn her name. But I did."

Anastasia shifted slightly, drawn in by the weight in Evelina's voice.

"The nobles didn't notice me, not really. To them, I was just another shadow, lingering in corridors I wasn't supposed to be in. But I saw everything." Henry's expression remained neutral, but there was something carefully measured in the way he listened. Evelina smirked.

"The Labouants had secrets, just like every noble family. Affairs, betrayals, debts hidden behind golden doors. But the real power wasn't in knowing those secrets—it was in knowing how to use them. And that's what my mother taught me."

Anastasia frowned slightly. "Did she ever regret it? Serving them?" Evelina shrugged, staring up at the ceiling as if searching for an answer she had lost a long time ago. "Regret? No. She understood the world too well for that. She never wanted me to be part of it, though. That was her mistake. Because I was already watching. Already listening. Already learning."

Her lips curled, not in amusement, but in something quieter. "She wanted me far from court, far from the nobles who would use me the way they used her. But instead, I learned how not to be used at all." The fire crackled, sending a sudden pop of sparks into the air. Henry studied her carefully before speaking, his voice lower than before.

"And did it work? Keeping yourself from being used?" Evelina met his gaze, smirking. "I'm still here, aren't I?" Anastasia exhaled, feeling the weight of the story settle between them, pressing against the walls of the cabin like something lingering long after it was spoken.

Anastasia's gaze drifted toward the far wall, something catching the firelight—faint, worn, nearly lost to time. She stood, crossing the room, running her fingers over the uneven texture of the wood.

Time remembers what the world forgets.

Henry stepped beside her, staring too intently at the inscription, his body unnaturally still. His fingers brushed against the carved letters—slow, deliberate, tracing as if recalling rather than reading. Anastasia glanced at him. "What?" Henry shook his head. "Nothing." Evelina did not challenge him.

That night, exhaustion weighed against them, pulling them toward restless sleep. Anastasia drifted but her mind refused peace. She saw a man, faceless, standing at the threshold of a grand hall, his silhouette unnaturally long in the firelight. A woman approached, her laughter brittle, broken, filled with something hollow.

"You are making a mistake." Her voice trembled, a warning curling at the edges. The man did not answer.

He stepped forward instead, the fire behind him growing taller, unnatural, twisting upward like grasping hands. Anastasia gasped awake, choking on her breath, her heart hammering. She sat up and Henry was watching her. It was a concerned look and she could tell he had been looking out for her whilst she slept.

The morning air was sharp, cutting through the cracks in the cabin like cold steel, pushing against their skin as they stirred from restless sleep.

Anastasia stretched, her limbs aching from the rigid wooden floor, the memory of her dream lingering like smoke in her chest—thin, suffocating, hard to ignore. Henry was already up, running his fingers along the door frame, his expression unreadable.

Evelina let out a frustrated sigh. "Alright, genius, any thoughts on how we get out?" Henry smirked. "I was hoping you'd magically summon a solution." Evelina rolled her eyes. "Magic is wasted on the undeserving."

Anastasia stepped forward, pressing her palms against the door, testing the weight. "Maybe if we push together, with force."

Henry tilted his head. "Or maybe we stop pretending brute strength is the answer and check for a weakness." Evelina crossed her arms. "Fine. You're the strategist. What do you suggest?" Henry ran his hand along the hinges, eyes narrowing. "These are old. Rusted. If we can loosen them, the door might slide free instead of breaking outright."

Anastasia glanced at Evelina. "Think you can pry them open?" Evelina smirked. "I can pry open an armored vault if I'm annoyed enough." Using the edge of a dagger, Evelina dug at the rusted metal, loosening it piece by piece as the cabin groaned under the pressure. The door shifted, but refused to give entirely. Henry gritted his teeth. "One more push—on three."

One. Two. Three.

The hinges cracked, and the door swung violently inward, the force sending Henry stumbling forward, catching himself on the frame. Outside, the forest stretched before them—damp, tangled, wild, and open. Evelina breathed out, relieved, shaking the dust from her hands. Anastasia tilted her head toward Henry. "You alright?"

Henry smirked. "What, worried about me?" Anastasia huffed, stepping past him. "Not particularly." Evelina grinned. "Shame. I was enjoying watching him suffer."

They left the cabin behind, stepping into the forest, ready to forget the suffocating hours trapped inside. The castle loomed against the horizon, its towering presence less like home and more like a silent judge, waiting for their return. Evelina rode beside Anastasia, studying her carefully.

"You look like you'd rather turn back." Anastasia exhaled. "Maybe I would." Henry pulled his horse beside them, the usual smugness in his expression faded, replaced by something more unreadable. "The court hasn't changed. Just the way you see it."

Anastasia knew he was right. Genevieve still schemed. The nobles still watched. She shook off the thought before it could settle, gripping the reins tighter. As they entered the palace gates, the whispers began like curling smoke, drifting into the halls, pressing against her ribs.

She felt eyes on her, felt the murmurs tighten around her like invisible chains. Genevieve was nowhere in sight, but her influence still lingered, sewn into every glance, every measured breath, every step Anastasia took.

Roland stood at the entrance of the great hall, tense, unreadable, jaw clenched, but his eyes—his eyes betrayed his relief. Anastasia met his gaze, unsure what to say, unsure if words could ever be enough to bridge the space that had grown between them. He exhaled, stepping forward. "You're back." She nodded. "I am."

His voice was lower now, quiet but edged with something unspoken. "You were gone longer than expected."

Evelina cleared her throat. "Would've been shorter if Henry hadn't led us into a collapsed shack." Henry scoffed. "Excuse me? That shack was a stroke of architectural genius." Roland ignored their exchange, his focus unwavering on Anastasia. "Are you alright?"

Anastasia hesitated, the weight of her dream, the words carved into the cabin, the unease curling in

her stomach all pressing in at once. She forced a
nod. "Yes." Roland studied her carefully, his
fingers twitching as if he wanted to reach for her
but wasn't sure if he could. "Good."

✳✳✳

While the garden air invigorated Anastasia as she
paced the stone path, the scent of damp earth
clinging to the fading light, Evelina remained
unmoved. Her arms were crossed, her expression
a closed book, mirroring her mood of the entire
day.

Anastasia finally exhaled, glancing sideways.
"You were harsh with Henry." Evelina arched an
eyebrow, unimpressed. "Harsh is generous. I was
restrained." Anastasia let out a dry laugh. "You
barely spoke to him unless you were insulting
him."

Evelina shrugged. "You say that like I'm
supposed to feel guilty." Anastasia turned to face
her fully, frowning. "Do you not trust him?"
Evelina didn't answer immediately. Instead, she
let the silence settle, dragging the conversation
taut before responding.

"I don't."

Anastasia studied her carefully. "Why?" Evelina sighed, brushing dust from her sleeve as if wiping away thoughts she didn't want to say aloud. "Henry is a ruffian. A vagabond. The kind of man who takes what he wants and expects the world to let him."

Anastasia shook her head. "That's unfair. He's reckless, yes, but he's loyal." Evelina gave her a sharp look. "Loyal to what?" Anastasia hesitated. "To us. To Roland." Evelina's lips curved, not quite a smirk, but something that resembled doubt.

"Henry will sleep with any woman he sets his eyes on, if she lets him. He's restless, careless, ruled by impulse. He has no regard for consequences."

Anastasia felt a flicker of unease curling in her stomach. "He's been loyal to Roland. To me." Evelina's expression didn't change. "Loyalty isn't the issue. Self-control is." Anastasia hesitated, watching Evelina closely. "What are you really trying to say?" Evelina sighed, rubbing a hand over her face before meeting Anastasia's gaze firmly. "You are a married woman, Anastasia, even if you weren't meant to be."

Anastasia swallowed. "I wouldn't..." Evelina raised a sharp eyebrow. "Wouldn't you?" The silence stretched between them, heavy with implications neither of them dared say outright. Finally, Evelina exhaled, shaking her head. "Just be careful. Henry lives in the moment. You don't have that luxury." And with that, she walked ahead, leaving Anastasia standing alone, uncertain if Evelina was right—or if she simply didn't want her to be.

✳✳✳

The candlelight flickered weakly against the pages of her journal, shadows curling over ink-dipped thoughts that refused to settle. Anastasia sat at her writing desk, fingers absently tracing the worn edges of the leather-bound book, but she hadn't written a single word.

Evelina's voice echoed in her mind, sharp and certain. "You are a married woman." She had known that. Of course, she had. But hearing it, saying it aloud, acknowledging it as more than a fact but as a binding truth, that was different.

Her marriage was complicated. Tied to duty, tangled in expectations she hadn't chosen, marked by a history still unfolding in ways she couldn't control. And Henry, Henry had nothing to do with it.

She wasn't foolish enough to think he had any intentions beyond what was fleeting. Evelina was right about him, he *was* a ruffian, restless, always chasing the next indulgence, never considering what remained behind. And yet....

Anastasia's fingers curled tighter against the journal. The way Henry looked at her sometimes—not like Roland did, not with duty or weight or quiet understanding. But with something else. Something unburdened.

She wasn't tempted. She wouldn't be. She was married. She repeated the words to herself, over and over. And still, they felt like something too distant to grasp.

The terrace was quiet, the lantern light casting warm pools of gold against the stone. The scent of rain still lingered in the air from the earlier storm, curling around them in damp traces.

Anastasia leaned against the railing, arms crossed, watching Henry as he stretched, exhaling deeply. He had that familiar ease about him—relaxed posture, lazy grin, the kind of confidence that made everything feel like a game to him.

"Evelina doesn't trust you," Anastasia finally said, cutting through the silence. Henry smirked, tilting his head slightly. "You say that like it's a shocking revelation." Anastasia narrowed her eyes. "I thought maybe it bothered you."

Henry scoffed, shaking his head. "Oh, come on, Princess. Do I seem like a man who spends his nights losing sleep over what Evelina thinks of me?" Anastasia rolled her eyes but didn't look away. "She says you're reckless. A ruffian. A danger to any woman who sets eyes on you."

Henry's grin widened. "Ah. So she's paying attention." Anastasia huffed a quiet laugh, shaking her head. "She thinks I should keep my distance." Henry studied her for a beat too long—not suspicious, not calculating, just watching her in that way he did sometimes, like he could see the thoughts shifting behind her gaze before she even voiced them.

"And do you agree?"

Anastasia leaned back slightly, tapping her fingers against the railing. "You haven't given me a reason to." Henry let out a soft chuckle, running a hand through his hair. "Yet."

Anastasia arched her brow. "Yet?"

Henry smirked, stepping closer—not in a threatening way, not in a way that made Anastasia wary, but in the way someone did when they wanted to test limits, to see how much space they could take up before being pushed away.

"Come now, Princess. You've heard the rumors. Surely you must know I have a talent for trouble." Anastasia didn't move, didn't shift, didn't step back. "That's exactly what Evelina warned me about."

Henry tilted his head, gaze flickering with something unreadable before settling into amusement again. "And yet, here we are."

The words lingered between them, stretched out thin in the evening air, laced with unspoken meaning that neither of them bothered to name. Anastasia exhaled slowly, pushing off the railing, stepping back toward the palace entrance.

"Don't get comfortable, Henry. You're still exactly who she says you are." Henry grinned, hands in his pockets, unbothered as he called after her. "And you're still here." Anastasia ignored the comment, ignored the way it made her pulse tighten for half a second. She wouldn't give him the satisfaction.

NINETEEN

The great hall was alive with laughter, music swelling beneath the chatter of nobles draped in silk and arrogance. Candles flickered along the walls, casting golden light over silver goblets filled with dark wine. The air was thick, too warm, too heavy, too laced with tension that only Anastasia seemed to recognize.

She sat beside Roland, her fingers curled lightly around her glass, listening, watching. Genevieve was at ease, her presence effortless. She smiled as she spoke, her laughter honey-sweet as she recalled stories of Roland before the weight of responsibility had settled on his shoulders.

"Do you remember, Roland?" she mused, tilting her head slightly. "When duty was just a distant thought—when you could laugh without measuring your words? Gods, those were the days, weren't they?"

Roland chuckled softly, shaking his head. "Those days made us reckless." Genevieve smirked. "Oh, but weren't they wonderful?"

Anastasia felt the shift—the subtle but undeniable push, the way Genevieve guided the conversation like hands steering a ship toward uncertain waters. She exhaled, offering a quiet smile. "Roland has grown into his responsibility. A leader cannot live in recklessness forever."

Genevieve turned to her then, slow, deliberate, her smile curving like the edge of a blade. "Oh, my dear, Roland has always been loyal to what he chooses. Are you certain you are among those choices?"

The words cut, sharp and precise, slipping between Anastasia's ribs before she could prepare for them. She expected Roland to correct her, to dismiss Genevieve's implication with his usual certainty. Instead, he was silent.

Anastasia's pulse tightened, her fingers curling against the edge of the table. The laughter around her continued, the banquet moving forward as though the world hadn't just shifted beneath her feet. She stood abruptly, ignoring the curious glances, ignoring the quiet murmur of whispers that followed her as she stepped away from the table, away from Roland, away from the weight settling in her chest.

Roland caught up to her quickly, his footsteps purposeful against the stone.

"Anastasia."

She didn't stop, didn't turn, couldn't—because the moment she did, she knew she would break.

"Anastasia, wait."

She halted, her breath uneven, her hands clenched at her sides as she finally faced him.

"Are you *truly* questioning my place here?"

Roland exhaled sharply, rubbing his temple as if trying to clear the tangled thoughts Genevieve had planted in his mind. "It's not that simple, Anastasia." She scoffed, shaking her head. "Then make it simple."

Silence.

Genevieve leaned against the far wall, watching through the sliver of an open doorway. She didn't need to hear the words. She saw the way Anastasia stiffened, the way Roland clenched his jaw, the way the space between them widened just slightly—just enough. A slow smile curled across her lips.

Roland clenched his jaw, exhaling sharply as he ran a hand through his hair. "Anastasia, don't do this." She scoffed, crossing her arms tightly over her chest. "Don't do what, Roland? Question why you hesitated? Ask why, after everything, you let her words linger?" His eyes flickered with frustration, with something heavier than simple irritation. "It wasn't about her."

Anastasia shook her head, laughing bitterly. "No? Because it certainly felt like it was." Roland stepped closer, his voice lowering. "You are twisting this into something it isn't."

"Then tell me what it is, Roland!" She snapped, her voice sharp, unraveling despite the control she desperately tried to keep. "Tell me why I had to sit there, listen to her, her of all people, question my place here and you said nothing."

Roland's silence stretched too long again. And that hurt more than anything. Genevieve tilted her head slightly from her position in the shadows, watching the moment unfold exactly as she had intended. It was almost too easy.

Anastasia sat on the edge of her bed, the silk sheets cool beneath her fingers as she ran her hand absentmindedly over the embroidered patterns. The fire in the hearth crackled softly, but its warmth felt distant, unable to touch the chill twisting in her chest.

She had never felt like an outsider in Roland's world until tonight. The weight of Genevieve's words pressed against her skin, wrapping itself around her thoughts like creeping ivy.

"Are you certain you are among those choices?" The worst part wasn't the question. It was Roland's hesitation. She wanted to believe it was nothing—that it had been a moment, a misstep, that his silence hadn't meant anything. But doubt was a poison that spread quickly, slipping into cracks, filling spaces that had once been solid.

Anastasia curled her knees toward her chest, staring blankly at the flickering flames, her mind racing through every interaction, every glance, every moment where she had been certain of Roland's loyalty.

Was she imagining this? Letting Genevieve's manipulation sink in too deeply? Or had something always been fragile between them, waiting for the right moment to break? She pressed a hand against her temple, closing her eyes, forcing herself to breathe.

"*I* am his wife." She whispered it aloud, as if saying the words would make them feel more tangible. But tonight, they felt more like a title than a truth.

Roland stood in the empty corridor, fists clenched at his sides, his breath uneven. The evening air had cooled, but the tension weighing on his shoulders burned hotter than any fire.

Genevieve's words had been calculated—precise, meant to strike at the cracks that already existed. And he had let them. He rubbed a hand over his face, exhaling sharply. Why hadn't he answered immediately? Why had he allowed her to walk away feeling uncertain about her place here?

Because a part of him—the part buried beneath duty and expectation—had wondered too. Not about his devotion to Anastasia, not about his feelings, but about the world she had been forced into. Had he made a mistake bringing her here?

Not because he doubted her—but because sometimes, love wasn't enough to protect someone from the weight of court.

The realization unsettled him. And Genevieve, standing somewhere in the shadows, had seen all of it. Roland gritted his teeth, shaking off the thoughts, straightening his stance. He would speak to Anastasia. He had to. Because if he allowed this doubt to fester—Genevieve would win. And that was something he refused to let happen.

Roland barely had time to compose himself before Evelina stepped into his path, blocking his way with arms crossed, her gaze sharp enough to slice through the lingering frustration clinging to him.

"You said nothing."

Roland exhaled, rubbing his temple. "Evelina, not now." She tilted her head slightly, unimpressed.

"That's convenient, isn't it? When exactly should I bring up that you left your wife questioning her place in court because Genevieve prodded too hard?"

Roland stiffened, jaw tightening. "It wasn't what it looked like." Evelina scoffed, shaking her head. "No, it was exactly what it looked like. She baited you, and you let her." Roland ran a hand down his face, his frustration shifting from Genevieve to himself. "I didn't mean—"

"It doesn't matter what you meant," Evelina interrupted, stepping closer. "What matters is that Anastasia walked away tonight feeling like maybe she wasn't chosen after all."

Roland's pulse tightened. That wasn't true. It couldn't be. Evelina's expression softened just barely—not with pity, but with understanding, with someone who had seen the damage hesitation could do before.

"Fix it, Roland. Or Genevieve wins." She didn't wait for a reply. She simply walked away, leaving him standing alone with the weight of the warning pressing against his chest.

The morning light pooled against the polished floors of the corridor, golden and deceptively warm. Anastasia walked with measured steps, her mind still tangled in the threads Genevieve had woven the night before. Genevieve stepped beside her without invitation, her presence effortless, like she had always belonged in whatever space she occupied.

"You left early last night," she murmured, her tone light, conversational, but edged with something sharper beneath the surface. Anastasia kept her expression neutral. "I wasn't enjoying the conversation." Genevieve chuckled. "Oh, dear, that isn't like you at all. You usually thrive under pressure." I did, Anastasia wanted to say. Until you made me doubt myself.

She exhaled, keeping her stride steady. "Some conversations aren't worth engaging in." Genevieve hummed, tilting her head slightly. "And yet, you walked away. Not Roland. Not the court. You."

Anastasia tightened her jaw. "Don't twist this into something it isn't." Genevieve's lips curved—not wide, not mocking, but pleased, as though she had already won simply by being in this moment. "Oh, but everything can be twisted if you know where the cracks are."

Anastasia stopped walking, turning fully to Genevieve, her gaze unwavering. "You should choose your words carefully." Genevieve smiled sweetly, folding her hands together. "And you should choose your battles wisely. Because you may find that some of them have already been lost."

Anastasia swallowed her anger, keeping her posture perfectly still. She would not give Genevieve the satisfaction of seeing her waver again. Genevieve leaned in just slightly, dropping her voice into something softer—not sympathetic, but intimate, conspiratorial.

"You know, I never wanted Roland to struggle like this. He was so much easier to love before duty weighed him down." Anastasia's stomach tightened, her breath catching for half a second. Genevieve smiled, sensing the reaction. "I only hope that when he finally realizes what he wants, it isn't too late."

Through the palace corridors, past the towering columns that once felt sturdy but now loomed too heavy, too permanent, pressing against her thoughts like weights she couldn't shake.

Genevieve's words curled inside her mind, latching onto every quiet doubt she had refused to name until now. "I never wanted Roland to struggle like this. He was so much easier to love before duty weighed him down. I only hope that when he finally realizes what he wants, it isn't too late."

Anastasia pressed a hand against the cool stone of the nearest wall, her breath uneven. She shouldn't let Genevieve affect her. She knew what this was—a deliberate game, a precisely planted seed meant to grow into uncertainty.

But the problem with manipulation was that it worked best when it fed off something that was already fragile. And tonight, for the first time, Anastasia realized—she wasn't certain anymore. She wasn't certain of Roland's love. She wasn't certain of her place here.

She wasn't certain that the battle she thought she had won was actually over. Anastasia exhaled sharply, straightening her posture, forcing herself to remember who she was, where she stood, why she had fought so hard to be here. But deep down—somewhere quiet, somewhere she would not acknowledge aloud—she feared Genevieve was right.

Anastasia barely noticed the footsteps approaching until Evelina was beside her, arms crossed, expression sharp with quiet assessment. "You look like you're about to make a stupid decision."

Anastasia let out a breath, shaking her head. "I'm not." Evelina arched an eyebrow. "That's exactly what someone about to do something foolish would say." Anastasia exhaled, pressing her fingers against her temple. "I just need a moment."

Evelina studied her carefully, her gaze flickering toward the distant end of the hallway—toward where Genevieve had disappeared, leaving behind nothing but the lingering echoes of manipulation. "She got to you."

Anastasia tensed. "She didn't."

Evelina scoffed. "You're standing in an empty hallway questioning yourself, and you want me to believe she didn't?" Anastasia swallowed hard, looking away. "She's good at what she does." Evelina let out a low chuckle. "Of course she is. She's been twisting words since the day she learned how to speak."

She softened slightly, stepping closer, voice lowering. "But here's the thing, Anastasia, Genevieve doesn't win unless you let her." Anastasia clenched her jaw. "And what if she's right?"

Evelina exhaled, shaking her head. "She's not. You already know that."

Anastasia wanted to believe it—wanted to shake off the doubt, to push past the hesitation, to silence the voice whispering in the back of her mind that maybe, just maybe, Roland regretted choosing her.

Evelina sighed, crossing her arms. "Come on. Let's find something stronger than tea." Anastasia huffed out a quiet laugh, despite the weight pressing against her chest. Evelina nudged her lightly. "And stop letting that venomous woman live rent-free in your head."

Evelina had led her to a private sitting room, away from the murmurs of court, away from the weight of Genevieve's presence lingering in unseen corners. A half-filled goblet of wine sat between them, untouched, the conversation pressing harder than any drink could.

Anastasia tapped her fingers against the armrest of her chair, her thoughts tangled, unruly. Evelina watched her carefully before exhaling. "You need to go to him." Anastasia scoffed. "Why? So he can be silent again?"

Evelina leaned forward, resting her elbows on the table, her gaze sharp. "You're letting this fester. And when something festers, it rots. You and I both know that's what Genevieve wants."

Anastasia swallowed, looking away. "Maybe she's right." Evelina's expression hardened. "You don't believe that." Anastasia let out a quiet breath, shaking her head. "I don't know what to believe anymore."

Evelina scoffed, sitting back. "Oh, for gods' sake, Anastasia. I know you're clever enough to see through this." Anastasia didn't answer, didn't meet her eyes.

Evelina sighed, rubbing a hand over her forehead. "Fine. Sit here, drown in your uncertainty, let Genevieve carve out space where she doesn't belong. But don't come crying to me when the damage is irreversible."

She stood, grabbing her goblet before shaking her head. "Or you could go to him now and force him to remember that you are his wife, not his regret."

Anastasia flinched slightly at the word, at the weight it carried. Evelina turned back toward the door, her voice lighter now, but pointed. "Your choice, Princess." Then, she was gone. And Anastasia was left staring at the wine that had grown warm.

TWENTY

Sleep did not come easily.

Anastasia lay in her bed, staring at the ceiling, the flickering candlelight casting restless shapes against the stone walls. The weight of the day clung to her, pressing into her ribs, curling tightly around her lungs like unseen hands.

People were watching. Whispering. Waiting.

Roland had warned her, but she hadn't needed his words to feel it. The air in the palace had shifted—heavier now, thick with quiet judgment, with questions no one dared ask aloud. She forced herself to close her eyes, willing sleep to take her. And when it did—it pulled her under fast.

She stood in a grand Georgian ballroom, the scent of beeswax and perfume thick in the air, clinging to every golden-framed mirror lining the walls. The chandeliers overhead glittered like frozen stars, their crystal droplets catching the light and refracting it into sharp, unnatural colors. The people moved around her in carefully measured steps, skirts swaying stiffly, hands gliding just barely against one another as they danced in precise, rehearsed motions.

And yet—the sound was wrong. The harpsichord notes were sharp, clashing against the sweeping violins in a melody that should have been elegant—but instead felt foreign, distant, like a memory she had never lived but somehow knew too well. She tried to dance, moving through the motions, letting her feet carry her across polished marble, but every movement felt too free, too fluid, too much of who she was—something the court did not understand.

The whispers started slowly, curling at the edges of the room like smoke. "She doesn't belong."

"Look at the way she moves. Not proper. Not controlled." She tried to ignore them, tried to steady herself, but their voices grew louder, layered with murmurs, with judgment, with veiled disappointment. Her heart pounded.

Then—Roland appeared beside her. His presence should have steadied her, should have reminded her that she wasn't alone, that she belonged here despite the lingering doubt.

He offered her his hand, his expression unreadable—but familiar. Safe. She reached for him—but just as her fingers brushed his, he vanished. The ballroom collapsed around her, melting into shadows, pulling her under into a different world—a world she knew. A world she had lost.

She was standing in London.

The neon-drenched street pulsed with a vibrant, artificial life. Sharp pinks and blues ricocheted off the wet asphalt, distorting the shapes of the buildings. The club music was a deep, insistent thrum that resonated in her bones, eclipsing the distant sounds of the city and the voices of the anonymous crowd.

The scent of vodka and cigarette smoke lingered in the air, mixing with the rain that had settled into the streets. This was home, her home, and she wanted to stay. She wanted to reach for the familiarity, to step forward, to let herself sink into the life she had lived before but the dream would not allow her.

The neon lights faded, not like a dimming flame, but like something ripped away too quickly, stolen before she had the chance to grasp it. And before she could fight it, she was back. Back to the time she was trapped in. Her breath hitched as she woke, the sheets clinging to her damp skin, the heavy silence of the palace pressing down against her like unseen hands. Her world was pulling in two directions and for the first time, she wasn't sure which one she wanted to follow

The sewing room smelled faintly of lavender and aged parchment, the scent curling into the dim afternoon light filtering through the tall windows. Evelina sat near the hearth, embroidery needle in hand, carefully threading delicate patterns into fine linen—her movements slow, precise, practiced.

Anastasia lingered in the doorway for a moment, watching, then stepped forward with a soft scoff. "I do not understand how you find this enjoyable." Evelina laughed, shaking her head without looking up. "It is expected of me."

Anastasia huffed, crossing her arms as she leaned against the nearest chair. "Expected, perhaps. But still tedious." Evelina finally glanced up, studying her for a beat before gesturing toward an empty seat across from her. "You do not always have to fight everything."

Anastasia held her breath for half a second, then slowly sank into the chair, folding her hands in her lap. "But I want to." There was no humor in her voice this time, only quiet exhaustion. Evelina set down her needle, leaning forward slightly, her expression softening just enough to reveal something close to concern. "Then fight for the right reasons, Ana." The words lingered between them, stretching across the candlelit room, pressing against the weight Anastasia had carried since the moment Roland had warned her—since the moment Genevieve had planted doubt in her ribs, twisting it into something she had not yet managed to pull free.

The door swung open abruptly, breaking the silence. Roland stood in the entryway, his presence filling the room as his gaze settled on Anastasia. His expression was tense. "The king has summoned his advisors." Anastasia straightened. "For what reason?"

Roland exhaled, shaking his head. "He wants answers for the unrest." The words settled heavily in the space between them.

Evelina sat back in her chair, arms crossing slowly over her chest. Anastasia met Roland's gaze, steady, unwavering—but deep inside, a quiet dread curled into her bones.

The chamber was heavy with the scent of wax and old parchment, the flickering candlelight casting uneasy shadows against the polished oak table where the king's most trusted advisors sat.

Anastasia sat beside Roland, her posture straight, her expression carefully measured—a deliberate display of control she had learned to maintain in rooms like this. The discussion had been restrained at first, murmurs of unrest, subtle remarks on the growing tension in the lower districts. Until Lord Percival spoke.

"The Queen has encouraged rebellion." The words settled into the room like a stone thrown into still water. Roland's jaw tightened, his fingers twitching slightly against the edge of the table. "That is not true."

Lord Percival smirked—not openly, but just enough to show his satisfaction. "She visits the lower districts, speaks to the people, listens to their grievances—and what do we find? Protests. Resistance. Discontent spreading like wildfire." Anastasia clenched her jaw, her breath steady even as her pulse picked up.

"Listening is not rebellion, Lord Percival." Percival turned his gaze on her, his expression calm, carefully composed. "But it breeds it, does it not?" Roland leaned forward, his voice firm. "You are twisting the narrative to fit your own agenda." Lord Percival shrugged slightly. "I am merely presenting the facts."

The room fell into tense silence, broken only when King George exhaled sharply, rubbing his temple before leveling Anastasia with a gaze that felt more like judgment than warning. "You are walking on dangerous ground, Princess." His voice was steady, cool, and authoritative. "You were brought here to secure England's future—not to dismantle its traditions." The words pressed against her ribs, heavy, decisive. She should have been careful in her response. She should have agreed, nodded, shown restraint. But she did none of those things. "A future cannot thrive if its people are suffering," Anastasia said quietly, evenly. "And England will not remain strong if it refuses to evolve." The silence that followed was suffocating

Anastasia barely had time to steady herself after leaving the council chamber before Roland caught up to her, his footsteps sharp against the marble floors, his expression set with frustration.

"What exactly were you trying to accomplish in there?" She didn't stop walking. "Speaking the truth." Roland exhaled, falling into stride beside her, his voice lower now, edged with urgency. "You are playing a dangerous game, Anastasia."

She turned to him then, eyes narrowing. "Because I refuse to sit silently while they twist the narrative to suit their fears?" Roland shook his head. "Because you are proving their fears right." Her pulse tightened, her hands clenching into fists at her sides. "You think I am encouraging rebellion?"

He hesitated—a fraction too long, just enough to sting. "I think you are making yourself a target."

Anastasia scoffed, stopping abruptly, forcing Roland to turn back to face her. "I will not apologize for listening to the people. I will not apologize for refusing to pretend their struggles do not exist."

Roland sighed, rubbing a hand down his face, his frustration shifting into something heavier. "I know that."

"Then stop acting like I am the problem," she snapped, her voice quieter now, more dangerous. "The unrest began long before I arrived. I am not the cause of it." Roland held her gaze, his expression unreadable. "But you are becoming the symbol of it."

Anastasia inhaled deeply, steadying herself. "Then perhaps the real problem is that they fear change more than they fear injustice."

Anastasia did not storm away from Roland, nor did she let the frustration push her into reckless action. She walked. Through the palace corridors, past the quiet murmurs of servants, past the looming portraits of monarchs long dead, past the suffocating expectation pressing against her ribs.

Roland's words echoed in her mind—"You are becoming the symbol of it." That was what unsettled her most. Not that she was feared, not that she was being watched, but that her presence—her very existence in this court—had shifted from obligation to rebellion, from necessity to danger.

She found herself near the sewing room again, drawn toward something stable, something not dictated by political games or suffocating duty. Evelina sat in her usual place, embroidery needle in hand, working as though the world had not just shaken beneath Anastasia's feet.

Evelina didn't look up immediately, but when she finally did, her gaze softened. "Sit."

Anastasia didn't hesitate. The chair was firm beneath her, grounding, pulling her back to herself—to who she was before doubt had settled so deeply. Evelina set down her needle, exhaling slowly. "You look like you've been fighting ghosts again."

Anastasia let out a quiet laugh, shaking her head. "No ghosts. Just men who refuse to see beyond their own fears." Evelina hummed thoughtfully, resting her elbow against the armrest, chin lightly pressed against her fingers. "And Roland?" Anastasia clenched her jaw, looking away. "Still convinced I am walking too close to danger."

Evelina scoffed. "You are walking exactly where you need to be." Anastasia hesitated. "But at what cost?" Evelina watched her carefully, studying the exhaustion tucked beneath the frustration, the quiet uncertainty hidden beneath sharp defiance.

Then, her voice softened—but did not lose its strength. "Fight for the right reasons, Ana." The words settled deep, curling into the spaces Anastasia had feared were breaking apart. She breathed in, steadied herself.

Anastasia didn't hesitate this time. She found Roland in his private study, his fingers curled around the edge of a map sprawled across his desk, his expression tense—as if he had been trying to piece together a solution to a problem that had no easy answer. The door shut behind her, the click of the latch settling into the silence.

Roland looked up, exhaling heavily. "I was wondering when you'd come." Anastasia crossed her arms, her posture steady, but the exhaustion lingered in the set of her shoulders, in the weight pressing against her ribs. "You hesitated last night." Roland sighed, rubbing a hand down his face before straightening. "Genevieve knew exactly what she was doing."

Anastasia's jaw tightened. "That doesn't make it any less damaging." Roland didn't respond immediately, his gaze flickering toward the fireplace, where the flames curled softly against the stone. For a moment, he looked as if he were somewhere else entirely—somewhere before this conversation, before this marriage, before the weight of duty had settled onto both their shoulders. "Genevieve wants you to doubt me."

The words were spoken calmly, but Anastasia could see the tension beneath them—the quiet frustration, the lingering hesitation. She took a slow breath. "She wants more than that, Roland." His gaze snapped back to hers, sharp, questioning. "She wants you." Roland's lips parted, then pressed into a thin line—no immediate denial, no sharp dismissal.

The silence between them stretched too long. Anastasia inhaled deeply, keeping her voice steady. "Did you ever love her?" Roland ran a hand through his hair, exhaling. "It doesn't matter." Her chest tightened. "It does." Roland studied her, his expression unreadable.

Then—finally—he spoke. "Once. A lifetime ago." The admission should not have felt like a wound. And yet, it did. Anastasia clenched her jaw, but she did not let the moment break her. "And if she tries to make you remember that? If she tries to win back what she lost?"

Roland straightened, the firelight flickering against his features as his expression hardened. "She won't." But Anastasia did not miss the flicker of hesitation in his voice—not the same hesitation that had betrayed him before, but something quieter, something more uncertain. She swallowed, the weight of the conversation pressing into her ribs. "Then prove it." Roland didn't answer immediately.

✳✳✳

The air held a sharp chill as Anastasia entered the palace gallery, the vast space feeling even more imposing under the evening sky. Her mind, however, remained trapped in the echo of her argument with Roland.

She didn't notice Genevieve at first. Not until she spoke. "You have made quite the mess, haven't you?" Anastasia stilled, turning slowly to face her. Genevieve stood beside one of the grand portraits, fingers brushing idly against the edge of the gilded frame, her expression poised—not mocking, but satisfied, as if she had been expecting this moment.

"You look tired," she mused, tilting her head slightly. "I can't imagine how exhausting it must be, trying so desperately to hold onto something that was never truly yours." Anastasia clenched her jaw, refusing to take the bait. "You underestimate me." Genevieve chuckled, stepping forward. "No, dear. I think perhaps you are the one underestimating me."

Anastasia exhaled, her patience thinning. "What exactly do you want, Genevieve?" Genevieve's smile was slow—not wide, not cruel, but deliberate, the kind of smile that spoke of carefully planned victories. "I want what was meant to be mine."

Anastasia's pulse tightened. "Roland is my husband." Genevieve hummed thoughtfully, folding her hands together. "For now." Anastasia took a slow breath, steadying herself. "You will not manipulate him the way you manipulate the court."

Genevieve's expression didn't waver. "Oh, darling. I don't need to manipulate him." The words settled like ice against Anastasia's skin. Genevieve let the silence stretch before speaking again, her voice softer now, more intimate, conspiratorial.

"He once loved me. And I can make him remember that." Anastasia refused to flinch. She refused to let Genevieve see even an ounce of hesitation in her expression.

Instead, she smiled—not sweetly, not warmly, but sharply, like a blade meant only for Genevieve to recognize. "Try, then." Genevieve's lips parted slightly, surprised—not by the words themselves, but by the calm with which Anastasia said them.

Genevieve knew better than to act too quickly. She was patient. Calculated. And tonight, she would wait for the perfect opportunity. She found Roland in the great hall, reviewing documents, his posture rigid, his focus unwavering—but she knew the weight of his thoughts. She had always known him too well.

She approached without hesitation, stepping lightly across the stone floor. "You look troubled," she murmured, tilting her head. "Thinking too much again, Roland?" Roland glanced up, his expression neutral. "What do you want, Genevieve?"

She smirked slightly. "That's a dangerous question, isn't it?" He sighed, setting down the parchment in his hands. "You're wasting your time." Genevieve stepped closer, lowering her voice just enough to press it softly into the space between them.

"Am I?" Roland finally met her gaze—steady, unreadable, unwavering. Genevieve expected hesitation. Expected that brief flicker of doubt she had seen in him before. But instead—Roland leaned back, his expression settling into something firm, something resolute.

"It doesn't matter what you're trying, Genevieve."
She arched an eyebrow, feigning amusement.
"You sound so certain." Roland exhaled slowly,
shaking his head. "I am certain." For the first
time, she saw no hesitation. No wavering. No
space for doubt. And that—more than
anything—was the moment Genevieve realized
she had lost something she could not get back.

She didn't show it, of course. She never would.
Instead, she smiled, easy and composed, tilting
her chin ever so slightly. "We'll see about that,
won't we?" Genevieve was nothing if not
adaptable.

She saw the shift in Roland's resolve, the way he
had brushed aside her carefully placed words.
She wasn't foolish enough to make the mistake of
trying again—not with him. No, if she wanted to
tear down Anastasia, she had to do it differently.

She moved through the palace corridors with
effortless grace, slipping into conversation where
it suited her, weaving doubt into places where it
would take root.

"She's passionate, yes, but does she truly
understand England?"

"I wonder if she realizes how delicate our
traditions are."

"Roland was so steady before—so certain. And now? Now, he seems... troubled."

Evelina wasn't one to indulge in gossip. She was sharp, observant, and more skilled than most at cutting through the layered politics of court without ever being caught in its web. Which was why, when she found Anastasia in the east wing, tucked away in the quiet of the garden corridor, her expression was not casual, not distant, but carefully measured.

Anastasia glanced up, sensing the weight in Evelina's silence before she even spoke. "You look like you have something to say." Evelina exhaled, crossing her arms. "You need to be careful." Anastasia frowned. "What are you talking about?" Evelina stepped closer, lowering her voice just slightly—not in fear, but in quiet urgency.

"Genevieve is playing a new game. She isn't trying to win Roland back anymore." Anastasia stiffened. "Then what is she doing?" Evelina's lips pressed into a thin line, frustration flickering in her gaze. "She's making sure no one trusts you."

Anastasia's stomach tightened. "Rumors?" Evelina shook her head. "Not quite. She's being smarter than that." She gestured vaguely toward the palace beyond them. "She's planting doubts. Questions. Soft, seemingly harmless observations that make people second-guess what they already believe."

Anastasia inhaled sharply. Evelina continued. "She's shaping the narrative carefully, so that when real accusations come, they'll seem obvious—like something people should have seen long ago." The weight of the warning settled heavily in Anastasia's chest.

This wasn't just Genevieve seeking personal satisfaction. This was a slow dismantling. A quiet destruction of her place here. Anastasia swallowed, straightening her posture. "She won't win." Evelina's expression didn't shift. "Not unless you let her."

The air beyond the palace walls was crisp, carrying the scent of damp earth and distant smoke from the town beyond. The streets were quiet this late, the world settled into uneasy stillness.

Anastasia walked beside Henry, her arms folded tightly across her chest, her mind still tangled in the confrontation with Roland, in the slow unraveling of Genevieve's tactics. Henry exhaled softly, kicking a loose stone as they strolled. "You look like you're plotting something dangerous."

Anastasia huffed a quiet laugh. "I'm always plotting something dangerous." Henry grinned, but his gaze flickered toward her more carefully this time. "Genevieve?" Anastasia nodded, the weight of her thoughts pressing deeper. "She's undermining me. Whispering doubt into places that should be solid. Evelina warned me, and she was right—if I don't stop her now, she'll make certain no one trusts me."

Henry sighed, stretching his arms behind his head as they walked. "You know, it's not just you that she's aiming at. Roland isn't blind to it either."

Anastasia clenched her jaw. "He should be doing more." Henry scoffed. "Oh, come on. You think Roland is going to suddenly become a tactician against Genevieve? You and I both know he's always been too slow in court politics."

Anastasia opened her mouth to argue—but something felt wrong. The hairs on the back of her neck prickled, a slow, sinking pressure settling in her gut. She stilled, scanning the empty alleyway ahead, the quiet stretch of road behind them. Henry noticed her hesitation immediately. "What is it?"

She exhaled softly, barely above a whisper. "We're being watched." Henry's posture shifted—not rigid, not panicked, but alert, prepared. He turned slightly, scanning the shadows that stretched between the buildings. "Relax," he murmured, voice low but firm. "I won't let anything happen."

And then figures emerged from the darkness. The moment Lord Percival stepped forward, Anastasia knew this was not a simple warning—this was a declaration. Rough hands kept her and Henry locked in place, their grips tightening with each passing second.

Percival's boots echoed against the cobblestones as he approached, his expression one of cold amusement. "Ah, Your Majesty. We've been watching your little excursions closely."

Anastasia's jaw tightened. "You are making a mistake." Percival scoffed, tilting his head. "*You* have made the mistake, Princess. Meddling where you do not belong. Speaking out when silence would have served you better."

Henry tensed, his arms straining against the men holding him. "Let her go." Percival barely spared Henry a glance. "And why would I do that, mercenary? You are just as guilty." Anastasia kept her voice steady, unwavering. "If you touch him—"

Percival laughed, sharp and short, before stepping closer—too close, enough that she could feel the venom in his breath, the weight of his satisfaction. And then—he spat in her face. The shock was brief, but fury followed fast, burning through her restraint like wildfire. Henry fought harder, breaking free just enough to land a sharp blow to one of the guards—but they were too many, too skilled, too prepared.

Anastasia lunged toward Percival, her hands curling into fists, but another set of hands grabbed her, yanking her backward with force enough to steal her breath.

Percival adjusted his coat, sighing as if the entire scene bored him. "Take them." The last thing Anastasia saw was Henry trying, failing, fighting, losing—his gaze meeting hers just before the night swallowed them whole.

TWENTY ONE

The night swallowed them whole. Anastasia felt the bite of cold air against her cheeks as rough hands hoisted her onto the back of a horse. The scent of damp leather and sweat filled her nostrils, choking out everything else—the sweet freshness of the evening, the distant perfume of wildflowers carried by the wind.

The ropes binding her wrists burned against her skin, too tight, unforgiving. Beside her, Henry twisted against his captors, his voice sharp with defiance. "You have no idea who you're crossing." A snort from one of the riders. "Oh, but we do." Then, the horses surged forward.

The pounding of hooves against the dirt road vibrated through Anastasia's bones, each brutal gallop sending tremors through her limbs. She lurched forward, head slamming repeatedly into the flank of the beast beneath her.

Each impact blurred her vision further. The world tilted—stars stretched into streaks, the trees melted into a single dark mass, the air hollowed out into nothing but wind and silence. Then darkness.

A sharp shake dragged her back. Anastasia gasped, her breath catching in her throat, her fingers twitching against the freezing stone floor. Henry's hands gripped her shoulders, his face close to hers, his expression set with concern, tempered by frustration. "Come on, Ana. Stay with me."

Her pulse was sluggish, her limbs numb from the cold. She blinked—slow, careful—her vision adjusting to the dim glow of candlelight spilling weakly into the cell.

The walls were rough-hewn stone, lined with cracks where moisture seeped in. The air was sharp with the scent of damp earth and old iron. To her left, outside the cage, a winding staircase twisted up to a wooden door, golden candlelight pushing through the thin space beneath it.

Aside from a single candlestick affixed to the wall, there was no other source of illumination. Shadows pooled into the corners, deep, unmoving. Anastasia sat up slowly, rubbing her wrists where the rope had cut into her skin. She was freezing.

She turned her gaze toward the right wall. A small hole gaped in the stone, just large enough to glimpse the neighboring cell. And through it—movement. A faint silhouette, shifting in the dim light. Anastasia hesitated, licking her dry lips before speaking.

"Hello?"

Silence.

Then—a sigh, quiet, resigned, but unmistakably familiar. "I wasn't imagining things. They've put someone else down here." Anastasia's chest tightened. She recognized that voice.

The barmaid.

Her breath hitched. "Is it really you?" A pause. Then—a quiet, dry laugh, weak but real. "I remember you. You stood up for me once." Anastasia exhaled, glancing toward Henry, who remained still—listening, assessing, waiting.

She turned back to the gap in the wall. "It's... nice to hear a familiar voice." The barmaid hummed softly. "Nice enough, I suppose. Though I wish it weren't under these circumstances." Anastasia shifted forward, peering through the hole as best as she could. "How long have you been here?"

A sigh. "A month. Maybe more. Hard to tell when the days blend together." Anastasia clenched her hands into fists. "Why?"

Silence—one that stretched just a beat too long. Then—the truth came, raw and unapologetic. "I'm carrying Lord Percival's child."

The words struck like a slap. Anastasia sucked in a sharp breath. "What?" The barmaid's voice remained steady, laced with exhaustion but not broken.

"He panicked. I threatened to tell you and the king, and he knew you'd actually do something about it. So he took me before I could."

Anastasia felt the guilt settle, thick and suffocating, twisting deep despite knowing it wasn't hers to bear. "I'm sorry." The barmaid exhaled, shaking her head faintly—even though Anastasia could barely see her through the narrow stone gap.

"You have nothing to be sorry for." The quiet between them felt heavier now. Until Henry finally spoke—his voice a sharp cut through the cold. "We're getting out of here."

FOUR MONTHS LATER

The cold had settled deep into Anastasia's bones. She had carved tallies into the stone wall with the edge of a broken spoon—thin marks, uneven, a record of days that blurred together into something shapeless and suffocating.

Four months in darkness. In silence. In cold that sank beneath her skin and carved itself into her bones like rot. Anastasia had kept track of time—at first, with careful precision, marking tallies against the rough stone, counting the days with a desperate need to anchor herself to something real.

Now, she wasn't sure if the markings even meant anything. The scratches on the wall blurred together, the lines uneven, smudged where her shaking hands had pressed too hard against the stone. The cold had settled into her ribs, crawling up her spine like fingers she couldn't pry off. The routine was always the same.

Wake, wait, endure, sleep, repeat.

Their captors never spoke beyond the necessities. They never hinted at the world beyond these walls. There was no trial. No escape. No promise that death wasn't waiting just beyond the next set of footsteps descending the stairs. Some days, Anastasia didn't feel like herself anymore. Some days, she wasn't even sure she remembered what feeling normal was.

Anastasia knew only the cold for so long. The bone-chilling, soul-numbing cold of her gilded cage. Then came the manor. Gargantuan, opulent, dripping with a decadent wealth that felt both obscene and mocking. Each shimmering chandelier, each meticulously placed antique, was a stark reminder of everything she had lost, everything she was denied.

Her brief excursions were the only breaks in the monotony. The heavy oak door would creak open, and a guard, face impassive and eyes devoid of pity, would gesture curtly. The only purpose of these brief freedoms was the most basic of human necessities. Yet, even these short jaunts were agonizing. The sheer scale of the place, the winding corridors that seemed to stretch into infinity, only amplified her despair.

Hope, though, a tenacious weed, still clung to the ravaged soil of her heart. With each outing, she plotted. She observed. She waited for a flicker of opportunity.

Today was like any other. The door opened, the guard gestured. She shuffled forward, her bare feet barely audible on the plush Persian rug. This time, however, she saw a window, unlatched. The world, bathed in the golden light of the late afternoon sun, beckoned.

Adrenaline surged through her veins, a fiery counterpoint to the years of icy confinement. Ignoring the guard's expectant stare, she lunged. A desperate, clumsy leap towards the window, her fingers scrabbling for purchase on the ornate frame. She almost had it. Almost tasted the freedom on the wind.

But the guard was quicker. A strong arm clamped around her waist, hauling her back with brutal efficiency. She struggled, her nails raking against his leather-clad arm, a silent scream tearing through her throat. She thrashed, kicked, fought with the ferocity of a trapped animal.

It was no use. Her body, weakened by deprivation and despair, was no match for his strength. He pinned her against the wall, his grip unyielding. The brief spark of defiance flickered and died.

With a grunt of exertion, he dragged her back towards the cage, her dreams of escape shattered on the cold marble floor. As she was pushed back inside, she caught a glimpse of herself in a gilded mirror.

The sight was horrifying. Her once vibrant eyes were now dull pools of exhaustion. Her hair, a cascade of gold that had once been her pride, now hung down to her knees, a knotted and matted mess. Years of neglect had turned it into a tangled ruin. Her gown, once a symbol of her elevated status, was now raggedy and torn, hanging off her emaciated frame like a tattered shroud.

She had started whispering to herself. Not in full conversations—not yet.

But muttering. Recounting things she remembered. Filling the silence with something other than the sound of her own heartbeat. Henry had noticed. He always noticed. But he never commented on it. Not directly, anyway.

Instead, he just watched—not with pity, but with understanding. The kind of understanding that came from someone who had spent long stretches of time in the same suffocating, unchanging reality. The kind that knew exactly where a mind went when it had nothing left to hold onto.

Anastasia paced, her arms folded tightly against her chest, her breath uneven, unable to sit still. Her limbs ached with exhaustion, but she couldn't stop moving.

She wasn't sure if she was restless or if the fear—the raw, all-consuming knowledge that she would die here—had finally begun unraveling something in her mind.

Henry watched her from his place on the makeshift cot, his exhaustion evident—but there was something else there too, something raw, something neither of them had ever acknowledged aloud.

She stopped.

"I don't want to die without feeling alive one more time."

Henry scoffed, shaking his head, but his voice lacked humor—only something hollow, something edged with something sharp and unspoken. A beat of silence stretched between them—longer than it should have. Heavier.

A shift in stance. A breath drawn too sharply. Touches that weren't meant to linger but did anyway. The air thickened, pulling tight, curling around them with something neither of them were willing to name. Henry—normally composed, sharp-tongued, quick-witted—let himself break. Let himself feel. No time for consequences. No space for hesitation. Only the frantic need to drown out the fear with something real. "We're going to die anyway." His voice was lower now, rougher, almost resigned.

Anastasia and Henry's breaths mingled in the frosty air as they pressed their lips together desperately. His rough hands roamed her body possessively, tracing over the thin layers of worn clothing that served as their only warmth.

She moaned softly against his mouth as the freezing temperatures made their movements frantic and urgent. Henry pushed her gently against the wooden board, his muscular frame pressing into hers. The sound of chain links clinking against the stone walls seemed to echo their desperation. He whispered harshly against her ear, "Anastasia... I need you. I need to feel something, anything, to escape this godforsaken place and the cold that's eating me alive." His voice was ragged with desire and a hint of something deeper, a longing that went beyond physical need.

Anastasia's heart pounded as she felt his urgency. She wrapped her legs around him, pulling him closer as they moved together in a rhythm dictated by their mutual desperation. As Henry's hands explored her body, she closed her eyes, and suddenly his face blurred into another's—Roland's.

The realization hit her like a punch to the gut. She missed her husband, missed his warm smile, his gentle touch, his presence that always made her feel safe and loved. Tears pricked the corners of her eyes as she clung to Henry, seeing not the prisoner but her beloved Roland.

"Roland..." she whispered softly, her voice breaking. Henry paused, hearing the name that wasn't his, and for a moment, he simply held her, understanding dawning on him. He knew she was imagining her husband, pouring out her longing and love for Roland onto him. He didn't care.

Anastasia moaned louder, her mind fully consumed by the illusion that she was with Roland again. The cold forgotten, they moved together with renewed fervor.

Their bodies moved together in the harsh, unyielding stone cage, seeking comfort in forbidden warmth. Anastasia's fingers dug into Henry's shoulders, imagining they were Roland's muscles beneath her touch. Henry responded with gentle passion, knowing he was filling a void left by another's absence.

Anastasia's breath hitched with a soft cry that was both a release of physical tension and an emotional plea for Roland. Henry held her tightly, feeling her body tremble against his, knowing that in this moment, he was merely a stand-in for the man she truly loved.

Afterwards, they lay entwined under the thin piece of cloth, their bodies still pressed together for warmth. Anastasia's eyes were closed, tears silently tracking down her cheeks as she thought of Roland. Henry said nothing, just held her closer, offering what small comfort he could.

Henry ran a hand through his hair, exhaling slowly, his breath pushing into the cold air like mist. The dim glow of the flickering wall candlestick cast deep shadows across his tired features, accentuating the sharp lines of his jaw, the exhaustion lingering beneath his eyes.

"If we make it out of this, let's pretend this never happened."

His voice was steady, but there was something raw beneath it—something unspoken, something fragile enough that neither of them dared acknowledge it too deeply. Anastasia huffed a tired laugh, leaning back against the rough stone wall, her body aching in ways she had grown used to.

"If we die, I'm telling everyone in hell."

Henry huffed sharply, shaking his head, but she saw it—the quiet amusement, buried beneath the resignation. The shared understanding that, after months trapped in this unrelenting cage, laughter, however fleeting, was the only real escape.

The first contraction came without warning. At first, the barmaid only shifted uncomfortably, pressing a trembling hand against her swollen stomach, her breath shallowing.

By the second, her face tightened with pain, her fingers curling against the wooden board chained to the wall—her poor excuse for a bed. By the third, she barely held back a whimper, her eyes squeezed shut against the inevitable.

The barmaid's pained breaths filled the damp air, sharp and uneven, each contraction pulling her closer to the inevitable.

Anastasia pressed herself against the iron bars, her fingers curling around them as she called toward the guards stationed near the staircase. "She won't make it alone," she said, her voice firm, laced with something close to desperation—but controlled. Calculated.

One of the men scoffed. "That's not my problem." Anastasia straightened, forcing herself into the role she had played so well in court—the queen, the authority, the woman who expected to be obeyed. "It will be your problem if this child dies because you refused to let me help."

The two guards exchanged a look—uncertain, hesitant. Percival had made it clear that Anastasia was to be contained. Controlled. But this? This was different. This was a complication. One of them sighed, shaking his head, before unlocking the cell door with slow reluctance.

"One hour."

It wasn't generosity. It wasn't mercy. It was pragmatism. They knew a dead newborn would bring consequences. They knew letting her assist was the lesser risk. Anastasia wasted no time, rushing into the barmaid's cell, dropping beside her with quick, steady hands, pressing her palm against her sweat-dampened forehead. "I'm here," she whispered, voice softer now, meant only for the woman struggling before her.

Henry remained behind the iron bars, watching carefully—his sharp gaze never leaving the guards, his presence a silent promise that they would regret it if they tried to intervene. There were no medical supplies. No trained midwives. No warmth beyond the flickering flame of the single wall candlestick.

Only her hands, her frantic whispers, her desperate attempts to guide the birth as best she could. Hours passed in brutal waves—pain, blood, strained cries that rang too loud in the confined space.

Then, the final moment. A baby boy, slick with sweat and life, his fragile cries piercing the silence. Anastasia lifted him carefully, cradling him against her chest, her breath uneven, her heartbeat wild with relief, with exhaustion, with something raw. And then, the quiet. It was too quiet.

Anastasia looked down. The barmaid wasn't stirring. Her breath was shallow. Then slowing. Then gone. Anastasia sat frozen, the weight of the infant pressing against her ribs. Henry leaned forward, pressing two fingers against the barmaid's pulse—a moment too long of waiting, of hoping.

Anastasia's throat tightened. "No, no, no—" Henry exhaled sharply, not with frustration, but with something final. "She's gone." Anastasia pressed her lips into a thin line, her fingers tightening around the baby's tiny body. She wouldn't let death win again.

Not this time.

Desperation fueled Anastasia's actions. She wiped the mucus from the newborn's mouth, her fingers slick and slick with the harsh reality of death clinging to the fragile form. She pinched his tiny feet, rubbed his back with a fervor that bordered on frantic. Time seemed to stretch and compress, each second an eternity. The baby was so small, so impossibly vulnerable.

Then, a flicker. A minuscule twitch in the corner of his lips. Anastasia redoubled her efforts, her breath catching in her throat. Another rub, another prayer whispered into the silence. Finally, a gasp. A tiny, shuddering inhale. And then, a cry.

Not a strong, robust wail, but a weak, fragile sound that resonated through the room like the first peal of a church bell. It was enough. It was life.

Tears streamed down Anastasia's face, tears of relief, of grief, of a profound and unexpected joy. She cradled the baby close, her own body trembling with the force of her emotions. He cried again, a stronger, healthier cry this time, and Anastasia wept with him, her sobs punctuated by soft murmurs of comfort and gratitude.

In that moment, something shifted within her. An emotion she had never truly known bloomed in her chest, a fierce and protective love that transcended anything she had ever experienced. This small, fragile creature, orphaned before he even drew his first breath, had claimed a piece of her soul.

She looked down at his tiny face, his eyes screwed shut in protest, and a name formed in her mind, unbidden and powerful.

"Arthur," she whispered, the name heavy with meaning. Arthur. After the legendary king who protected his kingdom, who rose above treachery and despair, who fought for what was right and just. Arthur. He would need that strength, that resilience. He would need someone to fight for him.

Anastasia knew then, with unwavering certainty, that she would be that person. She would protect him with everything she had, with every fiber of her being. His mother was gone, but she would be his shield, his guide, his kingdom. As Arthur continued to cry, his small fists clenched tight, Anastasia held him close. The air in the room, still heavy with sorrow, was now infused with a nascent hope.

The sun would rise again. And in the face of unimaginable loss, a new dawn had broken, heralded by the cry of a baby and the unwavering commitment of a woman ready to build a kingdom of love around him.

But darkness still lurked in the corners of the world. The scent of blood had barely faded from the air when the heavy doors to the chamber swung open, slamming against the stone walls with a force that sent a fresh shiver through Anastasia's bones.

Lord Percival stood in the doorway, draped in arrogance, his gaze cutting across the dimly lit room. "So this is the wretched thing she died for." Anastasia stiffened, clutching Arthur closer to her chest, her body instinctively shielding him from the venom dripping in Percival's voice.

Percival stepped forward, his boots echoing against the cold stone floor as he studied the newborn with barely concealed disgust. "Look at him. Weak. Useless. Just like his mother."

Anastasia's grip tightened. "He is a child. And he is innocent." Percival laughed, bitter and sharp, the sound twisting through the chamber like poison. "There is no innocence in filth. Do not be foolish enough to believe his blood won't betray him."

He leaned closer, his hand twitching as though he considered snatching the babe away, as though he might discard him like waste. But Anastasia's stance remained firm, unwavering. "You will care for him," Percival ordered, his tone cold and unforgiving. "I will not waste my coin or my time ensuring a whore's bastard lives past the week."

Anastasia's jaw clenched, fury bubbling beneath her ribs, fighting against the fear that threatened to paralyze her. "He is not vermin. He is your son." Percival's expression darkened, the cruel slant of his lips turning into something more sinister. "He is a stain upon my name. An unwanted consequence of foolish desire. And when the time comes, he will know it."

He took another step forward, lowering his voice to something sharp, edged with quiet malice. "But until then, I will see to it that he is your problem." Anastasia inhaled sharply, pressing Arthur against her chest, feeling the fragile weight of him, the warmth of his tiny breaths, the soft hum of life against her heart.

Percival turned on his heel, his presence leaving a chill in the chamber long after he disappeared. Anastasia looked down at Arthur, her fingers trembling as she traced his delicate features. "You are not him. You will never be him." She rocked him gently, soothing the faint whimpers that escaped his tiny lips. "You will be loved. And I will make sure of it."

They fed him with small bottles of milk provided by the guards at Percival's request. Despite his speech, it seemed he cared, even just a little, about his son. Not enough to love him, however. When the brutal nights descended, Anastasia and Henry huddled around Arthur, sandwiching his small body between theirs, sharing what warmth they had. Anastasia refused to cry. She wouldn't permit herself the vulnerability. Henry wept once, a fleeting moment of grief he concealed from her.

Beyond their confinement, the gang was fracturing. Animosity simmered, arguments stretched, and impatience laced every word. Lord Percival's relentless cruelty had bred resentment amongst his own men. Anastasia saw it first – the subtle shifts in demeanor, the slackening of their vigilance. The careless words. The growing sloppiness. It was a crack, an opportunity.

✳✳✳

The world suddenly erupted into chaos. The hideout, once suffocating in its heavy silence, now splintered apart as Roland and his soldiers tore through the fortified doors, swords unsheathed, armour gleaming in the flickering torchlight.

Shouts echoed through the stone corridors, steel clashing against steel, the heavy thud of bodies hitting the ground as Lord Percival's men scrambled to defend themselves. Anastasia barely had time to react before a soldier grabbed her, yanking her from the shadows, his grip firm yet careful as he pulled her toward the exit.

But something, someone, stopped her cold. Henry. Standing still. Not fighting. Not running. Not helping. Just watching. Her pulse hammered against her ribs, blood roaring in her ears as Lord Percival stepped forward, his blade glinting under the dim torches, his expression far too pleased for a man facing his downfall.

"You played your part beautifully, Henry," Percival mused, his voice thick with satisfaction. "I do admire your patience."

Anastasia felt the words before she understood them. Her breath hitched, fingers tightening around the infant cradled against her chest. "What does he mean?" Her voice was sharp and demanding but beneath it, deep inside, she already knew the answer. Henry didn't move. Didn't speak. Didn't deny it.

The silence was worse than the confirmation itself. Percival smirked, stepping closer, his blade tapping against his palm in amusement. "Oh, dear Princess, you still think you understand what's happening?" Anastasia turned to Henry, her breath uneven, pulse hammering, every fiber of her being screaming for him to refute it, to fight back, to say something that would make this not be true. "Tell me he's lying."

Roland stepped forward, blade raised, his voice low with warning. "We're done here." Henry tilted his head, watching them both, his eyes flickering between Roland and Anastasia as if debating whether to say more. Then, he smiled. Not cruel, not mocking. Just resigned. "I hope you make it out alive."

The confrontation erupted into pure violence, steel clashing, bodies twisting, Percival's men scrambling against the full force of Roland's army. Anastasia barely managed to keep Arthur close, shielding his tiny form against the frantic movement, breath uneven, limbs shaking from exhaustion and fear.

Roland's voice cut through the chaos, his grip firm as he grabbed her arm, shoving soldiers aside as he fought his way toward the exit. Henry wasn't stopping them. Henry was watching them go.

Outside, the cold night air slammed against her skin, crisp and brutal against the blood and sweat drying on her arms. Roland hauled himself onto a waiting horse, reaching for Anastasia, pulling her up behind him in one smooth motion. The baby trembled against her chest, his whimpers barely audible beneath the storm of fleeing men, clattering hooves, the final cries of battle fading behind them.

They rode fast and when the hideout was nothing but a blur behind them, swallowed by the night, Anastasia finally let herself breathe again. The wind ripped through the open road, whipping against Anastasia's face, dragging through her tangled hair, its sharp bite a cruel reminder that she was alive, that she had survived.

The baby whined softly, his breath uneven but steady, his fragile frame barely shivering beneath the thin blanket wrapped around him. Roland's grip tightened on the reins, his voice steadier than she expected. "We will figure out what to do once we return." Anastasia lifted her chin, her fingers smoothing over the baby's tiny back, steadying his breath, his pulse and everything aching inside her.

"I already know." Roland exhaled, shaking his head, his tone edged with resignation. "Anastasia—"

"I am not abandoning him."

The finality in her voice left no room for argument. Roland was silent for a long moment. Then finally he sighed. "Then he stays. But under one condition." Anastasia narrowed her eyes, waiting.

Roland met her gaze, serious, unwavering, sharp in the flickering moonlight. "When you return to your own time, the baby will remain here. As my heir." Anastasia's breath caught. "Roland—"

"It will spare me from marrying the princess of Prussia." The words settled between them, pressing against the space where uncertainty still lingered.

And beneath them, the quiet understanding that, despite everything, despite time, despite betrayal—Roland was still choosing her. Anastasia looked down at the baby, his tiny fingers curling against her arm. She nodded. "Fine."

Roland smirked softly, shaking his head. "You always were terrible at knowing when to walk away." And for the first time in months, Anastasia allowed herself to laugh.

TWENTY TWO

Roland thrived on order, his ability to command chaos solidifying his power at court. He was a master of navigating the treacherous landscapes of war, politics, and royal expectations, wielding a king's ruthless precision. Yet, Anastasia's vanishing act was something else entirely. It wasn't the familiar, manageable chaos he knew so well. Instead, it was a slow, insidious creep, a suffocating uncertainty that burrowed deep within him. It stretched through the palace's echoing silence like a persistent illness, a contagion he was powerless to eradicate.

The first reports arrived in pieces: a jumble of half-truths, fearful whispers from servants, and the hesitant words of knights. She wasn't dead, they said. But the silence that followed felt heavier than any confirmation of death. Death, at least, brought an end. This offered nothing. No resolution, no peace, only hanging uncertainty.

The first few days were filled with urgency. Roland sent scouts, informants, his best knights riding out in all directions, combing through villages, questioning merchants, tracking any possible movement that might lead them to her. But every lead unraveled too quickly.

Rumors led to dead ends, trails went cold within hours, people who claimed to have seen something recanted their statements, too frightened to be caught in whatever game was unfolding. Roland paced the war room until the stone beneath his feet felt worn from the weight of his steps, reviewing maps, circling locations, considering every possible connection Percival might have used but there was no clear path.

And the nights? The nights were worse. They were filled with sleepless hours, with the weight of exhaustion pressing against his ribs, with dreams of her that shattered the second he opened his eyes. He saw her in flickers—the way she had stood at the balcony, teasing him about duty; the way she had laughed at court's stiff traditions; the way she had challenged him in ways no one else ever dared.

And in those dreams, she wasn't missing. She was here. Alive. Real. But every morning, reality reminded him that she was gone.

The palace hum grew louder each day Anastasia remained missing, a nervous hum that threatened to overwhelm the court. Uncertainty festered, and advisors tightened their grip, each offering grim solutions. Some advocated for acceptance, while others, with thinly veiled ambition, pushed for strategic marriages to secure the kingdom's future. All waited for the king to face the unspoken truth. Genevieve, a constant, elegant fixture, lingered on the periphery of these tense dialogues, a patient shadow. When she finally dared to address him, her words were carefully chosen, devoid of malice, yet sharpened with a calculated pragmatism.

"Roland, you can't dwell on a ghost." He remained silent. She sighed and closed the distance between them, her gaze fixed on his face. "A kingdom isn't built on inaction." Still, he offered no response. Because she was wrong, and he wouldn't give her the satisfaction of admitting it.

Roland carefully steered clear of the locations that amplified the ache of her absence. He couldn't bear to revisit the gardens, now haunted by her laughter and the memory of her playful defiance of courtly manners. The east wing balcony remained untouched, forever echoing with her whispered musings on fate beneath the starlight. Even the training grounds felt hollow and incomplete, missing a vital, unspoken element that only her presence had provided.

Roland's charge was to safeguard her, and now doubt gnawed at him. Had he erred in bringing her here? Had he unwittingly delivered her into the jaws of the danger he'd vowed to prevent? He should have been more perceptive, foreseen Percival's desperation and the extremes to which it would drive him, fueled by Anastasia's unwavering defiance. Genevieve's question echoed in his mind: did Anastasia truly belong at court? If she were lost to him, could he ever find forgiveness?

The study was dim, lit only by sputtering candles that cast uneasy shadows across Roland's face. Genevieve found him there, his fingers clamped onto the edge of a timeworn map, jaw tight with a frustration that seemed to seep into the very air around him. He'd traced those ancient lines countless times, seeking an answer hidden within the faded ink. She stopped near the doorway, her arms crossed, offering a silent, watchful presence. "What if she does not return?" Roland didn't acknowledge her immediately.

He remained motionless, then finally expelled a slow, heavy breath. "She was not just anyone." Genevieve tilted her head, assessing him. "I hope, for your sake, that she comes back." A beat of silence stretched between them, filled with unspoken implications. "Otherwise," she continued softly, "I fear you may have lost yourself already." Roland remained transfixed by the map, the ink swimming before his eyes, its secrets obscured.

The study was suffocating. Roland leaned forward, his elbows pressed against the edge of his desk, his fingers curled tightly against his temples. Maps lay scattered across the surface, ink smudged where his hands had lingered too long over fading lines.

Every possible route. Every hidden passage. Every informant who had whispered false hope into his ear. All of them had failed. And now there was nothing left but silence.

Evelina bypassed the formality of a knock and entered. Her footsteps whispered across the floor, but the weight of her presence pressed down on Roland—a familiar intensity he knew better than to ignore. She carried the quiet burden of someone who observed too much and revealed too little. Stopping a breath away from his desk, she crossed her arms, her gaze a blend of sharpness and concern. "You're burning yourself out."

Roland remained fixed on his work, refusing to acknowledge the truth in her accusation. She sighed and took another step, planting her hands on the maps covering his desk, forcing him to look up. "You won't find her by destroying yourself." He released a controlled, frustrated exhale. "I can't stop. I won't." His voice was resolute, unyielding. "I should have protected her."

Evelina's eyes scanned him, noting the rigid set of his shoulders, the clenched jaw, the raw grief barely concealed. She leaned closer, her voice softer now, but no less firm. "She never asked you to be her shield." He started to protest, but she continued. "You think losing her means losing yourself."

Roland swallowed, his fingers digging into the parchment beneath them. A crack appeared in his carefully constructed wall, a sliver of vulnerability allowing the admission to escape before he could suppress it. "She belonged here. I know she did."

Evelina tilted her head, studying the lingering tension in his posture, the wavering edges of his conviction. Then, she posed the question that cut to the heart of his struggle. "Then why do you keep questioning it?" Roland said nothing, not because he didn't know the answer, but because he couldn't bear to voice it aloud.

Evelina placed a hand softly on his shoulder and then left him alone, closing the door gently behind her. Roland sat at his desk, ink pooling at the tip of his quill, the parchment stretched before him—empty, waiting, demanding something he could not quite give. The candle flickered beside him, its golden glow casting long, uneven shadows against the stone walls. The room was silent, save for the faint whisper of the wind curling against the window, pressing against the space that had once been filled with something warmer.

He had sent men across rivers, through forests, into villages that barely marked themselves on maps. Still, nothing. And so, he wrote. Not because it would bring her back but because the silence had become unbearable.

Anastasia, my search for you has been relentless, tireless, bordering on reckless. You've vanished, leaving behind a void where certainty once reigned, an echoing emptiness in places now devoid of meaning without you. The world is ignorant of your whereabouts, and so am I. Yet, I continue to search, not fueled by hope of resolution or faith in answers, but by the sheer refusal to accept this as the end. You were meant to defy them, to triumph. You were meant to be here. I cannot believe you left willingly. But doubt, unwelcome and persistent, whispers insidious questions. Did the court, the constant struggle, become unbearable? Did I fail you? Was I meant to shield you, or was my presence the very reason you needed protection? Genevieve claimed you were too gentle for this world. I desperately hope she was wrong. I pray you're still out there,

still fighting. And if you are, I swear I will continue
this search, even if it destroys me.

With all my love,

Roland.

He exhaled slowly, dragging a weary hand
down his face, fingers pressing against his
temples as if to quell the ache resonating deep
within. The nearby candle flickered, its flame
unsteady, a silent protest against the burden of
unspoken words. Roland folded the letter,
carefully concealing it. There, it would remain -
unread, unanswered, but eternally
remembered.

Genevieve stood by the window, her silhouette
outlined by the dying light of the evening sun,
her posture poised, composed—as if she had
already won whatever game she thought they
were still playing. Roland still sat at his desk,
his fingers curled against the edge, his jaw
locked, the letter he had written to Anastasia
tucked away in the drawer—unread,
unanswered, unseen by all but himself.

The silence in the room was a tangible barrier, a
heavy premonition of endings. Genevieve, as
always, broke it first. "The court is growing

impatient." Roland remained fixed, his gaze averted. The whisper of her gown against the stone floor marked her advance. "They question the wisdom of your...obsession." His fingers tightened on the desk, a subtle betrayal of his composure.

Genevieve's head tilted, her voice softening, though not in kindness. "A queen must be resolute, Roland. She must understand her position." Her words coiled around the absence Anastasia had left, a space once filled with laughter and a fierce, untamed spirit. Another step brought Genevieve into candlelight. "Perhaps she wasn't meant for this world at all." Roland's sharp exhale was an exercise in restraint, a visible struggle against burgeoning anger.

Genevieve, seizing the opening, pushed harder. "If she wished to be found, she would have been." That was the breaking point. Roland surged to his feet, the chair screeching against the floor, his posture rigid, his expression a mask save for the dangerous glint in his eyes, the resolute line of his jaw. "Enough," he bit out, the word a weapon. Genevieve froze, her hands neatly arranged, her face an exercise in control, though Roland detected a flicker of surprise, a crack in her carefully constructed certainty. The palace held its breath – servants stilled, guards shifted, a palpable tension settling into the very stones.

Roland's voice, now a low thrum of power, resonated with command. "You will not speak of her again." Genevieve's lips parted, a retort poised for release, but he cut her off. "You will not attempt to insinuate yourself into places where you do not belong." She exhaled slowly, her chin lifting, her gaze unreadable. Roland closed the distance, his next words delivered with the full force of his authority. "Leave." Finality hung in the air, absolute and undeniable. "You are no longer welcome here." She offered no pleas, no arguments. Only a knowing smile, one that hinted at a victory yet unseen, a game she still intended to win. Then, with measured steps, she turned and walked away – out of the study, beyond his reach, leaving behind the palace where she had once flourished in subtle manipulation. And she was gone.

The sword felt heavier than it should have in Roland's grip—not because of its steel, but because of the thoughts pressing hard against his ribs, each one curling into the spaces that had been left hollow since she was taken. The training grounds stretched wide around him, empty of soldiers, empty of sound except for the faint rustling of the banners overhead. The air was sharp with the scent of dirt, the faint flicker of torchlight barely stretching into the edges of the open courtyard. This was where he should have been focusing. Where he should have been preparing, strategizing, anticipating war before it reached his doorstep. But instead, he stood motionless.

Evelina stopped just short of him, arms folded across her chest, gaze cutting through him like the steel blade he had yet to strike against his opponent. "You don't know what to do without her." Roland's grip tightened against the hilt of his sword, his jaw clenching slightly. She wasn't wrong but he wouldn't admit that.

Evelina sighed, stepping closer, her voice lower now, weighted with something that felt more like quiet frustration than sympathy. "Genevieve is gone. The court is quiet. And yet, you still hesitate." Roland let out a slow breath, his fingers curling tighter against the leather-wrapped handle of his weapon, as if the tension in his body could be willed away through sheer force.

He had barely any time to respond when a door slammed shut and a guard came rushing over to the pair. "Ashbourne House, Your Highness. The princess has been spotted!" The words hit like thunder, crashing through Roland's chest, ripping through the suffocating quiet. For half a second, everything froze.

Evelina barely had time to react before Roland was shoving past the guard, his strides long, his breath sharp, his focus narrowing to a singular point, Ashbourne House. The name barely settled in his mind before instinct took over. Henry. His own kidnapping. The connections that didn't make sense but there was no time to untangle them now. Only one thing mattered. Anastasia. She was alive and he was going to get her back.

The courtyard erupted into movement. Roland's soldiers rushed to their horses, the sound of hooves scraping against stone filling the air. Roland mounted Dogweed, gripping the reins tight, his pulse hammering against his ribs. Evelina stood at the steps, watching him with the kind of expression that carried too many warnings.

He ignored them. He wasn't thinking about risk nor consequence. He was already gone.

With a sharp pull of the reins, Roland kicked Dogweed forward, the army following close behind, the night swallowing them as they raced toward Ashbourne. The doors to Ashbourne splintered apart, shattering beneath the force of Roland's men as they tore through the fortified hideout with brutal precision. Steel glinted beneath the flickering torchlight, unsheathed blades reflecting the violent eruption of battle. The air was thick with the scent of damp stone, of sweat, of blood.

Shouts echoed through the corridors, each one sharp with urgency, with aggression—Percival's men scrambling, unprepared for the reckoning that had finally arrived. Roland was at the head of it all. His sword cut through the air, his movements swift and deliberate as he pushed forward, each strike of his blade tearing through the resistance before him. Percival's men fought but they were losing.

Amidst the chaos, Roland saw her. Pulled from the shadows by one of his soldiers, her frame tense but unbroken, her arms wrapped tightly around an infant, her expression sharp with fear, with exhaustion, with something unreadable. He was moving toward her before he even realized it. Henry. Standing still. Not fighting, not running, not helping. Just watching. Roland's grip on his sword tightened, a new kind of tension settling into his muscles. Percival stepped forward, blade tapping against his palm, his smirk far too pleased for a man whose empire was collapsing around him.

"You played your part beautifully, Henry," Percival mused, satisfaction dripping from his words. "I do admire your patience."

The meaning hit Roland before the words did. Henry was connected to Percival. Connected to her imprisonment. Connected to everything. Anastasia's breath hitched, fingers tightening around Arthur who was cradled against her chest, her voice sharp and demanding. Roland stepped forward, blade raised, his voice low with warning, steady with fury. "We're done here." Henry tilted his head, watching them both, his eyes flickering between Roland and Anastasia as if debating whether to say more.

Then, he smiled. Not cruel or mocking but resigned. "I hope you make it out alive." Roland grabbed Anastasia's arm, pulling her toward the exit, shoving soldiers aside, fighting against the desperate last stand of those who refused to surrender. Henry wasn't stopping them. He was just watching them escape.

TWENTY THREE

The castle's towering doors shut behind her, sealing her back into a world she had feared she might never return to. Anastasia clutched Arthur closer to her chest, her breath steady but fragile, as she absorbed the familiar halls, the golden glow of the candlelight, the quiet murmurs of those who had awaited her return.

She was home. She had survived. And yet, survival did not come without weight. Without scars. Arthur stirred against her, his tiny fingers curling into the fabric of her gown, grounding her in the reality of this moment. He was safe. He was here, in her arms, where he belonged. And Roland had made sure of that.

Her thoughts barely had time to settle before a messenger approached her, bowing stiffly. "His Majesty, King George, requests your presence in the throne room." Her stomach clenched instinctively, her grip tightening around Arthur. She hesitated, barely allowing herself a breath before nodding. "Lead the way."

The throne room was eerily quiet when she stepped inside. King George stood near his throne, his back straight, hands clasped behind him, his expression unreadable beneath the warm candlelight. The room stretched wide, grand, filled with the silent weight of power, of duty, of expectations she had spent months trying to understand. She had never feared him but she had never fully understood him, either.

Anastasia stopped several paces from him, adjusting Arthur in her arms, pressing a soft kiss to his curls. "Your Majesty." George exhaled slowly, studying her with an intensity that bordered on something softer, something quieter than the usual sharpness he wielded.

"You are back." The words were deliberate, heavy with meaning. Not a question. Not an observation. A confirmation. She nodded. "I am." Silence stretched between them, thick, layered with unspoken truths. Then, finally, George stepped forward. "As much as we have had our differences, I am relieved you are safe, Anastasia."

She froze slightly, caught off guard by the sincerity beneath his words. Relieved? He had tested her endlessly, questioned her presence, challenged her existence within his court. But now there was no doubt in his voice. No hesitation in his stance.

"And I now know, truly, that you were the right one for Roland to marry." Her breath caught, fingers curling protectively around Arthur, absorbing the quiet weight of George's words.

She had never sought his approval. Had never needed it. But hearing it now, after everything, made it matter in ways she hadn't anticipated. George inhaled deeply, shaking his head slightly, as if recalling something private, something only he had witnessed.

"Roland was desperate to get you back." His voice was measured, but there was an edge to it. "His every thought, his every breath, his every action was driven by the need to find you. I have seen my son fight for his kingdom, for honor, for duty but never have I seen him fight for something as fiercely as he fought for you."

His gaze flickered to the child in her arms. He studied Arthur carefully, his brows furrowing slightly. "What is his name?" Anastasia swallowed, glancing down at Arthur, tracing her fingers lightly over his small back, her heart tightening at the quiet weight of the moment.

"Arthur." George was silent for a beat, the name settling in the air between them, heavy but whole. Then, with quiet certainty, he asked another question, one she had not expected. "Have you taken him in?" Anastasia hesitated, her fingers pressing gently against Arthur's tiny hands, feeling the warmth of him, the unspoken truth carried in his presence.

"He is mine," she answered, voice steady, unwavering. "I couldn't abandon him there." George inhaled slowly, something shifting in his expression. He took another step forward, his voice softer than before. "And I suppose that makes me his grandfather, then."

The words settled over Anastasia like something permanent, something whole, something final in the best way. George studied Arthur intently, as if searching for fragments of Roland within him, as if memorizing him, as if seeing him for the first time not as a title, not as an heir, but as a child.

"Arthur." His voice carried weight, certainty, something firm yet not unkind. He reached out, his large, calloused fingers brushing gently against Arthur's cheek. The boy blinked up at him sleepily, his tiny hands still clinging to Anastasia's gown, unaware of the significance of this moment.

"I am your grandfather." The words settled over Anastasia like something permanent, something whole, something final in the best way. George studied Arthur intently, as if searching for fragments of Roland within him, as if memorizing him, as if seeing him for the first time not as a title, not as an heir, but as a child.

Then, slowly, he stroked his cheek, gently and with reverence. And when he lifted his gaze back to Anastasia, his expression remained steady. Without hesitation, he placed a firm hand on her shoulder. Then, he kissed her forehead. "I truly am glad you are safe, Anastasia." His voice was low, sincere, carrying more weight than any royal decree ever could. Anastasia swallowed hard, emotions tangled between shock and quiet, overwhelming relief.

But then, the king smirked. "This does not mean I fully accept you in court yet, mind you." The tension broke, giving way to a quiet chuckle from Anastasia, a shake of her head, a moment of unexpected ease between them. "I wouldn't expect anything less.

✳✳✳

Despite the warm welcome, as the days passed, Anastasia remained chilled to the core, the cold a stubborn tenant in her bones. Perched by the window, her fingers clutched the sill, her unfocused gaze drifting past the city sprawling below and the castle grounds beyond. Instead, she was trapped in the liminal space between recollection and reality, the weight of her confinement etched deep within, eroding her certainty.

Fragments of memory surfaced: the cold, rough stone beneath her fingertips, the cruel bite of chains against her wrists, Henry's voice, smooth, insidious, weaving lies she had almost succumbed to. Her breath hitched, a painful pressure against her ribs. Then, the creak of a door splintered the silence, jolting her like an electric shock. Her grip on the sill tightened convulsively, her pulse surging as she whirled around, expecting a confrontation. But it was only Evelina.

The panic arrived subtly, uninvited. It wasn't a dramatic outburst, but a shadow lurking in the periphery. It manifested in the claustrophobia of closed rooms, in the unsettling dance of candlelight on rough walls, in the jarring echo of sudden noises – a book slamming shut, a raised voice, the ring of metal on stone.

Each minor disturbance threatened to drag her back: back to the chilling dampness, the insidious whispers, the inscrutable mystery of Henry's eyes. She clutched at her chest, struggling to regain her composure, to draw a steadying breath. But control was elusive, her grip on it weaker than it had ever been. This new vulnerability was a source of bitter resentment; she loathed the feeling of detachment, the sense of being fundamentally changed.

The nights were a torment. Sleep offered no respite, instead becoming a relentless replay of horrors she couldn't escape. Henry's lurking presence, Percival's chilling laughter against her skin, and the phantom cries of Arthur, swallowed by the memory of flight, all warred for dominance in her mind. She'd jolt awake, gasping for air that wouldn't come, her hands clenched into fists, nails digging into her flesh. Some nights, sleep remained elusive, and she'd simply sit, a solitary figure in the muted light of her room, watching the candle flame dance and the moonlight creep across the floor, a spectator to time rather than a participant.

Mirrors became forbidden territory, avoided like portals to some unseen danger, something within herself she couldn't confront. She had glimpsed her reflection once – a gaunt, exhausted version of herself, edges sharpened where softness had once resided. She was irrevocably altered, and the path back to who she was seemed lost.

Evelina saw. She always did. But she offered only silent companionship, a quiet presence that respected Anastasia's boundaries. She never pried, never forced unwanted conversations, never pressed for answers Anastasia wasn't willing to give. Instead, she would simply stand near, leaning against the doorframe, arms crossed, her voice unusually gentle. "Healing doesn't happen quickly," she'd say. Anastasia only exhaled, her hands trembling in her lap, offering no response.

Anastasia's love for Arthur bordered on reverence. She cherished the heat radiating from his small body, the gentle rhythm of his breathing as he nestled against her. His tiny fingers, gripping hers with surprising strength, seemed to know instinctively that she would always hold on. His wide, trusting gaze filled her with a joy that was laced with a chilling fear. This love came with a crushing weight of responsibility, a terrifying vulnerability. Was she capable of protecting him? The thought of failing him, of losing him to the world's harsh realities, haunted her. Even in moments of peace, the insidious "what ifs" slithered into her mind, casting a shadow over her joy.

Dawn was her refuge, the only time the world felt truly her own. The palace slumbered, and the air hung light and sweet, free of the day's demands and the ever-present burden of her history. During these stolen moments, she cradled Arthur, kissing his forehead and losing herself in the quiet pulse of his life. Her fingers danced over his miniature hand, tracing each knuckle, captivated by his unwavering trust, his immediate and fearless grasp. He reached for her without question. But despite his faith, doubt lingered within her. She knew firsthand how easily trust shattered, a lesson etched deep in her soul.

The exhaustion was bone-deep, unlike any she'd encountered before motherhood. Arthur's cries, sharp and insistent, shattered the fragile peace, a suffocating weight pressing down on her. Panic was now an unwelcome shadow, quickening her pulse, stealing her breath, making her hands tremble as she reached for her son. It wasn't a lack of love, but a terrifying uncertainty about herself, about whether she could mother him while piecing herself back together.

Understanding the truth of Henry's betrayal did nothing to ease the shock. He had been her trusted friend, her confidant, and the self-loathing was a constant ache. How could she have been so blind? How could she have believed in his fabricated persona? She was trapped in a loop of their last conversation, dissecting his words, his tone, the sickening realization that their entire relationship had been a lie. It was the falsity of their shared history that cut the deepest.

Roland offered silent support, never demanding she revisit the trauma of Henry's betrayal. Yet, she sensed his contained rage, directed not only at Henry but also at himself, at a failure they both felt but couldn't articulate. This unspoken burden hung heavy between them.

They were irrevocably changed. A chasm had formed, filled with unsaid words and uncomfortable silences. Roland's protectiveness, a constant watchful presence, both irritated and comforted her.

Anastasia knew she couldn't remain paralyzed by the past. She refused to let it choke the life out of her. She would move forward, even if progress was slow, even if the path was unclear. She had to. For herself, and for Arthur.

✱✱✱

Roland stood in the war room, a map spread before him, the parchment wrinkled with age, edges curling slightly under the weight of his touch. His face, etched with grim concentration, mirrored the severe lines of the countryside traced by his fingers. He moved deliberately, a ghost of hesitation flitting across his features when his hand hovered over a place long forgotten: Ashbourne's neighbor. Their attention had been consumed by Ashbourne, but nestled beyond its borders, obscured by time and neglect, was an old farmhouse, a name whispered in his memory - the Cameron Farm. A sudden, cold weight settled in Roland's chest as he absorbed this revelation, and he pivoted sharply, heading directly for Anastasia.

The candlelight danced, casting shadows on Anastasia's face as she absorbed Roland's words. Her arms remained crossed, a visible shield beneath her furrowed brow, but the tension in the air wasn't apprehension. It was anticipation, a coiled spring ready to unleash. The silence after Roland's final word hung heavy, a moment for comprehension to solidify into resolution. Then, it broke. Anastasia straightened, her chin lifting with newfound resolve. "We're going." Roland watched her, his gaze searching for any flicker of doubt. He found none. "Are you certain?"

Anastasia's breath escaped in a sharp gust. "No. But waiting won't tell us if we should." Roland continued his assessment, a silent calculation before he finally nodded. "We'll leave at dawn." Anastasia's head snapped back, her frown deepening. "No. We leave now." The urgency in her voice brooked no argument. Roland's raised eyebrow was a mere acknowledgement, not a challenge. He understood. Stalling had yielded only frustration in the past. This time, they refused to surrender another precious moment.

The air crackled with unspoken tension as they rode, the winding road vanishing into a landscape veiled in mist. Each breath was a crisp reminder of the encroaching evening. Dogweed, a solid anchor beneath Anastasia's hands, moved at his usual, unhurried pace, as if understanding the gravity of their mission. Beside her, Roland sat rigidly, his eyes constantly darting towards the distant farmhouse. Silence held them captive as they passed Ashbourne House, its looming presence sending a shiver of dread through Anastasia.

Its crooked towers and imposing stone walls were perpetually cloaked in shadow, untouched by sun or time. Anastasia forced her gaze forward, refusing to dwell on the past and the horrors she had endured within those walls. She was no longer the trapped woman she once was. A gentle pressure from her knees urged Dogweed onward. This time, she would be resolute. This time, she would not fail.

The farmhouse, entangled in the forest's verdant grip, appeared less destroyed than simply forgotten. Vines, like grasping hands, softened its outline, and the roof sagged wearily under the weight of countless storms. The once-ochre walls, now muted by ivy and the relentless passage of time, retained a ghostly echo of their former vibrancy. A rusted gate, its iron bars askew with neglect, guarded the entrance. Roland, dismounting, pushed it open, the hinges screaming in protest – a jarring sound after years of unbroken silence.

Anastasia followed, each footfall muffled by the mossy ground. A prickle of unease danced on the edge of her awareness, but her breath remained steady. Touching the wooden doorframe, she sensed not emptiness, but a suspension, a place frozen in time. The heavy door groaned as she turned the handle and pushed it inward, revealing a preserved tableau.

Inside, the house held its breath, untouched by the decay one might expect. Dust lay thick, but the furniture stood as if waiting for its owners' return. The dining table was still set, its plates heavy with the ghost of forgotten meals. Beside the cold hearth, a rocking chair held a faded quilt, a silent promise of warmth abandoned.

The air, thick with the scent of aged wood, carried a whisper of lavender - a fragile echo of Lucinda, a lingering memory. Anastasia moved slowly, her fingers tracing the contours of an old desk, the spines of unread books, the tarnished surface of a dusty mirror. Roland watched, silent, as she absorbed the stillness, allowing it to seep into her bones. They would not leave until they found it, until they unearthed the secret buried within these walls, until they uncovered the truth.

The groaning staircase seemed to resent Anastasia and Roland's intrusion, its aged wood complaining with every step. Dust, thick and undisturbed save for their passage, coated the banister and hung heavy in the air. The upper floor echoed the house's state: untouched, eerily still, as if time itself had paused. They moved with deliberate caution, their eyes darting across faded portraits and forgotten trinkets – fragments of a life left behind. Then they entered Lucinda's room. It wasn't opulent or grand, but possessed a poignant intimacy. It whispered of a life lived within these walls, its secrets woven into the very fabric of the room. In the corner stood a tall, imposing wardrobe. Anastasia traced the delicate carvings etched into its wooden surface before slowly pulling open the doors. An aroma of aged fabric enveloped them, revealing a jumble of old dresses, lace collars, and folded linens. But something was amiss. The back panel of the wardrobe was subtly uneven, its placement almost unnatural. She pressed against it, her fingers seeking a hidden latch, until with a soft click, the false back loosened. Behind it lay a treasure: five leather-bound diaries. Anastasia's breath caught as she lifted the first one, its worn spine fragile in her grasp. She opened it and Lucinda's words leaped from the past.

March 3rd, 1782

Dear Diary,

I saw the first signs of spring today—the frost has begun to melt, and the fields breathe again. Father complains that the mud will ruin his boots, but I have never minded the way the earth shifts beneath my feet when the seasons change. Teddy visited. He brought that ridiculous dog of his. I think he is growing too attached to the idea of belonging somewhere outside court. I do not blame him. Mother says I ought to think about my future, but I find that future terribly boring if it only consists of what she expects of me.

July 17th, 1783

Dear Diary,

Edward came again today. He lingers too long, but I do not mind. He speaks in riddles sometimes, his thoughts too tangled to follow easily, but when he talks about his dreams, I understand. He wishes for escape. For freedom from expectation, from duty, from everything that ties him to this world. I do not think he knows that I understand more than he expects.

September 4th, 1784

Dear Diary,

Time is an odd thing. It moves too quickly when we wish for stillness and too slowly when we beg for change. I have studied it long enough to know that movement is *not always linear. Edward does not believe me, but I know better. There are ways. Paths that do not follow the rules set before us. Elsmere is quiet, forgotten by most, tucked away where eyes do not linger. If I am to step beyond the limitations of this time, that is where it must happen. The key is finding the way. The method. The moment when time folds instead of stretches. And I think I am close.*

Anastasia's breath shuddered as she pressed her fingers to the ink, the weight of Lucinda's words settling deep within her. She looked up at Roland, her eyes sharp with newfound understanding. "She planned this." Roland lifted his gaze from the open diary, his expression unreadable. "She knew how to do it." The ensuing silence crackled with possibility.

Lucinda's diary lay open on the creaking floorboards, its pages fragile beneath Anastasia's fingertips. The ink had faded slightly, but the words remained sharp, haunting in their clarity. She ran her thumb over the edge of the page, absorbing every detail, every thought Lucinda had left behind. Time travel. Elsmere. Edward. She turned to Roland, her voice steadier than she expected. "We need to find Edward."

Roland studied her, his stance firm, his expression unreadable. "Lucinda trusted him." Anastasia nodded. "Which means he knows something. He must have known what she was planning." Roland let out a slow breath, glancing around the room—the remnants of a life abandoned, frozen in time.

"If he's still alive." Anastasia hesitated, considering. "If he isn't, then we find what he left behind." Roland moved toward the doorway, his voice deliberate. "Then we start with the farmhouse records. Someone must have known where he went." Anastasia cast one last look around Lucinda's room, at the wardrobe that had held so many secrets, at the bed that had been left untouched for decades, at the house that had stood silently, waiting for someone to return. She swallowed down the uneasy feeling curling in her chest. "Let's go."

The instant they entered the castle, pandemonium seized them. Gone was the courtyard's familiar tranquility, replaced by a cacophony of shouting, the frantic thud of soldiers' boots in the corridors, and a frantic chorus of voices. A wave of dread washed over Anastasia, a cold, constricting fear that tightened its grip with every breath.

Roland, ever the pragmatist, dismounted first, his keen eyes assessing the turmoil. Something was terribly amiss. Before they could seek clarification, the heavy doors crashed open, and

Evelina burst out, her face drained of color, gasping for air, her eyes wide with terror. She seized Anastasia's arm, her grip trembling. "Arthur! They've taken Arthur!"

The world lurched. Time seemed to splinter. Then, Roland exploded into action. A raw fury emanated from him as he surged forward, his stride long and purposeful, his soldiers instinctively falling into formation behind him. The castle trembled with his rage.

Anastasia's fingers dug into Evelina's arms, anchoring her. Though her own chest heaved, she maintained a semblance of calm. "Tell me everything. Now." Evelina, pale and trembling, shook her head. "He said... he said to go back to the start."

The words hit Anastasia like a physical blow, stopping her cold. They weren't a threat, nor a boast, but something stranger, unsettling. *'Go back to the start.'* The meaning eluded her, yet a cold dread constricted her chest. She refused to yield. Instead, she transmuted the fear into something harder.

Determination hardened her gaze. Courage surged through her veins. A thirst for vengeance consumed her. With a sharp pivot, she marched toward the war room, her steps firm and resolute despite the chaos threatening to overwhelm her.

The war room buzzed with nervous energy, his soldiers fixed on Roland as he stood at the head of the table. Anastasia's abrupt entrance cut through the tension, her presence immediately dominating the space. "Evelina says Henry told them to 'go back to the start'," she declared.

Roland's face betrayed nothing, but a flicker of understanding, or perhaps calculation, passed through his eyes. "The start?" he echoed, his tone hushed with thought. Then, with a sharp exhale, understanding clicked into place. "I mentioned to Henry that I met you at Elsmere."

Anastasia's surprise was evident. "You told him that?" Roland's jaw tightened. "A partial truth. Enough to be dangerous." A brittle laugh escaped Anastasia, her expression hardening into a cold, almost cruel mask. "Of course it's Elsmere." She gripped the back of a chair, steadying herself. "Poetic, really. Perhaps this time, I'll finally get to go home." Roland's gaze turned steely. Wheeling back to his troops, he barked, "Prepare for war."

Anastasia advanced quickly, interrupting the order before it could take hold. "No," she declared. Roland swiveled toward her, his eyebrows drawing together in confusion. She locked eyes with him, unyielding. "I need to be the one to end him."

A weighty quiet enveloped them. Roland scrutinized her—not with skepticism or hesitation, but simply evaluating the depth of her determination. At last, he gave a slow nod. "Then we set out at once. Just you and me." No forces. No diversions. Only the two of them, heading back to Elsmere—the place where everything started, and where it would at last conclude.

TWENTY FOUR

The sky was dark, painted in heavy strokes of deep indigo, the stars barely breaking through the thick clouds stretching across the horizon. The wind had picked up, curling into the folds of Anastasia's cloak as she urged Dogweed forward, her grip firm on the reins, her pulse steady despite the storm brewing beneath her ribs.

Roland rode beside her, his gaze locked onto the road ahead, his expression unreadable. He had been silent for most of the journey, but it wasn't the kind of silence that bred uncertainty—it was the silence of someone sharpening their resolve, cutting away distraction until only purpose remained.

Elsmere lay ahead, shrouded in mist, its outline barely visible against the night. It was a place of forgotten histories, of secrets buried in time, of choices that had led them both here. And waiting within its shadows, Henry.

They stopped just short of the abandoned manor, its ivy-covered walls looming in eerie stillness, the stone cold beneath the faint glow of moonlight. Anastasia slid from Dogweed's back, landing softly against the damp earth, her breath curling in the chilled air.

Roland dismounted just as quickly, his movements sharp, controlled, his sword resting at his hip. He turned to her, his voice low, measured. "Are you sure?" Anastasia didn't hesitate. "I have never been more certain of anything in my life." Roland nodded once, then drew his sword. They moved forward. Into the trap. Into the final confrontation that would decide everything.

Henry was waiting. Of course he was. He stood at the center of the hall, Arthur cradled in his arms, his posture calm, his expression unreadable. Anastasia felt the rage coil in her gut, sharp and unrelenting, but she forced herself to breathe—to focus. She would not allow emotion to cloud her resolve.

"You have no idea what you've done." Roland's voice was deadly, his presence carved in fury. Henry smirked, shifting Arthur slightly in his hold. "Haven't I?"

Anastasia stepped forward, her voice controlled, steady. "Let him go." Henry didn't flinch. "Go back to the start," he murmured, gaze flickering between them. "Tell me, does it feel familiar?" Anastasia's breath hitched, her mind racing, searching for meaning but Roland was already moving.

Roland tightened his grip on his sword. "Speak plainly." Henry laughed softly, shaking his head, his expression shifting—not cruel, not mocking. Simply resigned. "You always think you see everything so clearly, but neither of you understand. Not really." His gaze flickered between them, his voice lowering. "This was always meant to happen. You were always meant to come back here. She was always meant to choose." Anastasia swallowed, forcing herself to keep her stance firm, refusing to let his words dig too deep. "Choose what?"

Henry's smirk faded slightly, replaced by something more calculated, something more deliberate. He adjusted Arthur's weight, the baby completely unaware of the tension rippling through the air, his small hands curled into his blanket, trusting the arms that held him even if they did not deserve it. Henry watched Anastasia closely, his expression shifting just enough to unsettle her.

"You always believed you were different, that your arrival here was an accident. But it wasn't, was it?" His words slithered through the room, pressing against the edges of something she had never dared to question. "Did you ever wonder why it was you? Why Lucinda left behind the knowledge for only you to find?"

Anastasia's breath hitched, her pulse hammering against the confines of her chest. "What are you saying?"

Henry exhaled, almost disappointed in her lack of understanding, as if she should have pieced it together long ago. "She knew what she was doing, Anastasia. You were never meant to be just a traveler. You were meant to be the reason this world changed."

Roland stiffened beside her, his stance adjusting just slightly, his grip shifting against the hilt of his sword. "Enough of this." Henry didn't react. His gaze remained locked onto Anastasia, waiting not for permission, but for realization.

"You think time moved at random? That it chose you without thought? That Lucinda's actions were born of mere curiosity?" He let out a quiet, almost pitiful laugh. "She didn't choose Elsmere because it was forgotten. She chose it because it was the safest place to start over."

Anastasia felt her throat tighten, the weight of his words sinking deep, pressing against truths she hadn't dared confront. Lucinda hadn't just traveled through time. She had built something. She had chosen her players.

"You think you know who I am." His voice was measured, controlled, carrying the weight of something long buried, something carefully concealed. "But you never did."

Roland tensed beside her, blade still raised, but he did not move. Not yet. Not until Henry said the words that hung heavy between them, the words Anastasia wasn't sure she was ready to hear. She wasn't ready, but Henry wasn't waiting for readiness.

Henry exhaled, gaze flickering between them. "You're searching for Edward." His lips curved into something close to satisfaction. "You don't need to. He's standing right in front of you."

The words landed like stone against her ribs. Anastasia's breath caught, pulse hammering, refusing to believe it, refusing to entertain the possibility. "That's not possible."

Henry tilted his head, that unbearable calm still lingering in his posture, like he was waiting for her to catch up. "Lucinda called me Edward. It was my middle name, and I preferred it back then."

Anastasia's mind raced, the pieces shifting, rearranging, clicking into place. Edward Ashbourne. Henry Ashbourne. The same person. The breath in her lungs vanished, leaving only a cold void in its place. "No."

"Yes."

Henry's voice remained patient, unwavering, carrying the weight of a truth that had waited decades to surface. "She loved me once, just as I loved her." His fingers curled tighter against Arthur's blanket, his gaze turning distant, lost in something neither Anastasia nor Roland could see. "Until I doubted her. Until she decided I was not worthy of the path she had chosen."

Roland shifted beside her, his voice sharp, cutting through the thick quiet. "Lucinda abandoned you."

Henry's gaze darkened. "I thought she would return. I waited ten years for her, believing she'd come back, believing she would prove me wrong." His jaw tightened, his voice lowering into something dangerously thin. "She never did."

Anastasia swallowed hard, her mind struggling to keep up with the weight of truth crashing against her. "You searched for her."

"I scouted." Henry nodded once, slow, deliberate. "Watched the manor. Studied the changes. Then one day, I saw the same flash that appeared when she left." His eyes found hers then, locking her in place, freezing the world around her. "And you came through."

The words tore through her like fire. Henry had known. From the beginning. The moment she stepped into this time, he had known she was connected to Lucinda somehow. And he had gotten close to her—not out of friendship, not out of loyalty, but out of necessity. Because she was his key to understanding the secrets Lucinda had taken with her.

Everything, the kindness, the companionship, the promises, they had never been real. They had been calculated. Planned. Designed. To get her to trust him.

"I befriended you. Trusted you. I- I *slept* with you." Roland's breath stilled beside her. She felt it—the sharp intake, the pause, the quiet tension curling into something unreadable. The moment stretched unbearably long. Then, her voice cracked against the silence.

"Roland, I- I was desperate."

The words were sharp, defensive, almost pleading. "For any sort of contact. For anything real."

Roland turned to her, his gaze unreadable, but not cruel. He studied her, weighed the words, measured them not as judgment but as understanding. Then, he shook his head.

"It doesn't matter now." His voice was steady, unwavering. "Arthur is more important."

Anastasia exhaled, barely managing to release the weight pressing against her chest. Roland stepped forward, sword still raised, voice firmer now.

"And we're taking him back."

Henry's smile did not fade, even as Roland stepped forward, even as the promise of bloodshed hung thick in the air. He had expected this. He had planned for it. And he had prepared for the moment Anastasia would be forced to choose.

He adjusted Arthur in his arms—not carelessly, not cruelly—but deliberately. Anastasia's entire body tensed at the movement, her breath catching, her instincts screaming. But she did not lunge. Not yet. Henry's gaze flickered between them, measuring their reactions before speaking, his voice quieter now, sharper, laced with something close to satisfaction. "You think this ends with my death but you're mistaken."

Roland's fingers twitched against the hilt of his sword, his stance shifting, every muscle coiled with restraint. "We're done listening to your riddles."

Henry let out a slow breath, unbothered, gaze settling on Anastasia. "You were meant to change this world. Lucinda ensured that. And I gave you every opportunity to trust me, to let me guide you, to help you understand what she had stolen from me."

Anastasia shook her head, the fury curling in her throat nearly unbearable. "Lucinda didn't steal anything from you. You betrayed her."

Henry's jaw tightened slightly, but his smirk returned, small but certain. "And yet, here we are." He shifted Arthur again, this time more deliberately, more dangerously. Anastasia stepped forward instinctively, her heart hammering, her vision narrowing. "Don't." Henry's expression darkened, the smile fading completely now. "Then listen carefully."

The room seemed to still, the very air pressing down, holding them hostage. Henry exhaled slowly, deliberately, before delivering the words that would change everything. "If you kill me, you will never find the final piece. The final truth Lucinda left behind." His grip on Arthur did not tighten—he did not hurt him, did not threaten him physically—but his presence alone, the way he held him, was enough. Enough to make Anastasia understand that this wasn't just about vengeance. It was about knowledge. About power. About deciding what mattered most.

Roland stiffened beside her, his voice colder now, sharper. "You expect us to bargain with you." Henry tilted his head, considering. "Not bargain. Just understand." His eyes flickered back to Anastasia, watching her closely. "You need me." Anastasia felt every inch of her body reject the thought, every part of her screaming to fight, to end this, to tear Arthur from his grasp and leave Henry's corpse to rot in the ruins where he had twisted his own fate beyond recognition. She knew she couldn't. She had to force herself to listen to him.

Henry exhaled slowly, watching her with that unbearable certainty, his voice deliberate, edged with something dangerously close to satisfaction. "You have spent all this time searching for answers." His words were measured, carrying the weight of knowledge Anastasia had been desperate to find. "Searching for the way home. I have it."

Roland stiffened beside her, his fingers twitching against the hilt of his sword, but he did not speak. Not yet. Anastasia swallowed hard, forcing herself to meet Henry's gaze, to hold onto the fire threatening to consume her. "An incantation."

The word felt foreign on her tongue, strange and powerful in a way that unsettled her.

Henry nodded, slow, deliberate, savoring the moment. "A spell tied to time itself. A way to bridge the gap, to step between worlds. It was meant for her use alone, but I studied it. I held onto it, waiting for the moment it would serve me." He paused, letting the weight of his words settle. "And now it will serve you."

Roland's grip on his sword did not waver, his voice sharp as steel. "And what do you want in return?" Henry smiled, thin, measured, knowing. "You take me with you." The air in the room shifted, everything pressing inward, heavier, suffocating. Anastasia's breath caught, the demand crashing into her like ice. "No." Henry raised a brow, calm, patient. "Then you don't go home."

Silence stretched, thick and unbearable. Anastasia's fingers curled tightly into fists, her mind racing, her thoughts colliding into one another in chaotic, violent motion. She had spent so long fighting for this. So long searching for the truth, so long unraveling the mystery Lucinda had left behind, so long clawing through time with nothing but the fragile hope that somehow, somehow she could return.

And now it was within her grasp but the price was too high. Her voice cracked against the quiet. "You're asking me to give you what she refused." Henry exhaled, gaze unwavering. "Yes." Roland shifted beside her, his expression unreadable, his thoughts locked behind the cold calculation of a warrior ready to end this at a moment's notice. He spoke carefully, his voice edged with quiet warning. "We could kill you now and take it ourselves." Henry laughed softly, shaking his head just slightly. "And lose your only guide? You're playing a dangerous game, Roland."

He turned back to Anastasia, gaze narrowing slightly. "You want to go home? Then you take me with you." Anastasia swallowed hard, staring at him, staring at Arthur, staring at the choice that was curling around her like a vice.

The moment hung suspended in the air, time stretching, twisting, narrowing into the impossible choice Henry had placed before her. Anastasia's breath came sharp and uneven, her pulse hammering against her ribs. Every instinct in her body screamed at her to take the incantation, to agree, to escape—to go home. But not like this. Not with him.

She lifted her chin, resolve settling deep in her bones. "No."

Henry barely had time to react before Roland struck. He moved like a blur, a force of fury and precision, his sword slicing through the thick, suffocating air. Henry, caught off guard, stumbled back just enough for Roland to wrench Arthur from his grip, twisting, stepping away, passing him into Anastasia's waiting arms.

Arthur wailed, his tiny voice piercing through the chaos, but Anastasia barely heard it over the sound of clashing steel. She held him tight against her chest, pressing desperate kisses to his forehead, whispering assurances into his soft hair. "I've got you, I've got you, I've got you." She didn't know if she was saying it for his sake or her own.

Roland and Henry clashed, their swords ringing through the open doorway as they moved into the gardens. The wet earth churned beneath their feet, the scent of crushed leaves rising into the chilled air as blades collided in fierce, unforgiving strikes. Roland fought with fury, with purpose, with the weight of something far greater than revenge. And Henry fought with desperation. With the knowledge that everything he had planned, everything he had waited for, was crumbling beneath Roland's blade.

And then, Anastasia saw her.

At first, it was only a flicker, a shift in the air, a presence that made the world feel heavier, thicker, charged with something beyond understanding. Anastasia stilled, her breath catching, Arthur still pressed against her as she turned her head slowly.

She knew before she even saw her face.

Lucinda.

Her grandmother.

A sob tore from Anastasia's throat, raw and unexpected, and before she could even think, she ran forward. Lucinda met her halfway, pulling her and Arthur into a tight embrace, pressing a kiss to Anastasia's temple, whispering words too soft for anyone else to hear.

"My brave girl."

Anastasia wept against her, clutching her desperately, Arthur squeezed between them, his cries quieting as Lucinda stroked his back. She pulled away only slightly, brushing her fingers against Anastasia's tear-streaked cheek, her gaze impossibly warm. "I knew you would find your way here."

Anastasia shook her head, still struggling for breath, still struggling to understand. "You were here all along?"

Lucinda smiled, sad but proud. "I was always watching."

She lifted her hand, placing two fingers against Anastasia's forehead, and then the words came to her. The incantation. The way to open the house, to make it travel through time, to bring it back to where she belonged.

Lucinda sighed, her expression softening. "You know what you must do." And then, she was gone. Fading like starlight, dissolving into the quiet hum of the air, leaving behind only the lingering warmth of her touch. Anastasia knew. She understood.

She had to leave Arthur and Roland. She had to take Henry with her, had to stop him from hurting them, had to make sure the fight ended here. It didn't matter what happened to her, only that they were safe.

And in that moment, as she turned back to the gardens, watching Roland fight for her, watching him fight for their son, she knew the truth that had been waiting in the depths of her heart all along.

She loved him.

Truly, deeply, irreversibly loved him.

She stepped forward, her voice sharp and commanding as she shouted through the chaos. "Stop!" For the briefest second, they did. Roland and Henry both hesitated, blades raised, muscles coiled, their breath heavy in the cold air.

Anastasia swallowed against the lump in her throat, her voice steadier than she felt. "I love you, Roland." Roland's body stilled completely, his sword lowering just slightly, his gaze locking onto hers with something unreadable—something raw, something that cracked through the walls between them.

She took a slow breath, voice unwavering. "And because I love you, I need to do this." She turned to Henry, expression cold, sharp. "You can come with me." And then, she spoke the incantation. The words curled in the air, weaving through the walls of Elsmere, wrapping around them like a pulse of unseen magic. The house trembled, the glow returning, stretching through the ruins, pulsing with the same energy that had first pulled her into this world.

Henry's gaze flickered, a glimmer of evil curling in the depths of his irises. Roland saw it. And in that instant, he knew he would not let Anastasia leave with Henry. Henry lunged, sword raised, fury spilling into his every movement. But Roland was faster. He struck.

"I love you too, Anastasia Cameron. Always remember that." He quickly placed a hand on her face and then on Arthur's, holding off Henry with his other hand. And then he shoved Anastasia backward, Arthur still in her arms, pushing them through the glowing doorway, into the house, into the spell, into the moment where the past and the present collided.

"No!"

But it was too late. The light swallowed her whole. And then, she was gone. Roland knew it instantly, could feel the absence as the house settled into silence, as the glow faded, as the time that had once held Anastasia in his world released her back into her own. Anastasia collapsed onto the floor, Arthur clutching tightly to her chest, her breath coming ragged, uneven, desperate. She was home but at what cost?

TWENTY FIVE

The house was eerily silent, dust settling in the air, the weight of time pressing against its broken walls. Anastasia lay where she had fallen, Arthur curled into her chest, his tiny fingers gripping the fabric of her cloak as though he could sense the shift—the difference between the world they had left and the one they had returned to.

Her breath came uneven, ragged, her pulse thundering beneath her skin as the reality of it crashed into her, she was home. But she was alone. Roland was gone. Roland was never coming back.

A sob tore from her throat, sharp and unbearable, shaking through her body as she clutched Arthur closer, burying her face into his soft, warm skin. She had fought so hard to get back. She had fought so hard to return but it had never been supposed to be like this.

The home she had stepped into all those months ago, the ruined, worn house that had first swallowed her into its secrets remained unchanged, as though it had waited for her, knowing she would return. The walls were still faded, the floorboards still creaked beneath her shifting weight, the scent of rain-soaked wood still clung to the air. She had been here before. But not like this.

She forced herself upright, her legs weak beneath her, her body still trembling, her mind struggling to catch up to everything that had happened. She glanced down at Arthur, checking him, running her fingers lightly over his face, his hands, his tiny chest rising and falling with steady breaths. He was safe. That was all that mattered in the moment.

She swallowed hard, pressing another kiss to his forehead, whispering against his skin. "It's just us now, my prince." Arthur whimpered softly, his fingers grasping at the collar of her cloak, too young to understand the words, too young to know that his world had just shifted in ways neither of them could fully comprehend. "Just us against the world."

She inhaled deeply, steadying herself, forcing herself to move. She had to get out. She had to step into the real world, had to see it with her own eyes, had to confirm that everything was as it should be, that time had settled, that history had corrected itself, that nothing had shattered beneath the weight of her return. And she had to go back to her grandmother's house. She had to see it one last time.

After everything she had learned, after everything she had uncovered, she owed it to herself, to Lucinda, to Roland, to Arthur, to walk through the doors and breathe in the memories that had always lingered there. She adjusted Arthur against her chest, pulled her cloak tighter around them both, and stepped out of the house. The world awaited.

The air outside was crisp, the sky painted in muted hues of gray, stretching endlessly above the quiet fields that surrounded the worn house. The world felt the same, unchanged, unmoved by the storm that had raged within her.

Anastasia stepped forward, her boots pressing against damp earth, Arthur nestled against her chest, his warmth grounding her even as everything else felt impossibly uncertain. The streets stretched ahead, familiar yet distant, modern yet untouched by the whirlwind of time she had just emerged from.

Her breath was uneven, her pulse steady but heavy. As she walked, every step carried the weight of memory. Roland, the castle, the war, Henry, her grandmother. And yet the world around her continued forward, indifferent to her absence, unaffected by her return.

She reached the edge of town, the familiar roads leading toward her grandmother's house, tucked away in the quiet corner where it had always stood, where it had waited for her. The moment she saw it, her chest constricted. It looked the same.

The same cottage-like charm, the same weathered stone pathway, the same white-trimmed windows that had once held so much warmth. She swallowed hard, forcing herself to move, forcing herself to cross the threshold, forcing herself to step inside the space that had once been her safe haven.

The door creaked slightly as she pushed it open. Silence greeted her, thick and unmoving. She took a slow breath, adjusting Arthur in her arms, pressing a hand lightly against his back as she stepped further inside.

The scent of aged books lingered, mixed with faint traces of lavender, a perfume so delicate, so familiar, that it sent fresh tears streaming down her cheeks. Her grandmother had been here once. Lucinda had lived here. Had loved here. Had built an entire future from the remnants of time itself. And now Anastasia was standing at the edge of it, at the crossroads between past and present, holding the only piece of her old life that truly mattered.

Arthur whimpered softly, his tiny fingers curling into her cloak, pressing against her as though he understood, as though he knew the weight of the world had just shifted beneath them. She pressed her forehead to his, whispering against his skin. Arthur cooed, his small voice echoing through the quiet space, settling into the walls of the home that had always been hers. And for the first time since she had returned, she let herself breathe.

The days passed, then the weeks, stretching into months as Anastasia pieced together the fragments of her new life. The weight of history pressed against her, but she refused to let it bury her. She fixed up Elsmere, restoring its walls, clearing its overgrown gardens, shaping it into something alive again, not just a relic of the past but a place she and Arthur could call their own.

And she had found her own path, too. It hadn't been easy navigating a world that had continued on without her, learning how to settle back into a society she had once belonged to but now felt so foreign. But she had done it. She had chased the dream she had left behind before she ever stumbled into history, before she ever met Roland, before time had ever shifted beneath her feet.

She had become a historian. It was almost poetic, studying the past while carrying the deepest secret of time within her own bones. She lectured at universities, worked on restorations, published research on long-forgotten figures. And though she never breathed a word about Elsmere's true story, she knew the truth lived within her, a quiet whisper of the life she had left behind.

She learned to navigate the quiet moments, the ones where the ache in her chest was sharpest, where memories clung too tightly to the edges of her thoughts. But she did not let them break her. Instead, she focused on Arthur, on the way his laughter filled the empty halls, the way his tiny hands reached for hers, the way his eyes, so much like Roland's, sparkled with wonder when he discovered something new.

Arthur's first steps came on a golden afternoon, sunlight spilling into the great hall where Anastasia had been sorting through old furniture. One moment he was holding onto the edge of a chair, steadying himself with tiny fingers, and the next he let go.

Her breath caught as he took his first uncertain step forward, then another, his determination visible in the furrow of his brow, the way his lips parted in concentration. He wobbled slightly, but she was already there, arms open, waiting for him.

When he reached her, collapsing into her embrace with a delighted giggle, she laughed, pressing kisses to his cheeks, tears slipping down her face before she could stop them. "You did it, my prince."

His first words came not long after, small, broken syllables forming the first fragile attempts at speech. She cherished every one, holding onto them like precious treasures, watching with awe as he pieced together meaning from sound.

Then came the nights, the quiet moments where time slowed, where she tucked him into bed, brushing the soft curls from his forehead, whispering stories that belonged to another life. A heroic prince, a fierce beast, a daring rescue.

Arthur listened with wide, eager eyes, absorbing every detail, his tiny hands clutching his blanket tightly. But tonight was different. Tonight, as the story neared its end, his small voice, barely more than a whisper, asked the question she had dreaded. "Where Daddy?"

She inhaled sharply, the ache pressing hard against her ribs. He was too young to truly understand. Too young to know the depth of loss that settled in the spaces between them. But he felt it. Somehow, he felt it. She swallowed down the wave of emotion, reaching out and placing her hand lightly over Arthur's heart. "Daddy is here. Always."

Arthur blinked up at her, his small fingers reaching to touch her hand, as if trying to understand. She forced herself to smile, pressing a lingering kiss to his forehead. "Sleep now, my love." She stepped out of his room, closing the door softly behind her, holding herself together just long enough, just until she was alone.

And then, she broke. She sank onto the edge of her bed, sobs wracking her body, shoulders shaking as she pressed a trembling hand to her lips. She missed him. She missed him so much she could hardly breathe.

She let out a shaky breath, her voice barely above a whisper. "Arthur took his first steps today." Silence greeted her, cold and empty, but she pressed on, staring at the darkened space in front of her as if he could hear her, as if he could still sit beside her the way he used to.

"They were small, wobbly, but he was determined. He kept trying, even when he stumbled." She sniffed, blinking hard against the tears burning in her eyes. "He's just like you." She swallowed, pressing her hands against her face, trying to steady herself, but the weight in her chest refused to ease.

"His first word was Mama, just a little sound, barely more than a whisper, but it was real." Her voice cracked, raw, broken. "You would have

413

been so proud of him." She exhaled sharply, forcing herself to continue, forcing herself to speak into the silence, to fill it with something other than grief.

"He's starting preschool soon. I keep thinking about how nervous I'll be when I drop him off, how much I wish you could be there. How much I wish—" She stopped, the words too painful to finish, the ache curling into her ribs like a vice.

She bit her lip, stared at the ceiling, imagined him there, imagined him listening. "I miss you." Her voice was barely audible now. "So much it hurts." She lifted a shaking hand, pressing her fingers to her lips before blowing a soft, lingering kiss into the air.

"I love you."

Then, finally, she let the sobs take her. She curled into herself, clutching her own arms, shaking beneath the weight of everything she had lost. And though there was no answer, no warmth to hold her, no strong arms to catch her as she broke, she swore, for just a moment, she could feel him there.

Her breath trembled as she lifted her hand to the empty air, pressing her fingers to her lips before blowing a soft, lingering kiss to the space where

he should have been. And then, she closed her
eyes.

Anastasia stood at the edge of the garden, her
hands wrapped securely around Arthur's small
fingers, the warmth of his grip grounding her in a
moment that felt surreal, delicate, fleeting. The
air carried the scent of damp earth, mingled with
the faint aroma of wildflowers that had begun to
bloom along the stone pathways she had worked
so tirelessly to restore.

Arthur, dressed in his tiny blue jacket with his
backpack slung loosely over his shoulders,
bounced slightly on his feet, eyes wide with
excitement, oblivious to the storm of emotions
twisting within her chest. His curls, light much
like Roland's, framed his face in soft waves, his
cheeks rosy from the crisp morning air, his
expression so full of eagerness it nearly shattered
her.

Today was the first day. The first step forward.
Preschool awaited him. A world beyond Elsmere,
beyond her. And though she had prepared for
this moment, had told herself repeatedly that this
was just another milestone, another beautiful
moment of growth, it didn't make letting go any
easier.

She swallowed hard, adjusting his backpack straps for the third time even though they were already secure, her fingers trembling slightly as she tugged the fabric into place. Arthur looked up at her, blinking curiously, sensing something in her silence. His small hands reached for hers, gripping tightly, the innocence in his eyes calming the storm inside her in ways words never could.

The drive to the preschool felt both impossibly long and too short. The streets blurred past them, familiar yet distant, unchanged by the weight of history she carried within her. Arthur filled the quiet with his own excited chatter, his voice bright as he listed all the things he hoped to do, play with blocks, paint a picture, make a friend.

She listened, absorbing each word, holding onto them like fragile glass, afraid of what would happen when she finally let go. When she finally had to watch him step into the world without her at his side.

As they pulled into the preschool parking lot, she felt the weight of reality settle fully onto her shoulders. The building loomed ahead, painted in soft, inviting colors, the sound of children's laughter spilling into the open courtyard. It was warm, welcoming, everything she had hoped it would be for him. But still, she hesitated. Arthur, however, did not.

He stared at the entrance, his small body still for just a second, taking it all in. Then, he turned to her, eyes bright with determination. She held her breath, waiting for him to cling to her, waiting for the hesitation, waiting for the fear. Instead, he reached for her. Not to pull her back, not to beg her to stay, but to hug her. Fiercely, fully, with all the trust and love his tiny frame could hold.

She knelt down, pressing her lips to his soft curls, inhaling deeply, absorbing the warmth of him, memorizing the way he fit in her arms, knowing he wouldn't be this small forever. Tears burned the edges of her eyes, but she blinked them away, forcing herself to hold onto the moment as long as possible.

His tiny fingers loosened, his steps steady, confident, filled with quiet courage as he turned and walked through the doors. She stood frozen, watching him go, watching the world claim him in ways she hadn't yet prepared herself for.

Arthur thrived in the world she had built for him.

His preschool days were full of laughter and discovery, his confidence growing with each passing week. He made friends easily, his bright spirit drawing people toward him. There were playdates filled with wooden train sets and messy finger paintings, afternoons spent running through Elsmere's gardens with tiny feet pounding against freshly restored stone paths. He was happy and that was all Anastasia had ever wanted. As she watched him from the kitchen window one afternoon, playing with his best friend Oliver, their laughter carrying through the open air, she felt something settle deep within her heart.

Anastasia sat on the cold floor of her study, candlelight flickering against the walls, casting eerie shadows over the old books that lay scattered around her. Her hands trembled as she traced the faded script of a centuries-old journal, searching, hoping, praying for something, anything, that could bring her back to him.

She had tried everything. Every spell, every whispered incantation, every desperate plea. But nothing worked. The original spell, the one that had torn her from the past, had vanished from her mind the moment she cast it. Like time itself had erased it, ensuring she would never find her way back.

She had scoured her grandmother's belongings, digging through forgotten letters and old journals, finding fragments of knowledge but never the answers she needed. The truth settled heavily in her chest, an ache that had grown unbearable over time. Roland was gone. And no magic, no twist in time, no desperate attempt would bring him back.

But one day, she had worked up the courage to search for his grave. She had told herself she wouldn't, that she couldn't. That knowing would be too much. But curiosity, heartbreak, something beyond reason had pushed her forward. And when she finally typed his name into the search bar, the results had shattered her.

There was a family memorial statue. Three figures. One for her. One for Roland. One for Arthur and beneath it, a tomb holding her "body" and Roland's. It had been enough. More than enough. She never looked again after that. She knew what she needed to know, he had died that night. She hadn't saved him. She hadn't been there when he fell.

But now, she was ready to face it. The graveyard was quiet, lined with rows of stone markers that stretched endlessly beneath the crisp autumn sky. Arthur held tightly to Anastasia's hand as they walked, his small feet carefully stepping over pebbles, his fingers curling around hers in quiet curiosity.

Her fingers traced along the cool, worn edges of headstones as she walked, reading names that had long since belonged to history until she reached the one she knew. Evelina Marybeth Westcott. Her chest tightened. And beside her name, Harper Isabelle Lovelock. Anastasia exhaled softly, pressing a careful palm against the stone, absorbing the names, the certainty that they had belonged to each other, even in death.

They had never married, not in the way society would recognize. But they had built a life, one away from prying eyes, on the outskirts of the estate, in a quiet home filled with books and laughter and a love neither had ever dared to dream of.

Evelina had become a woman of quiet influence, her presence undeniable even as she had remained apart from court, her sharp mind respected, her wisdom sought after by those who once whispered against her.

Harper had thrived beside her, her hands still rough from years with the horses, her laughter still quick, her devotion unwavering. And when the years had stretched too long, when time had finally demanded its price, they had left together, neither lingering without the other. Their story had ended as it had begun. Hand in hand.

Anastasia smiled softly, eyes damp but not sorrowful. She let her fingers linger against the stone for just a moment longer before stepping back, exhaling. Then she looked up and there it was. The tomb and the statue. It was impossible to miss. Large, imposing, crafted with delicate detail, a dedication to the ones history had chosen to remember. She held Arthur's hand as they stepped forward, her breath caught in her throat as her gaze fell upon the inscription.

"In Honour of our dear Prince and Princess of England, May Their Souls be at Peace."

Something inside her cracked. She fell to her knees, a sob tearing from her throat as the weight of closure she hadn't wanted, but had desperately needed, settled around her. Arthur, sweet, loving, innocent, pressed his tiny hands to her cheeks, his wide eyes filled with confusion as he patted her face, trying to comfort her in the only way he knew how.

She pulled him close, clutching him tightly, pressing frantic kisses to his soft curls. He was all she had left. The only remnant of the life she had lost. But he was enough. He had to be.

Back at the manor, the walls felt suffocating, the air thick with a presence she couldn't shake. Arthur waddled into the living room, clambering onto the sofa, settling into the cushions with his usual ease. Anastasia walked through to the kitchen, moving on instinct, her mind numb, her heart heavy. She reached for the apple juice, pouring it into a cup, the routine grounding her, keeping her tethered to the present, forcing her not to spiral into the memories clawing at the edges of her mind.

Suddenly, a sudden, blinding, consuming flash of light filled the manor. She gasped, the cup slipping from her fingers, juice splattering across the floor as she stumbled back, panic flaring in her chest. It was happening. But nothing had changed. She was still here. Still trapped in her time. Then she heard him. "Angel! Are you here?" She turned sharply, her breath lodged in her throat, her body frozen as she stepped out of the kitchen and into the hallway.

And there he stood. Roland. Whole. Alive. Here. The world tilted beneath her feet, her heart crashing against her ribs as she surged forward, throwing herself into his arms, gripping him as though he would vanish if she let go.

And then they kissed. Deeply. Desperately. The kind of kiss that unraveled the months of aching distance, of lost time, of quiet devastation. Arthur waddled toward them, his small hands reaching curiously, eyes wide with wonder at the man standing before them.

Anastasia pulled back just enough, gasping against the force of her emotions, her voice trembling as she whispered, "Meet your dad."

Roland's breath hitched, his gaze dropping to Arthur, his expression shifting, something breaking, something rebuilding, something too raw to name.

Then he picked him up, holding him securely, pressing kisses all over his tiny face, swinging him in the air, laughing through tears. Arthur giggled, gripping onto Roland's collar, his small fingers curling into the fabric, like he had known him all along, like he had always been waiting.

Roland wrapped his arms around them both, burying his face in Anastasia's hair, breathing deeply, holding them as tightly as he could. And for the first time in what felt like forever, they were whole.

The End.

Printed in Dunstable, United Kingdom